# ghost moth

# ghost moth

Michèle Forbes

Weidenfeld & Nicolson
LONDON

First published in Great Britain in 2013
by Weidenfeld & Nicolson
An imprint of the Orion Publishing Group
Orion House, 5 Upper St Martin's Lane, London WC2H 9EA

An Hachette UK Company

1 3 5 7 9 10 8 6 4 2



A CIP catalogue record for this book is available
from the British Library

978 0 29787 044 9 (cased)
978 0 29787 045 6 (trade paperback)

The Orion Publishing Group's policy is to use papers that are natural, renewable and recyclable products and made from wood grown in sustainable forests. The logging and manufacturing processes are expected to conform to the environmental regulations of the country of origin.

www.orionbooks.co.uk

*To my father, Ernest, with love*

# 1

*August 1969*

THE SEAL APPEARS FROM NOWHERE, an instant immutable presence in the sea – although he must have been swimming silently beneath the surface for some time without her knowing. Katherine shudders in the water; her thoughts are moving like fast cold spikes inside her head. Where has he come from? Is he lost? Has he come to feed? The seal's heavy muzzle thrusts toward Katherine; his nostrils – two dark inlets – flare: He is taking in her smell, her fear. His stiff eyebrow hairs, beaded with sea drops, crisscross the thick shadowy skin of his dark, wide head. Battle-scarred, his snout slopes to an ugly dull point where his long wiry whiskers afford him the seductive familiarity of a family dog. But it's his eyes – the eyes of this wild animal – that terrify Katherine the most; huge, opaque, and overbold, they hold on her like the lustrous black-egged eyes of a ruined man.

Briefly the seal's lips roll to display his sharp conical teeth, strong enough to dismember a large bird, she thinks, strong enough to rip her flesh. Her panic rises. If she turns her head away from him to look for help, even for a second, God knows what he'll do. He may strike. Seals startle easily, someone once told her, their behaviour as unpredictable as human love. Yet if she remains where she is . . .

They tread the cold sea together, Katherine and the seal. Above them, sandpipers drop their miserable cries as they fly. Splinters of high voices peak on the blue wind. In the distance, there is the low mechanical churr of a train. Around them, the sea continues its cool lamenting slap.

A sudden thought. Is he alone? Are there more seals? Are there cows or pups to aggressively protect?

The bobbing sea confuses the distance between them. It feels as though he is moving closer to her with every swell. She is keenly aware of her quivering limbs, of her too-quick breathing, of the saltwater in her mouth: a jagged dark fear filling her up. Her mind shrinks to the size of one thought: He may kill me.

Out of this fear there is the sudden impulse to reach out and touch him. Like the only way to stop the white panic of vertigo is to jump. To finish it. To decide to finish it. Or by reaching out, by touching, she might just connect with him, soothe him, soothe herself, make it mean something. Madness, she knows. But his heavy beauty is suggesting just this.

She doesn't do it.

She hears her husband, George, calling out for her from the shore, his voice travelling like a lone seagull's cry, searching for her. But she doesn't respond. Transfixed by the seal's gaze upon her, by this odd and uncomfortable gift of him, by the fear of the ever-opening sea, she remains.

The seal is the first to move. He shifts his head a little, as though he is beginning to lose interest in her, and he snorts abruptly, spraying her face with seawater, the spiky claws on his fore flipper breaking the surface of the water as he moves. He turns his head, creating thick dark wrinkles around his neck. But after his black eyes casually scan the horizon, they return to her. His eyes, those eyes, brimming black liquid pools, stare into her. They are asking something of her; they are waiting for her to answer him.

The sea blasts an icy wash over her body.

She hears George calling her again. This time, the sound of his voice is pitched with relief that he has spotted her in the water. His voice pulls at her. 'Katherine! Katherine!' he calls. Does he see the seal beside her? Does he see him? 'Katherine! Over here!'

A new spiral of fear kicks in at the sound of her husband's voice. What if George cannot reach her? What if he frightens the seal and provokes it? She feels her stomach lurch, as though she might get sick. Reflux burns her throat. Her chest tightens. The eyes of the seal still hold on her. The heft of his body is now remarkably still, his bulk buoyed by the obedient sea. That big grey head.

Against her common sense, she turns her body to look for George and sees him wave to her from the rocks, beckoning her to come to him. She opens her mouth, but she cannot find her voice. Instead, her mouth fills with seawater, a thick glide of salt blue into pink. She swallows some, spits out the rest.

When she turns back, the seal is gone. She hangs in a quiver of cold sea.

---

That morning, George had casually announced that he had taken a day's leave due to him from his job at the Water Commissioner's Office. Katherine, surprised by George's uncharacteristic spontaneity, had nonetheless decided it opportune to pack a picnic and take their girls – Maureen, Elizabeth, and Elsa – and baby Stephen out for the day to Groomsport beach. After all, the girls are already on their summer holidays and the weather is holding up so beautifully, she had thought.

By early afternoon, the Bedford family were well on the road from their home in east Belfast, their bottle green Morris Traveller winding its way through the fourteen miles of unremarkable countryside away from the city toward Groomsport town. Apart from Bangor and the small village of Ballyholme, there was only the occasional farmhouse to be seen, some scattered clusters of whitewashed buildings here and there, and one or two forsaken churches whose crumbling stone walls had long since exposed their sacred interiors to a disinterested sky.

Katherine let her head rest back on the warm leather of the car seat, her body heavy, as though the hot August sun were inside the car with her. She looked out of the window and saw the world passing her by. She watched as the mottled hedges of hawthorn and gorse, the trees, and telegraph poles moved briskly into and then out of her view. Glancing beyond the low hills to the east, she caught a glimpse of sea. The blue sky offered a singular white cloud, as though it knew how to be summer.

Stephen was fast asleep on her lap, his plump, hot body rounded like a basking pigeon. Elizabeth and Elsa were jostling with each other beside her in the back of the car, whacking each other with a flat palm when they spotted a blue car on the road and sticking out their tongues at each other when they saw a brown car. Katherine's eldest daughter, Maureen, sitting in the front, was talking to her father as he drove, finding points of interest along the way. To Katherine, Maureen sounded older than her fourteen years, so amiable and agreeable was her tone, so ladylike and pleasantly curious. As her father drove, he occasionally lifted a hand off the steering wheel to point to a particular building or a stretch of land, and Maureen nodded her head and smiled politely and said that they had learned that at school, and her father said really, had they? Only when Elsa or Elizabeth stretched through the gap between the car seats to punch Maureen had she lost her composure to bark at her younger sisters and roll her eyes at them.

Katherine pressed her body against the car seat with some difficulty to adjust her position. Her skirt had crumpled up underneath her thighs and her nylons felt damp. She arched her lower back to ease Stephen's weight forward a little, being careful not to wake him, then, raising herself slightly, pulled her skirt back down to her knees.

'Everybody all right?' Her voice squeaked, as though she had forgotten how to use it. George responded with a 'Fine, thanks,' while Maureen did another little bobbing motion with her head. Elizabeth remained firmly scouring the road for blue cars, but Elsa turned to look at her mother.

'Are we nearly at Groomsport, Mummy?' Elsa smiled.

Katherine looked at her nine-year-old daughter, Elsa. Elsa was the only one of her children who looked like her. Maureen, Elizabeth, and Stephen all carried their father's swarthier complexion and his hair's blue-black sheen. To Katherine, in the squat, shadowy light of the car's interior, Elsa looked translucent, a child starved of sunlight, her creamy skin melting into the gold of her hair, and all of her features – eyes, nose, and mouth – as gently placed as butter into warm milk.

'George!' Katherine called to her husband in the front of the car, 'We're nearly there, aren't we?'

'Yes, love, another few minutes,' George addressed the clear rectangular slice of his wife in the rearview mirror, then shifted his gaze back to the road.

Katherine and Elsa gave each other a wide smile, as though they had secretly known the answer all along, and then Elsa turned quickly to stick her tongue out at Elizabeth.

'No, that wasn't a brown car.' Elizabeth shook her head.

'It was so!' Elsa replied.

'It was dark grey, or maybe purple, but it wasn't brown.'

'Mummy, wasn't that car brown?' Elsa looked to her mother, but Katherine was careful not to take sides.

'I didn't see what colour it was, pet.'

'It was brown,' Elsa insisted.

'It-wasn't-brown,' Elizabeth pronounced her words very precisely to indicate to Elsa that she was putting an end to the argument. Then with a regal glide, she turned to look out of the window again. Elsa stuck her tongue out at the back of Elizabeth's head.

As they approached the town, the car passed a long iron railing fronting a factory. Fast, fat slices of sun fell across Katherine's face, making her feel nauseous. She breathed deeply and squinted in the glare of the sunlight. 'Oh look,' she said quietly, turning her head away from the sun, 'there's a brown car!'

But no one paid any attention to her remark. Maureen and George were still chatting in the front of the car and Elsa and Elizabeth were now both engrossed in reading *Nurse Nancy and the Forgotten Parcel* from a Twinkle comic.

As though, all along, he had simply been pretending to be asleep, Stephen stirred, already pointing at something. His eyes were barely open, but he had caught sight of trees and rooftops and people, all of them worthy of his regard. He yawned and rubbed his eyes, then, pointing into the air again, he said to his mother 'Mama, mooon.'

'Where's the moon, darling? There's no moon!'

'Mooon dere,' he said emphatically, and, standing shakily on his mother's lap, pointed out of the car window.

'Does Stephen think that the moon is out, Mummy?' Elsa smiled, amused at her little brother.

'It's been all the talk of the moon landing in the house over the past few weeks.' Katherine kissed him. 'Can you see the man on the moon, my pet?' she teased Stephen affectionately. 'Is he still there?' Stephen clapped his hands gleefully against Katherine's forehead. Katherine hugged her darling boy and, rubbing her lips against his cheek, she spoke into his skin. 'And are you going to be an astronaut when you grow up and fly in a rocket to the moon?'

Stephen squealed with delight.

'No, he'll get a proper job like his father!' George remarked quickly, lifting his head to smile at Katherine in the rearview mirror.

Katherine laughed and turned back to Stephen, settling him once more on her lap.

'And will you take me to the moon with you when you go?' she whispered.

'Mooon dere!' Stephen said with a deeply earnest expression on his face. He pointed to the air again.

Elsa bent her body over toward Stephen and, moving her face close to his, said in a high, baby voice, 'There's no moon in the daytime, silly billy.' She shook her head at Stephen. 'No moon in the daytime.'

The way she pulled a face at Stephen made him laugh; his eyes became wide with delight and his laughter rippled like a warbling bird inside the car. He loved Elsa. He loved her. He wanted her to pull that face again. Elsa pulled that face. He threw his head back this time as he laughed, and Elsa laughed, too.

Maureen turned her head around from the front seat of the car to see what was going on. She couldn't help but smile.

George parked the car under a large ancient sycamore in a small concrete enclave just off the main Groomsport Road. The shade was welcome relief to Katherine.

She swung her legs out of the car and lowered Stephen onto the tarmac of the car park, where he immediately staggered into a little circular jig of excited anticipation. The three girls barrelled out of the car behind them and grabbed the bags and towels from the boot.

Groomsport – a small town of tidy streets, neat gardens, and well-scrubbed telegraph poles – was full of Union Jacks that day, for it was still the Protestant marching season in Northern Ireland. The flags hung languidly outside the shops and houses, however, as the breeze was too light to lift them. On the corner of the concrete enclave were a cluster of modest souvenir shops, the doorways of which were decorated with buckets and spades and plastic windmills tied with coloured string.

George, Katherine, and the four children followed the dusty brown path from the car park down to the beach. Banked high on either side of the path were mounds of dry marram grass, which brushed gently against their shoulders and arms as they walked.

Other digressions wound off the main path, like snail trails in a morning garden, created by eager day-trippers in their search for a private spot. A young man with untidy fairish hair moved briskly toward them along one of these smaller paths, looking down at his watch as though he were timing himself on his journey. He gently bumped against Katherine as he passed.

'Someone's in a hurry,' muttered George behind Katherine. But Katherine just smiled – it was too nice a day to complain about anything or anyone – and turned to watch the young man until he reached the car park and was gone.

From where they stood at the top of the sandbanks, the sea stretched before them like a cloth of blue jewels. Below them, a dirty spray of stones and shells echoed the gentle curve of the beach. Bunches of dank seaweed were caught between the rocks that jutted out into the sea from the flat yellow sand. The blue sky was dotted with a trail of pearly clouds that moved across it like floats in a slow parade.

Katherine had packed a flask of tea, some ham sandwiches for herself and George, and raspberry jam pieces for the children. There were also some chocolate biscuits, a small bunch of bananas, and four packets of Perri crisps. There was a bottle of diluted orange squash and some plastic cups.

George carried a bundle of blankets and towels to a spot on the beach sheltered by a modest sand dune. There were already several families farther down on the western side of the shore. A young girl in a red polka-dot swimsuit could be heard screaming 'Tom! Tom!' as she ran after a boy who was flying a blue kite. Katherine stopped to look at the two children for a moment, taking in the full sweep of the bay.

'We'll sit here, shall we? We'll get a lovely view of the bay if we sit here.'

George responded by spreading the blankets out. Katherine sat down with Stephen, who began to squirm, unsettled by the feel of the sinking soft, dry sand giving way beneath his feet.

'Get changed and go for a swim,' she said to the girls; 'then you can eat.'

Maureen, Elizabeth, and Elsa looked at the other children on the beach, who were skipping excitedly at the edge of the waves, but seemed reluctant to make a move themselves.

'Go on!' Katherine urged them.

Maureen was the first to organise herself and change into her swimsuit beneath one of the towels, slipping off her slacks and blouse, making sure no one could catch a glimpse of her underwear. Elizabeth and Elsa stood watching Maureen, as though they might glean some secret meaning or girlish code by the manner in which she undressed beneath the towel.

When Maureen was ready, Elizabeth and Elsa swiftly moved to catch up with her, until all three of them were in their black swimsuits and gingerly making their way toward the sea. Katherine watched her daughters move like three wading birds pecking at the sand with their spindly legs. A moment later, she turned to her husband.

'George, would you like some tea?'

'Yes, love.'

'Can you take Stephen for me?'

Katherine began to unpack the picnic bag, laying the sandwiches and cups on the blanket.

She poured them both a small cup of black tea, pushing George's cup into the sand beside him and then taking a quick sup from her own. They both sat silently for a moment. A light breeze shifted a thin whisper of sand around them.

Suddenly, throwing the remains of the tea from her cup into a nearby clump of beard grass, Katherine got up and, lifting her skirt, began to take off her nylons. George released Stephen gently from his hold to see if the child would stand unsupported on the soft sand. He turned and frowned a little at Katherine.

'What are you doing?'

'Going in for a swim.'

'You may want to use one of the blankets to cover yourself,' George said, turning to see if anyone was watching his wife undress.

'There's nobody looking.'

'Just for your own comfort . . .' George's voice trailed off as he reached out to catch the teetering Stephen, 'I've got you, buster,' he said, then turned to Katherine again. 'Katherine, I think you *should—*'

But Katherine ignored George. She pulled her white swimsuit quickly up over her body, fixing the straps over her shoulders, and left her clothes on the blanket as though they were the flimsy traces of a delicate skin.

Just a few steps short of the sea, Katherine stopped to look around her. The headland to the east of Groomsport bay narrowed into a slender spindle of rock, which curved in toward the shore like an arm enfolding the belly of sand. Rocky outcrops jutted here and there at its tip, reachable only when the tide was out. To the west, children could be seen searching for stickleback fish or velvet fiddler crabs in the salty pools near the small pier. The children's backs were bent, their flanks to the sun, their little plastic buckets swinging in the thin breeze.

The sea offered its familiar slide and sway of grey-blue waves, which occasionally slapped together and spurted out pieces of white foam. Mind, sea, and sky seemed all one. Katherine felt slightly revived by the sea breeze and by the quick sup of hot tea from the flask ('Nothing quenches a thirst more than a hot drink on a hot day,' she remembered her father saying).

Katherine heard Stephen calling her and looked back toward him. She watched as George lifted Stephen up into the air, up over his head into the wide blue. Stephen's limbs became rigid like the spokes of an invisible wheel. George then suddenly relaxed his arms and the child, squealing with excitement, plummeted down onto his father's chest.

Katherine looked at George and took him in, watched him for a while; then she turned and walked into the sea.

The water sliced into her, cold and invigorating.

She had always been a cautious swimmer, never quite conquering the skill of being able to put her face in under the water as she swam, never quite mastering the backstroke. But now she swam like a young girl, with sprays of seawater flying from her hair as she tossed her head purposefully from side to side. Keeping a keen eye on how far she was travelling from the shore, she soon passed out beyond her daughters as they played amid the salty waves.

A tingling rush surged through her body from the water's cold, but the impudent sun was a hot fist on her forehead. Seagulls flew above her, one of them holding a whole slice of white bread in its beak. Treading water for a moment, Katherine watched as the seagull with the bread suddenly flapped its wings to change direction, three other seagulls in hot pursuit. Katherine's eyes followed the birds as they flew toward the rocky outcrops east of the bay, where the spill of sun on the sea was like a big flat pearl.

Katherine decided to swim toward it.

Were they her daughter's squeals or the call of the seagulls on the wind? She could not tell. She swam on until she was no longer able to hear them nor to see George or Stephen on the shore.

Eventually, exhaustion caught up with Katherine and her breathlessness forced her to stop. She treaded water again, trying to gauge how far she was from the beach. A little too far out for comfort, she thought. Just a little. But look, she said to herself. Look at the sun on the sea. Listen to the lap of the water. The calm of this glassy blueness. A little bowl of paradise. She took it all in.

Closing her eyes, she lifted her face to the sun, cutting herself off. The full, hot, bright sun closing her off from everything else in the world. *I am only where the sun touches me,* she said to herself, *I exist only where the sun touches me.* She listened to the sound of the sea as it moved around her. The soft sound of the sea filled her head like music. A slow, infinite rhythm calming her, transporting her.

Then suddenly out of the deep, that great gunmetal grey head appeared beside her.

---

Now the air is charged with his absence. She cannot see the seal, but she can sense him near her. Her breathing is so sharp, it hurts her chest. She turns her head quickly from side to side. Where is he?

'Katherine! Katherine!' She hears George calling her again from the rocky outcrop. She struggles to swim toward him, making jerky movements in the sea, her breathing now taking on a frantic pace.

She spits out more seawater and tries to find her breath. Her heart thuds in her chest cold and hard, yet a traffic of hot sparks speeds through her body. She thinks of everything under the surface of the water. Just under the surface. Just right there. Any amount of things to pull her down. Ready to rise up and take her at any moment. She tries to blot out that thought, but she can't – the deep of the swollen sea beneath her opening up, revealing its great height, upon which she now hangs, down from which she might fall. The sea's great salty depths. It is *all* she can think about.

She calls out to George, but her fear reduces her voice to a small sound. She feels something against her leg. Is that the seal underneath her? Are they his breathy bubbles beside her?

She emits a cold, sharp shriek. 'Wheeeerrrree-is-heeee?'

George hurriedly pulls off his shoes and socks and hastily rolls up the ends of his trousers. 'Katherine!' he shouts to her. He slips off his leather belt. He wraps it around his hand, moving gingerly toward the edge of the rocks. The gelatinous sea algae is slippery underfoot. He spreads his toes to secure his step, but the rough, abrasive rocks that pierce the algae dig into the soles of his feet and unsteady him. He kneels down on the rocks and stretches out an arm to Katherine, leaning his upper body forward in order to give him more reach. With his free arm, he throws his belt toward Katherine. It is a thin, miserable length and will not reach her. He needs to move closer. *She* needs to move closer. But he sees that her panic is tiring her. Briefly, her face slips under the water and the top of her head becomes a smooth brown orb in the blue sea.

George quickly abandons his belt on the rocks. He crouches down, shifting his upper torso farther into the sea, as though he were edging his body through a low tunnel. Katherine's head appears up out of the water. George leans into the sea to grab her, but she is still too far away for him to reach her.

George heaves himself back up and rips off his shirt. He twists it into a rope and whips it into the sea. He turns sideways and submerges his upper body as much as he can. The cold sea bites at his chest. The jagged rocks cut his skin.

'Hold on to the shirt! Grab the shirt!' George calls to Katherine. The sea spray slaps his face. Katherine's head slips under the water again and disappears completely this time. When her head reemerges, her eyes are rolling.

The floating shirt and Katherine are only inches apart.

'Grab the shirt!' shouts George, furious at himself for not

being able to swim. This time, she seems to understand and her eyes fix on George. Her hand feebly reaches for the shirt. She finds it. Then the dark, wide head rises up out of the water beside her, disappears again. The shock awakens fresh panic in her and she pulls on the shirt. George is jerked forward but manages to cling to the edge of the rocks. He thrusts his free arm out and grabs hold of Katherine, pulling her toward him.

Katherine thrashes an arm, then a leg onto the rocks as though she were blind, but clumsily falls back into the water, scraping her legs. They begin to bleed beneath the sea. She grabs hold of George again as, this time, he flings his arm robustly around her waist. Finally he heaves her out of the water and throws his arms around her.

'I thought I'd lost you.' George hugs her. 'I couldn't see where you had gone.' He kisses the top of her head.

Katherine tries to catch her breath.

'You okay?' He keeps his arms around her.

Katherine gasps for air.

'What happened? Did something happen?' he asks her, loosening his hold on her.

Katherine breathes deeply for a moment, then coughs violently. 'I should have stayed nearer the shore,' she splutters.

'You sure you're okay?' George looks at Katherine.

Katherine nods her head a little. 'I went out too deep – that's all.' She bends her torso over to catch her breath again. 'I started to panic – I'm not as good a swimmer as I thought I was.'

'What possessed you to swim so far away from us?'

'I don't know – I'm sorry – I wasn't thinking.' Katherine clears the last of the seawater from her throat. Her body is shaking. She feels something prickling her legs. 'Oh,' she says almost casually as she looks down, 'I'm bleeding.'

'We'll get you sorted out, love.' George lifts his sopping shirt from the rocks and, wringing the seawater from it, he gently dabs Katherine's legs where they have been cut. Then he stands and brushes back her wet hair from her face. 'That could have been nasty, Katherine.'

'Oh, George! You're bleeding, too.' She touches his shoulder, where clear ribbons of seawater are infused with blood.

'It's nothing. Only a few scrapes. You sure you're all right?'

'Yes, I think so. It was the seal that panicked me.'

'The seal?'

'The seal – I was terrified he would hurt me—' Then she stops and looks into George's eyes. 'Didn't you see him?'

'No, love, I didn't.'

'Right beside me.'

'No, love – no, I didn't.'

'But he was just there—' Katherine looks out at the wide sea, then back to George. She cannot believe that he did not see the seal. She feels confused, stressed. But she is out of the water now. She's safe, thank God. Urgently, she wraps her arms around George's torso, her face turned to one side, her cheek flush with the curve of his chest. His skin icy against hers.

'He was right there,' she says quietly.

Something is happening to her. Something has happened to her in the water. She thinks of the seal's eyes.

'You're shivering,' says George. 'C'mon, let's get you warm.'

Katherine lifts her head. 'Where's Stephen?' she asks, with an urgency in her voice.

'The girls have him,' replies George reassuringly. 'He's fine.'

George reaches out and gently takes Katherine by the hand. She moves with him. They walk at a measured pace together back across the sand toward the children. A salty sea breeze begins to rise, whipping occasional strands of Katherine's hair up and across her cheek as though they are urging her on.

Out in the broad silver sea, a last flickering movement; then all is still.

'Okay, Mummy, you're out.'

Wrapped in towels in the back of the car, Katherine struggles a moment to regain her concentration on the game in hand.

'Oh, right, Elsa . . . but I haven't guessed who you are yet.'

'You were miles away, Mummy.' Elizabeth's voice is very matter-of-fact.

'I thought I had one go left.'

'No, Mummy, you don't.'

'You've used up your ten gos already,' Maureen informs her sympathetically.

'No, Mummy has one more go,' says Elizabeth.

'No, she doesn't.' Elsa makes a sharp face.

'Mama-go-dere!'

'Are you Ringo Starr?' Katherine asks.

'Mummy, you can't guess!' Elsa's temper is rising.

'Gregory Peck?'

'Let her have one more go,' chips in Maureen.

'That's not fair. And I told you, I'm *not* a singer,' Elsa says firmly.

'But you said you were singing.'

'No, I didn't *mean* singing.'

'What *did* you mean?' Elizabeth asks.

'Alan Ladd.'

'No, Mummy.'

'He never sang,' Elizabeth adds.

'I didn't *mean singing*, stupid.'

'Have manners, Elsa.' Katherine's voice sounds vacant as she straightens her back against the car seat.

'Dada dere!'

'Are you dead or alive?'

'Mummy, you asked that already.' Maureen looks out of the window.

'Did I?' Katherine shakes her head, unable to remember.

Elizabeth gives her mother a gentle reminder. 'He's alive.'

'Now that's three more gos you've had!' Elsa's cheeks flush a stubborn red.

'We saw this person on television last week in a film. He was wearing a funny hat and whistling in a train station.' Maureen is losing patience with both Elsa and her mother.

'Oh, yes – Ray Milland,' says Katherine with relief.

'Maureen, that was too much of a clue to give to Mummy!'

'It was taking her ages to guess.'

'But when you said wearing a funny hat and a train station and whistling, that just gave it away.'

'Dada dere!'

'Well – so!' Maureen turns away from Elsa.

'Oh, look,' says Katherine flatly, 'your father's back with the ice cream.'

The ice cream is recompense to the children for cutting the day short, as George is eager to get Katherine warm again and back home.

Sitting with the car window open, Katherine can hear voices travelling from the far end of the street, the way summer air seems to hold sound on a long leash. Under the canopy of the ice-cream shop, a man buys a candy floss for his daughter. Plastic buckets hanging from the shop door tap together in the breeze like dull wind chimes. The shop window still displays the front page of the *Belfast Telegraph* from almost a month ago, a large blurry black-and-white photograph of two astronauts with the words 'Footprints on the Moon' underneath it.

Katherine, not wanting any ice cream, eats one of the leftover jam pieces from the picnic bag instead. Stephen stands on his mother's lap. He holds a small dripping ice-cream cone in his hand, but his eyes are intensely fixated on the motion of his mother's tongue. He grips her arm, his mouth imitating hers, biting on nothing. Katherine scoops a small dollop of butter and jam from the bread onto her finger and pops it into his mouth.

'Mummy, my arms and legs are itchy,' says Elsa.

'Really, love?' Katherine's voice is hardly audible.

'Mummy?' Elizabeth rubs the back of her hand across her mouth as she speaks.

'Yes?'

'D'y remember when you were an opera singer before you got married?'

'Well, not a proper opera singer, Elizabeth. It was just

a hobby,' says Katherine, making an effort to engage in conversation.

'That was in the olden days, wasn't it, Mummy?' Elsa has a serious expression on her face.

Katherine smiles gently and nods her head.

'Daddy keeps telling us that you were so good that you could have done opera singing for your real job,' Elizabeth says respectfully.

'I know he does.' Katherine glances briefly over at George.

George turns around to Katherine from the front seat of the car. Unusually, his large arms are bare. His wet shirt is in a canvas bag in the boot of the car, so he wears only his vest and trousers. 'Well, that's the truth of it, isn't it?' he says to Katherine and bites on his cone.

Katherine remains silent.

'Well, why didn't you, then?' Elsa chirps.

'Sorry, love?' Katherine says quietly.

'Why didn't you do opera singing for your proper job?'

'Your mother had a family to raise.' George offers Katherine a paper napkin to wipe Stephen's face, but she refuses it with a shake of her head and uses instead the edge of her towel.

'Tell us again about the stage,' says Elizabeth.

Katherine knows how much the children enjoy the familiarity of the stories she tells about her amateur musical-theatre days, but, cold and shocked after her encounter with the seal, she now struggles to find the energy.

'Well . . . there were lots of different sets to show different places . . . there were street sellers' baskets and wooden wheelbarrows for the marketplace and—'

'But the fruit in the street sellers' baskets wasn't real fruit, was it, Mummy?' Elsa delights in the pretence of it all.

'That's right, love. It was only rolled-up paper painted to look like fruit.' Katherine continues slowly. 'And there were lots of fancy costumes and—'

'But you already had a proper job anyway,' says Elizabeth, interrupting her mother as she bites on the end of her cone.

'Oh, yes – a very exciting job as an accounting clerk in the Ulster Bank.' Katherine attempts humour. The girls smile. 'That was when I was walking out with your father, but when we got married, I had to leave.'

'"Walking out,"' Maureen repeats, laughing to herself.

'Nanny Anna said that that's how people used to talk to each other in the olden days.' Elsa takes over the conversation with an authoritative tone.

'What do you mean?' Maureen makes a disparaging face at Elsa.

'She said people didn't talk like we talk now; she said people sang everything in them days.'

Maureen starts to laugh at Elsa. 'No they didn't.'

'Yes they did!' Elsa glares at Maureen, then shoves her tongue down into the end of her ice-cream cone. Maureen starts singing in a mock operatic style, 'Can I have another ice cream please, Mother!'

Now Elizabeth begins to laugh.

'Shut up!' Elsa says sharply to her sisters, embarrassed now that she may have been fooled a little by Nanny Anna.

'Manners, Elsa,' says George.

'That didn't sound like opera singing to me,' Elsa snaps at Maureen.

'How would *you* know what opera singing sounds like anyway?' Maureen snaps back.

Conscious that Katherine is still tired and distant, George wants to lighten the tone. 'I'll have you all know, young ladies, that your mother was the finest singer the length of the Castlereagh Road!'

The three girls chime together, 'We know, we know!'

Katherine fixes the towel around her shoulders. She feels removed from all the chat in the car, as though something is pulling her away from it.

'Mummy?' Elizabeth sparks with a new thought. 'Maureen saw a plop floating in the water.'

It takes Katherine a moment. 'She saw what?'

'I did not!' Maureen is instantly annoyed that Elizabeth has mentioned this. 'It was seaweed, a lump of seaweed! I *thought* it was something else, but when I looked at it again, it was *seaweed*!' Maureen says the word *seaweed* very emphatically. She shakes her head at Elizabeth.

'But you said it was a plop. You said!'

'I only *thought* it was one, but it wasn't.' Then changing the subject quickly, Maureen says, 'Mummy, can I have a packet of crisps?'

Katherine doesn't answer.

Maureen registers her mother's solemn mood and so rummages in one of the picnic bags to get the crisps herself.

'Whose plop was it?' Elsa has apparently not followed the course of the conversation at all, her imagination having been so arrested by Elizabeth's initial image.

'It wasn't a plop. It was nobody's plop!' Maureen replies, exasperated.

'Easy girls,' George chips in. He looks at Katherine to check on her.

'Can I have a packet of crisps, too?' asks Elizabeth gently. She has clocked Maureen's reaction to their mother and now is a little concerned.

'And me,' says Elsa.

Maureen throws a packet of crisps from the picnic bag to each of her sisters.

'Wouldn't surprise me,' says George, attempting to draw Katherine out of herself. 'I've found a few things floating in there myself. Haven't I, Katherine?'

Katherine doesn't answer.

'Like what, Daddy?' Elsa becomes interested now.

'Only last summer, I went in for a swim—'

'Daddy, you can't swim,' Elsa chirps.

'Ssssh! Let daddy tell.' Maureen is beginning to doubt her own judgment about the seaweed.

'Elsa's right, he can't swim.' Elizabeth has found the little paper pouch of salt in the middle of her bag of Perri crisps and is biting it open.

'My arms and legs are really itchy,' Elsa complains to the air, scratching herself.

'—and just as I was coming back to shore, just by the shingly part of the beach, I lifted my head up out of the water and there bobbing up and down right in front of my eyes, was – a hand! You remember this story, don't you, Katherine?'

Katherine remains quiet.

'Ugh!' Maureen grimaces. Elizabeth and Elsa's expressions are held in a curious, hardened stare.

'Can you believe it,' continues George 'a hand.'

'A human hand?' asks Maureen, checking.

'Oh yes.'

'That's horrible, Daddy.'

'So, I thought that I had better get out of the water quickly and go tell the police.'

'Pl-op,' shouts Stephen.

'But just as I stood up in the sea, the fingers of the hand started to wriggle. Like this!' George moves his fingers ominously, imitating the severed hand. The three girls visibly shrink back. Their grimaces are identical now.

'I was petrified. I began to move quickly out of the water, but the hand began to move quickly, too.' George ripples his fingers. 'The hand began to quiver and turn and then it began to swim! I moved as fast as I could, but the hand was swimming after me. I got out of the water and began running up the beach. I looked around and the hand was running after me, and then suddenly the hand jumped off the sand and grabbed me like – THIS!'

George flings his wriggling hand out and grabs Elsa by the shoulder. Elsa's body jolts and then she screams. All the girls scream. Then Maureen laughs. Elizabeth shakes her arms out in front of her as if to free herself from the fright. Stephen gives a nervous cry at all the commotion, but he is comforted by

Katherine. After a few moments, the noise settles and the air in the car becomes once again a natural quiet.

George is disappointed that his story hasn't raised even a smile from Katherine, so subdued has she been since her swim. He turns to her. 'Darling, what's wrong? You okay?'

'Yes. Yes. I'm okay.' But Katherine's sense of preoccupation is growing even as she speaks to George, intensifying moment by moment.

'Maybe rest when you get home. You had a bit of a panic getting out of your depth in the water, love; it's bound to have shaken you a little. You had a bit of a shock.'

'Yes, perhaps you're right,' Katherine says. 'George?'

'Yes?'

'Are you *sure* you didn't see the seal?'

'No, love, I didn't see it. This place isn't really known for seals. Maybe it was seaweed or driftwood or something . . .'

'I love seals,' offers Elizabeth; 'they're so cute.'

'Maybe it was somebody's big gy–normous plop!' Elsa giggles.

'I don't understand it . . .' Katherine mutters to herself. 'How could you not have seen the seal? He was right in front of you . . . He was right there . . .'

'How are your legs?' George asks.

'They're still really itchy,' says Elsa.

'No, Elsa love, I wasn't talking to you. I was talking to your mother.'

Elsa frowns. George immediately registers his daughter's mood and responds to her. 'Well then. And how *are* your legs, Elsa?'

Elsa's frown tightens.

Katherine, says in a faraway voice, 'George, let's go home. I really want to go home.'

George takes her in. 'Okay, love,' he says tenderly, and starts the car. 'Everybody ready?' His voice lifts cheerily, but he receives a low groan as an answer from the children. Flicking the right indicator on, George now steers the Morris Traveller off from the side of the road, narrowly missing a passing car as he does so. He gives the horn a toot, then drives on.

Katherine shivers and adjusts the towel around her shoulders again with one hand, trying to hold Stephen with the other. Everyone in the car is quiet now. Stephen snuggles into Katherine as she lets her head rest back against the car seat.

Soon all of the children drift into their own world. George hums to himself as he drives.

Sitting wrapped in her towels, Katherine feels as though she is still in the cold, deep sea. Thoughts are lapping all around her now, stirring up from the deep, rising to the surface. Thoughts she now cannot stop. She closes her eyes. Thoughts of someone that she has blotted out throughout her married life but which – if the truth be told – have never gone away.

Thoughts of *him*.

As the Bedford family car turns the sharp bend onto the street where they live, Katherine sees Mr. McGovern standing outside his grocer's shop in his white nylon shop coat. She gives him a small wave from the back of the car. Mr. McGovern waves back to her as though he is putting up his hand at school, his arm long, his palm flat to the air.

When the car pulls to a stop in their driveway, George turns to Katherine.

'You look very pale, love.'

'I'm fine. I just feel very tired, that's all.'

George carries in the picnic bags and the blankets and asks Maureen, Elizabeth, and Elsa to help with the swimsuits and towels. Their reluctance makes them pick poorly at the items, like magpies at clumps of moss. Maureen carries one towel only, holding it disdainfully from one corner, as it is damp, sandy, and streaked in jam. Elizabeth takes only *her* swimsuit. Elsa trails the biggest towel along the ground, gathering pieces of dirt as she goes.

'C'mon, girls, smarten up there now.' George is half jovial, half annoyed. He lifts Stephen, who is chewing on a jam piece that he has found on the floor of the car, and takes him into the house. Maureen and Elizabeth answer their father with a sullen look, but their tempo remains unchanged. As they walk, they deposit thin trails of silty sand, as though they are spilling out of themselves.

Stephen heads straight for Katherine, who is standing in the kitchen, still wrapped in towels. With a piping complaint, Stephen grabs at her.

'Okay, pet, just give me a moment,' she says in a daze.

'Mama up!' Stephens pulls on Katherine as though she is a bell rope.

'Wait now.'

'Up!'

The telephone rings in the hall and Elizabeth goes to answer it. A moment later, she calls to her father, 'Daddy, it's the station!' George drops the bag he is carrying on the kitchen floor and rushes to take the telephone from Elizabeth. His work as a retained fireman makes frequent demands on his free time, a fact that has always bothered Katherine, as if – she often complains – his job as a civil engineer isn't demanding enough.

Maureen enters the kitchen, carrying a bag from the car. Katherine turns to her.

'Maureen, take Stephen for me, will you?'

Without waiting for Maureen's reply Katherine moves swiftly out of the kitchen, as though propelled by some pressing need. She passes George in the hall and goes upstairs.

'Come here to me, mister,' she hears Maureen call after Stephen.

Upstairs, Katherine walks quickly into her bedroom and closes the door behind her. Laundry has been left on the end of the bed. George's shirts are ironed and hanging on the handle of the wardrobe door. Katherine opens the wardrobe, kneels down, and, rummaging through the blankets and linen that are stored at the bottom of it, eventually pulls out a small box covered loosely with a cloth. She pulls the cloth off the box and opens it. Inside the box there is something covered in waxy paper. She opens the paper and reveals a small porcelain statuette of an old man, a needle and thread in one hand, a piece of cloth in the other. The smooth, bald head of the statuette had broken off when she had let it slip from her hands the day George was helping her move out of her mother's flat. She holds both pieces in her hand and looks at them.

As she lifts the paper in which the statuette had been wrapped, she feels the jolt it gives. She opens it out. She invites it in. It is a music sheet containing some of the music and lyrics from the opera *Carmen*. Before she sang at every rehearsal, she would take out her little handheld mirror and her lipstick from her handbag and ease orange-red across her lips. Then, folding her music sheet in half – this piece of paper in front of her – she would push it against her mouth to remove the excess. Scattered all around the page like a swarm of orange-red insects are her rosebud lipstick kisses. A sheet music full of kisses, little signals of orange-red love, each one a promise that she would nurture the spirit of her dreams until they came true. She reads: *'Si tu ne m'aimes pas, Si tu ne m'aimes pas, je t'aime; Mais si je t'aime, si je t'aime prends garde a toi!'* She looks at the bottom of the music sheet where a short translation of the lyrics is written in a very neat hand: 'Love you not me, love you not me, then I love you—' But she cannot continue reading. Her mind flashes with an image grim and disturbing. No, don't go there (and yet she feels the need to). No, not that. She blots it out.

The bedroom door opens and George steps a little into the room. 'Katherine, you should get dressed, love. You'll catch your death—' He is stopped in his tracks when he sees what Katherine is holding in her hand. He knows immediately what it is. 'That was the station—' he says to her, but he cannot hide his anxiety at what he sees.

'I gathered that,' says Katherine quietly.

'There's been a lot of trouble in the city.'

'Oh.'

'So they've called me in – I've been instructed to liaise with two other retainees before touching base.' He stands looking at Katherine. 'Please, Katherine, don't . . . please. Let it go.'

Katherine looks at George, her eyes now filling up with tears.

'No, don't, Katherine . . . please . . . I can't . . .'

The telephone rings again. George turns away from Katherine and leaves the room to answer it.

Katherine gathers herself up off the floor, not bothering to put away the porcelain statuette or the music sheet. She blindly follows after George. She catches up with him in the hall.

'What time will you be back?' she asks him solemnly.

George puts the telephone down and looks at Katherine. 'I've no idea. I won't know how bad things are until I get there.' He walks into the kitchen. Katherine follows him.

'But they'll be able to tell you at the station, won't they? They'll be able to brief you before you go?' she says.

'Katherine, you know only too well it's not that simple.'

'Do I?' Katherine's tone is harsh.

'Yes, you do!' George glares at Katherine. Then, checking himself, he lowers his head. He pushes past Katherine to get the car keys from the kitchen table.

'And why do you have to liaise with two other retainees?' Katherine pursues George, her tone becoming more strident. 'When did this start?'

'Any uniform's a target now! Aren't you aware of what's going on?' He grabs the keys.

'But there's always trouble around this time of year,' she snaps. 'Always trouble around the Orange marches – and then all that trouble with the Apprentice Boys' parade in Derry – you just expect it.' She's almost shouting at him now.

'This is different – something's building. I don't know – it's – it's very tense in the city.' Georges tries to steady himself.

'You're overreacting, George! It'll all blow over as usual and we'll all be back to complaining about the unemployment and the weather and—'

'How the hell do you know!' George barks at Katherine, pushing past her toward the front door.

Suddenly, Stephen walks into the corner of the kitchen table with a wallop. After a moment of silence – the air heavy with what is to come and his mouth having fallen open like that of a drowning fish – he pitches into his cry. Katherine lifts him up in her arms, rubbing and kissing his head. His cry is piercing and he squeezes his eyes tightly at the unfairness of it all, making two deep, wet creases around his mouth, as though it is melting with saliva.

'So what time will you be back?' Katherine follows George, Stephen in her arms.

'I told you, I've no idea.' George strains to talk over Stephen. 'Let me see the situation first – see how many of us have been called – I don't know.' He addresses Katherine over his shoulder as he moves. Katherine pursues him back out into the hall and stands in front of him.

'Then you'll ring me.' Katherine is biting at her words now.

'If I'm near a damn telephone!'

'Of course you'll be near a *damn telephone,* George. You'll have to be in contact with the station. You'll—'

'Mum!' Maureen calls from upstairs. 'Elsa's not feeling well.'

Stephen is still crying. He is feeding off the energy around him. The pitch of his cry is getting higher.

'Mum!'

'Wait!' Katherine shouts up to Maureen over the crying.

'Don't just walk off like that!' she shouts at George now. George stops.

'"Walk off?"' He repeats her words sharply. Then he turns squarely to Katherine. His face is hard, incredulous.

'Don't just walk off without—' Katherine is becoming increasingly agitated. 'Don't just walk off like that George – don't!' Her words, like her thoughts, are fragmenting now.

George turns away from Katherine. His lips are tight with anger. He says nothing. Katherine persists.

'George!'

George turns to Katherine and thrusts his head in toward her, the blood draining from his face.

'What exactly do you expect of me, Katherine? What exactly is it that you want from me? How exactly do I disappoint you?'

It all comes out in a rush. There is a moment's silence. Katherine looks startled.

'What? What do you mean, George?'

George holds his look at Katherine; then, almost immediately, he moves away from her again. 'Nothing, I mean nothing. It's nothing.'

'George, don't say that. Talk to me!'

George opens the front door.

'Mum!'

'George, come back! Don't walk away from me like that! Talk to me!' Katherine moves quickly onto the front steps.

'Mum – Elsa feels sick.'

'All right!' Katherine snaps at Maureen. 'George!' She moves down the steps. Stephen is still crying in her arms. 'George, what do you mean?'

George turns abruptly to Katherine, 'You *know* what I bloody mean!'

Katherine stops and looks at George. She says nothing.

George holds a hard stare. 'You know *exactly* what I bloody mean!'

He swings away from Katherine and, opening the car door, adds between gritted teeth, 'And I have a bloody job to do!'

Stephen is pulling at Katherine. His back is arched and his head is thrown back. His face is red. He is crying to the sky.

'George,' Katherine says quietly, and watches as he drives away.

Slowly, she walks back into the kitchen with Stephen's body squirming on her hip. He kneads his tiny fists into his eyes as though he were rubbing them out. He flings his head on Katherine's shoulder again, a sleepy, sad cygnet tired of holding his height.

It was true that the very life events that should have brought Katherine and George closer together as a couple seemed to have edged them further apart.

Katherine remembers that even on their wedding day, a pensiveness had followed them like a dust breeze at their backs, creating around them the sound of an almost-detectable pulse. She remembers the church small and quaint, like a doll's house. There were lilies in wide vases, settled in their symmetry, giving out a creamy, heady scent. There was the smell of frankincense and myrrh. There were white ribbons on the ends of the pews. Six tall candles graced the altar. As she walked up the aisle, the congregation passed their coughs along the pews as if passing a collection basket. She wore two rows of neat pearls around the lace neckline of her white silk wedding dress. George waited at the altar for her, shifting nervously from foot to foot. The priest had the pink glossiness of a skin not used to daylight.

At the reception afterward, they danced together as tentatively as they had danced the first night they had met at the Belfast Palais de Danse, introduced to each other on the grand staircase by a mutual friend, who then fled to recover a dropped glove by the circling glass doors. But, by the end of their wedding day, it had felt as though they were still waiting for the wonderful thing to happen.

Ever since Katherine had known George, he had always exuded a sullen determination in the way in which he approached things – a sense that life was a series of tasks that had to be done. This trait in him she had found attractive when they first met, as though it offered her stability and reassurance. However, since their honeymoon, she had noticed that there was a different edge to his determination. There was a darker, more destructive quality to it.

Katherine remembers the evening they moved into their new house (this small semidetached two-bedroom house in which they have lived now for fifteen years). George had walked out to the back of the property, brimming with new purpose, taking in the unfamiliar surroundings with a deep breath, and rolling his shirtsleeves up to his elbows. But, ten minutes later, he had returned to the kitchen full of irritation. With his shoulders hunched and his brow furrowed, he had pulled roughly at the stacked cardboard boxes in the hallway, tripping over a rolled-up offcut of linoleum that they had purchased for the new house, and had then stomped back out to the garden with a large spade clutched firmly in his hand. Katherine had followed him, and had found him savagely hammering the back lawn with the edge of the spade.

'It's full of fucking turnips!' he had said, glaring at her red-faced, as though it had somehow been her fault that he had found them. 'There must be hundreds of them!'

'Surely not hundreds,' she remembers saying, but George could not be humoured.

'I'll have to grow a bloody new lawn from seed,' he had muttered through jagged breaths, and then had resumed his frantic digging. He had stayed out all evening, until the last lip of daylight had slipped into dusk, and had then worked on into the night. She had called him to come in to eat, but George had insisted he stay outside and dig. So she ate alone.

The rest of the evening was spent quietly unpacking and placing their shared things about the house. In the back room of the house (which opens out into, and is really part of, the kitchen), she installed the two-bar electric fire that had been given to them by her mother, plugging it in to test if it still worked – why wouldn't it? The little fan whirred above the red bulb and made the light flicker through the scratched painted coal shapes (it was all pretend) and released the smell of heated dust into the evening air. Across the back of the brown leatherette sofa, which they had picked up from a secondhand furniture shop three days before, she placed a grey woollen throw with mint green edges. It slid off the sofa immediately, as easily as syrup off a hot spoon (as she had predicted it would – she remembers having made a mental note to sort it out; she had yet to get around to it). On the brown linoleum, which had been included in the price of the house, she placed a rug with regular little patterns of green-yellow flowers caught in serrated borders of crimson and blue. With some effort, she hung the long, heavy drapes, which she had made herself, either side of the back door, covering its glass with a milky net curtain. The drapes would come in useful for the winter – she realised she was a little ahead of herself hanging them in summer – and she fussed over their tidiness so that they fell on either side of the door like two long pillars of burned honey.

On the mantelpiece above the electric fire she placed a favourite and edge-worn photograph of herself with her father in Tollymore Forest, a place they had regularly visited on holiday when she was a child. Beside it she put an ever so slightly out-of-focus photograph of herself and George on their honeymoon in Mexico. Under a Latin American sun, they stood together, George's arm placed awkwardly around her shoulders. Their flimsy salt white straw sombreros were pushed back a little on their heads, so that they squinted into the new light with an embarrassed awe.

Finally, after checking that George's supper was still warm enough, she unpacked a sheet and two blankets and, leaving a light on in the kitchen, took herself up to their cold new bed and lay listening to the *thwat-thwat-thwat* of the garden spade outside, wishing that the first evening in their new home together had held a little more tenderness.

And the turnips kept coming. Just when George thought he had dug up the last of them, more would appear like stubborn, blank, disembodied heads. They forced their way up through the lawn and flagged their long, slender turnip tops. To her, the turnips were an unexpected harvest, and whether they were boiled, roasted, diced, or mashed, she made sure that every one of them was eaten. 'Think of the starving black babies of Africa,' she would say to George as she handed out yet more bowlfuls of turnip.

After many seasons of frenzied digging, the reluctant turnips disappeared, leaving the soil dry-brown and broken. Yet George, for months after, would stalk the garden, head low, like some horticultural vigilante, eyes intent on finding just one more, finding the one he had missed, ready with his spade. She would stand watching him from the kitchen window, see the sweat break out across his forehead and down his temples. He would walk slowly across the stunted earth as though he were trying to stalk and kill something. Buried things that he needed to unearth and destroy. Buried things that he needed to empty himself of. Too many buried things.

In time, the garden became theirs and the grass grew back without George's having to sow one single seed. It gracefully became a verdant cradle for their young children, Maureen and Elizabeth, where on summer afternoons they would sometimes be found among the long and tender new blades, curled, baby-fleshed, asleep, like soft blackberries having fallen from the bush. Katherine had often said that she would have made pies from them and eaten them. And George had seemed more at ease, more sure of his step. Becoming a father had been good for him, Katherine had thought. Since Maureen and Elizabeth had been born, he had been happier.

It was when Elsa was born, however, that she saw George's irascibility rise again. More intensely this time. Perhaps because Elsa was born at home, perhaps because of that, she kept telling herself, George had appeared more vunerable and had begun to behave as though he believed that the whole house was under siege.

Outside the window of the bedroom, where she was in labour with Elsa, bees had made a hive. With the impending birth, the busyness of the bees had barely been noticed. But that evening, as contractions began and she felt herself opening, as a freshly healed wound might be opened, reopened, accidentally, irreversibly, the bees night-gathered. She felt the impending force of her baby's descent as a thousand honey-laden bees hummed a melodious and rhythmical welcome song, a droning lullaby for the buttery baby. Daylight had soberly nudged its way in and Elsa was born. George had stood at the bedside of mother and baby as though he were a visitor in his own house, respectful and distant, his tender attention tempered by puzzlement that he could father a child so fair, so golden.

After the birth – her thighs blood-streaked and purposeless from the long labour – Katherine had wept from exhaustion and joy and had kissed the blue-hued skin of her pointy-headed baby. But George, it seemed, could only worry about the bees.

'The bees have to be killed; the hive has to be destroyed,' George had announced with a defiant anger.

'Bees? What bees?' Katherine had said, holding their new baby, the cadences of labour still fresh and warm.

And so the bee killer had been called in to smoke the bees out, a little man in a big hat. 'I'll put on my bee suit for protection,' the man had said to George like a child reading aloud, as though, in a final act of courtesy, he himself dressed up as a bee to do the deed.

For weeks after Elsa's birth, dead bees could be found all over the house, singular, sad, furry, redundant cases. Their still wings a thin transparent film, the colour of gently caramelized onion. Light, dried bodies semaphorically cut short and with the quietness of their purpose frozen. They lay around the house in corners, behind cupboards, reminders of a cruel and unnecessary demise. Some were even found outside, scattered by the fuchsia bush that grew by the coal shed. Under the cardinal purses of sickly nectar, they were little dark dots of death.

By eight o'clock, Stephen is settled and Maureen and Elizabeth have their faces washed, their teeth brushed, and are clambering willingly into bed. The paper blind in their bedroom is pulled closed, but the curtains are left open so they can still see in the milky evening light without having to turn on their bedside lamp.

Unusually, no decade of the Rosary is said that evening. Katherine has seen clearly, despite the curtailment of the picnic, how tired the day has made them all. She herself feels curiously emptied.

Before she goes in to say good night to the girls, Katherine slips into her own bedroom, taking care not to wake Stephen, who is fast asleep in his cot in the corner of the room. She tidies away the towels and her white swimsuit, which she had left on the floor (she had had to find her warmest clothes to wear, so chilly had she felt since her swim). She kneels and picks up the broken pieces of the statuette, which are still lying by the wardrobe, and wraps them in the paper that has the lyrics from *Carmen* written on it. She places the paper parcel back inside the box and she covers the box with the cloth. She places it deep in at the back of the wardrobe and closes the wardrobe door. But this time, the statuette doesn't feel hidden enough. It still feels visible. Present. If she had a key for the wardrobe door, she would lock it. Keeping everything in. Layer upon layer. Skin upon skin.

Katherine goes in to kiss Maureen and Elizabeth good night, their bodies heavy now with approaching sleep. Then she turns to Elsa.

After George had left for the station, Katherine had found Elsa lying on top of her blankets in bed like a small sea animal exposed by a departing tide. Elsa had said she felt nauseous and dizzy. Katherine had placed a glass of water by Elsa's bedside table.

Now she sits Elsa up in the bed and brings the glass of water to her lips.

Elsa wants to sleep, but the heat of her body is keeping her awake. Her own skin has hidden it from her until now, and now it is sheer intensity. The delay of sunburn, how it fools us. Katherine cannot believe how burned Elsa's body is. The back of her limbs and torso are still white, but the front of her body is an increasing red. Katherine helps Elsa stretch back out on top of the blankets, a rubric in her white cotton vest and pants, as though she is an offering to the gods. Elsa's arms and legs are splayed in her effort to avoid them making contact. She feels her skin might split and crack in the bends of her arms and around her knees. Nothing is turning down the temperature of her veins. Even the air above and around her body is rippling and eddying like a mirage, shimmering purls of hot air. She is a road on a hot day, giving it all back. *Make it stop, Mummy, Please, make it stop.*

But all Katherine can do for Elsa is to give her skin a momentary distraction. Katherine dabs clumps of cotton wool soaked in calamine lotion along the length of Elsa's arms and legs and across her throat and chest. The cotton wool has drunk the lotion in and is loath to share. Elsa's red skin is becoming patchy. She looks like an Indian fakir, her body caked in chalky paint.

Elsa does not say too much; her voice has lost its pace. And so the bedroom is quiet, as though it is the quietness that heals, and maybe it is. The delicacy of the child's downward gaze, the glassiness of her stare, her body preoccupied with her burning skin. The sun has altered her, making her a peculiar child, and now, as it dips in the pearly evening sky, her skin has ignited in its absence. Poor Elsa, Katherine thinks. It's her fair skin; it's her golden hair. Maureen, Elizabeth, and Stephen – none of them got burned by the sun.

'How did you get so burned, pet?' asks Katherine.

'When you went swimming, I pretended I was a starfish. I lay in the sand, waiting for you to come back. I wanted you to see me.'

'Oh, Elsa.'

'But you were ages – Daddy was worried.'

'I'm so sorry, love.'

Katherine sits beside Elsa, as she does not sleep. They are quiet and still together again. Elsa gradually calms as Katherine gently strokes her hair.

'Mummy? . . . Mummy?' Elsa's voice croaks.

'What is it, love?' Katherine replies, slowly turning her head to Elsa.

'Can I have some more lotion?'

'Of course . . . here, pet.' Katherine pours the calamine lotion onto a fresh clump of cotton wool and presses it gently against Elsa's skin. The simple action brings Elsa relief. Katherine looks at her daughter and smiles at her. Elsa's face is immobile, as though it is a fake face and she is just looking out of it, and she does not smile back. Perhaps, Katherine thinks, she could distract Elsa a little more with some easy conversation. Perhaps she could even distract herself after the strange day she's had.

'Do you know what you remind me of, Elsa?'

'What?' Elsa replies.

'You remind me of the way, when I was little, I used to wait and watch for moths in the garden of our old house.'

Elsa casts her eyes up to look at her mother. Katherine continues to dab the wet lotion-soaked cotton wool against Elsa's skin.

'Well – it was a patch of grass beyond the garden of the old house, the one we had before we lived over the chip shop. I would sneak out there at night in the summertime when everyone else had gone to bed. I don't know how I heard about the moths, how I knew they might be there. I think I remember my mother telling me that they were attracted to the plants that grew among the grasses there – the nicotiana, honeysuckle, the night-scented stock . . .'

Katherine's voice, though tender, has a settled, dark quality to it. She places her hand gently on Elsa's forehead. 'Anyway, I remember the first time I saw them, I couldn't believe it . . .' Katherine takes a deep breath. 'Oh, they were beautiful, so they were, Elsa. Pure-white moths rising and falling above the grass, as if they were dancing, moving toward me, hovering over me. I remember lying down in the grass on my back in my white nightdress – just like you are now, just in the same shape that you're making. I somehow believed I would be irresistible to them, that I could trap them, as though I were a light in the dusk.'

Katherine brushes her hand over Elsa's hair.

'And sometimes, believe it or not, they would actually settle on me; one or two of them, maybe more, they would settle on me if I kept really still. And then I would tilt my head up to look at them, but their white wings would blend into the white of my nightdress, so that it looked as though we were all the same. Then suddenly they would fly away from me, up above me again.'

'We learned at school that moths are moths because they shed their old skin.' Elsa's voice sounds gravelly. 'That there's a new them hiding inside a little case that comes out when it's ready.

Meta-mor-phosis is what it's called. We learned that from Sister Marion.' Elsa seems pleased with herself for remembering what she had learned in biology class.

'Yes, love, yes, that's right,' Katherine says gently.

'Maybe I'm having meta-mor-phosis right now, Mummy. Maybe I'll get a new skin.' Elsa attempts a little smile, but it hurts.

'I've no doubts, Elsa. Your sunburn will be sore for a little while, but then it'll get better.' Katherine strokes Elsa's hair again. She can now feel a dark swell rising within her. 'And d'ye know, pet, one night a whole swarm of moths came; a whole swarm of pure-white moths covered me from head to toe. I couldn't believe it. I remember thinking, This must be what it feels like to be in Heaven.' Katherine's voice falls almost to a whisper. She turns and dips her head to look at Elsa. 'My mother scolded me for lying in the damp grass in my nightdress . . . but my father said I must be very special for that to have happened, for me to have seen so many of them, for them to have covered me like that. He called them "ghost moths." He said that some people believed that ghost moths were the souls of the dead waiting to be caught, and some people believed that they were only moths.'

'And what did you believe?' Elsa stares at her mother, eager to hear what she has to say.

But Katherine does not answer. Ever since her encounter in the cold sea that day, the thoughts of *him* have continued to grow with every hour. Memories flooding through her veins like an electric river. Something she cannot seem to stop. A searing, biddable tide flowing through every part of her, gathering force and pushing her to the edge of a precipice.

# 2

*August 1949*

HER APPOINTMENT WITH HIM that night had been an impromptu one. There was the understanding, made clearly by Mr. Boyne's secretary, that any appointment for a costume fitting for any of the drama or musical groups rehearsing had to be scheduled in as and when the tailors' rooms were available, either outside of regular business hours or when a last-minute cancellation might arise. In fact, there was a notice clearly stating this on the rehearsal room door. And so when Katherine had been informed of her fitting by a slightly flustered stage manager, she was told to go immediately.

Boyne & Son, Men's Tailors and Outfitters, occupied part of what had at one time been a large Edwardian house on High Street in Belfast. The building had been acquired by Mr. Boyne, whose tailoring business now occupied two of its four floors – the cutting and fitting rooms on the second floor, his own office on the first. The third floor he sublet as a rehearsal room throughout the year and that was where Katherine had been rehearsing *Carmen* with the Rutherford Musical and Dramatic Society, which next month they were to present at St. Anne's Church Hall for four performances only. On the ground floor at the back of the building was an accountancy firm and at the front was a photographer's studio.

Katherine made her way down the stairs from the rehearsal room to the tailors' rooms. As she rapped the ribbed glass panel of the door with her knuckles, it shuddered with a loose twanging sound. The door was opened almost immediately by a grey-haired, powdery stick of a woman, whom Katherine assumed to be Mr. Boyne's secretary. The woman indicated a door on the other side of the room to Katherine and then turned to the large record book at her desk without a word.

Katherine made her way through the line of young tailors as they worked fastidiously at their sewing and loosening and cutting. At the end of the room, she passed a young woman, barely in her twenties, sitting with her back to the tailors, her hair clipped, tucked, and netted. The hard chair on which the young woman sat was either too low to allow her to work comfortably at her table or the table was too high, for she was perched on top of four large leather-bound ledgers. The young woman wore a biscuit-coloured blouse with an ivy pattern on it and sat so still in her dedicated accounting and leather-warming duties that it seemed that the ivy had grown on her while she sat. As though it had wound its way along the barren floors, creeping up the walls, where years of pulverous submission could be found nesting in every tongue and groove, and had wrapped itself around her. The stillness of her body belied the furious activity of her hand, which moved with such speed and evenness across the page that Katherine wondered what on earth the young woman could be writing. Was she documenting every single move that every tailor made at every moment in the room? A stenographer mother hen upon her roost? Assimilating each detail without her even having to lift her head? Was the young woman's intent to do the right thing and at the end of every day to take the ledgers to Mr. Boyne for his inspection? To allow him to see – as he ran his sweat-tipped fingers over the recently vacated surface of each leather-bound ledger – that everyone was working as they should be, that all was present and correct, that he was right to look so satisfied with his business?

Katherine reached the door that the grey-haired woman had indicated to her and pushed it open, moving to stand just inside the door frame. It was darker in this anteroom than the room from which she had come, but her eyes adjusted quickly.

A tailor was sitting at the worktable at the far end of the room. His head was bowed over a logbook and his shoulders were slouched. His right arm was bent, his elbow placed on the table, his head resting on his softly folded fist, his shortish fair hair sticking up untidily. His other arm was hanging loosely by his side. His table lamp was the only source of light, casting rich coppery shadows around the room.

Katherine coughed in an attempt to distract him from his work. When that failed to get his attention, she offered a cautious 'Excuse me,' but still he did not move to address her. She stood in the doorway of the room for at least thirty or forty seconds before he eventually lifted his head up off his hand. He looked at her with a curious, solemn intensity, as if he were concentrating on something else entirely, as if he were trying to retrieve the detail of something lost. His eyes wandered lazily from her and moved slowly to the space behind her.

Moments passed before the tailor visibly roused himself and turned his head to look around him, to where a clue might lurk as to the nature and purpose of this woman who had appeared in the room. Katherine noticed how his hair was dishevelled only on one side of his head. His hair on the other side was perfectly neat. There was also a deep red mark across his cheekbone, stretching down to the cusp of his jaw. It dawned on her then that he had been sleeping – his head on his hand – and that she had woken him by her presence in the room.

With a quick intake of breath he said, 'Yes,' not as a question as to why she should be standing there in front of him but as confirmation that he was remembering his appointment, gradually. He stood up from his worktable and made his way over to a chestnut cabinet on which were stacked boxes of ribbons and rolls of lining and fabric. His shoelaces were untied, as though he had intended to slip off his shoes before sleep had overtaken him. His trousers were creased around his calves. He pulled open the top drawer of the cabinet and took out a small black notebook that had two long black ribbons attached to its spine. Katherine chanced conversation,

'I'm Katherine Fallon. I'm here for the fitting.'

'You are,' he said simply. He turned to her. His movements toward her were full of the effort of efficiency now that she had woken him from his sleep. His disorientation had made a boy of him.

'If it's a bad time, I can always come back,' she said.

'No, that won't be necessary.'

The tailor didn't wear his measuring tape around his neck, as seemed customary with the other tailors, but instead took out of his trouser pocket a small tan leather case. He bent his knees and knelt at her feet. Without measuring anything for a moment, he opened his small black notebook, which he then placed on the floor beside him, and glanced at his notes. Quietly, he stretched out his tape measure in front of her as though she were a foreign visitor to his country and he were offering her a welcome garland.

'Rehearsals going well?' He looked up. He appeared almost doleful to her from where he sat hunkered, still like a boy, still wearing the asymmetry of his sleep on his face, in his eyes, in his hair. He smiled tentatively at her. It was difficult for Katherine to judge exactly what age he was. She guessed that he was perhaps in his late twenties, but that youthful, boyish quality of his could well be making him appear younger than he was – she was not sure. He gently raised the tape measure to her waist. She automatically lifted both her arms upward and outward a little.

'Oh fine.' She felt her initial flush of giddiness wane, and the very brief conversation between them came to a halt.

The clock in the far corner of the room ticked. The tailor stretched his hand around her waist to catch the tape measure in his left hand. He pulled the tape measure gently, teasing it from the small tan box that housed it. The back of his left hand brushed ever so lightly against her hip. The tailor conveyed, she thought, none of the impatience that some of the seamstresses in the past had shown her at similar fittings for other shows, nor none of the rudeness that one particular senior tailor had displayed to her by merely looking at her coldly over the top of his pinze-nez and flicking scant figures into the large book spread out before him like a dissected animal on a labouratory slab.

The tailor checked the markings on the tape and, releasing it, sat back and noted the measurements in his small black notebook with his left hand, so that as he wrote, his hand slowly swallowed the ciphers of her shape. He rose from his sitting position and, lifting the tape measure, encircled her hips, taking particular care not to pull the tape too tightly. He then measured her waist to her hip and jotted both measurements down in the black notebook.

'Could you please face away from me,' the tailor said quietly.

The wall to which she turned was covered with designers' drawings of costumes from different dramatic productions; *Othello, La Bohème, Troilus and Cressida, La Traviata.* Various certificates lined the wall, including one from the Royal Academy of Tailors' Association, which said on it 'Award of Excellence.' To the right of these, beside the chestnut cabinet, there were spools of thread on small shelves, wound and waiting, colours as varied and rich as ripe fruit – purple, blue, damson. These spools, side by side, were already a tapestry. Boxes of buttons were stacked along a higher shelf, numbered randomly in black ink. Some of the boxes had been torn open, revealing tiny landslides of navy satin circles and round nut-coloured shapes. One box revealed a spill of checkered red buttons, each one with a painted cornflower on its surface, the blue delicately and exquisitely speckled with pink and maroon. They were like drops of meadow in a tweed red prairie.

Then sweeping back her hair a little, and revealing to the world her pale, undiscovered skin, the tailor measured her from the base of her neck to the centre of her back. She felt the nub of pressure from his fingers against her spine. His touch was as light as a barely spoken prayer. But the more still she was, the more intense it felt. In response, her breath released itself in a loud sigh – she could not help it. Out of her embarrassment, she quickly turned her head to look somewhere else, anywhere else in the room. Over the chestnut cabinet there was a framed newspaper clipping containing a photograph of Princess

Elizabeth on her visit to Northern Ireland in 1946. The princess was shaking the hand of a woman in a bonnet, a bonnet so simple that it was just a black-and-white arc around her face, its black ribbon elegantly tied under her chin. The princess had an uncertain smile. The woman in the bonnet looked at the camera with a soft intent. The woman in the bonnet seemed to be looking straight at Katherine. Katherine concentrated hard on each and every detail of the newspaper clipping as she felt the tailor's hand move once again across her neck. She slowly became aware that her arms were still held upward and outward, as if waiting for him to return to her waist, as if offering herself. She lowered both arms, but no sooner had she done so than he raised both of her arms up again, gently placing his thumb and index finger on each side of her wrists. This time as she held her arms out, they began to tremble a little. She stayed as still as she could, staring at the picture of the woman in the bonnet.

'Who is the lady in the photograph?' she asked quickly, her own voice startling her a little in the quiet room. 'The lady shaking the princess's hand?'

'I've no idea,' the tailor said simply. 'I put the clipping up there because I like her hat. That's a great hat she's wearing, don't you think?'

Katherine stared at the clipping again but felt too flustered to determine whether it was a great hat or not. As she stared at the photograph, the tailor walked around in front of her and circled the tape measure around her back and under the swell of her upper arms; the slick of the tape grazed her left breast. His face was very close to hers. The smell of cedarwood, almonds.

'I would have called that a bonnet,' Katherine said, not looking at him.

'Pardon me?'

'Her hat – I would have called her hat a bonnet.' Katherine glanced up at the tailor. He smiled at her.

'Would you now?' he said.

She turned her head away from him and looked over again at the spools of thread, feeling a small pulse of adrenaline course through her. The clock ticked and the tailor continued to gather her piece by piece, placing one end of his tape measure in the centre of her lower back and pulling it down to the floor, then measuring her from her waist down to her knee. He stood in front of her and stretched the measuring tape from her right shoulder to her left. Then as he moved behind her to measure the full width of her back, he put his lips very close to her ear and said almost in a whisper, 'By the way, Miss Fallon, you woke me from a very deep sleep.'

A week later, she was running up the stairs of Mr. Boyne's premises, flushed and breathless. Window-shopping on her way to rehearsals, she had lost track of time and was now late. The clack of her heels echoed around the empty stairwell. Everyone else, she assumed, was already in the rehearsal room. Just as she approached the third return, she looked up and saw the tailor coming down the stairs toward her. She did not think of stopping but could feel her heart suddenly banging in her chest. It was all the running, she thought to herself, and climbing all the stairs so quickly; it was all the running and climbing that had made her heart beat so fast.

She went to squeeze past him and was willing to offer him a perfunctory 'Good evening' when she realised that she could not move, for the tailor had blocked her way. One of his hands rested on the balustrade; the other hand's palm was spread flat against the wall. His body was angled a little, as though to let her past, but he was not giving her enough room to do so.

'Miss Fallon,' he said softly. She lifted her eyes to look at him. 'I'm sorry,' he continued. He was staring at her intently. 'I'm Thomas McKinley . . . Tom . . . I should have introduced myself at our first fitting.' He reached out to shake her hand in a gauche, almost childlike manner. She automatically responded, shaking his hand and feeling the warm, wide expanse of his palm. Wondering how such hands, such large hands did such precise and delicate work, pinning, threading, sewing.

'Tom,' she repeated quietly, her heart still thudding in her chest, 'I'm Katherine.'

'Yes, I know your name. I have it written down in my black notebook under "*Carmen*."'

Despite only staggered pools of light on the stairwell, she held Tom McKinley's gaze more firmly now than when they had first met in the tailors' rooms. Now, his fair hair was neater, his eyes a brighter blue, his complexion fresher. Katherine noticed how his smile widened his features with a keen grace. She pulled her hand from his; in the strange configuration their bodies had created on the stairs, their handshake felt to her both puerile and slightly desperate.

Tom McKinley placed the hand he had just offered to her back on the wall beside him and spread it slowly. He did not move otherwise. Was it the air in the stairwell that felt tense and thick with heat, she wondered, or just the air within her lungs? She felt her cheeks reddening as her thoughts raced. In the ghostly light, his body cast a broad, featureless shadow of swollen blues on the wall behind him. As she stood close to and a little below him, her shadow was completely immersed in his, so that she could no longer see what mark she made on the world. What made him stay so long and so close to her?

She looked up at Tom. The way he looked back at her, she felt, was as though he was already well familiar with her and perhaps, having stolen her every measurement at their first meeting, he was. And perhaps, for all she knew, he reassembled her over and over again in the privacy of the tailors' rooms, when the starless evenings had sent all the junior tailors home and the world had become a quiet black.

'It's bad luck to cross on the stairs.' Tom smiled at her as he spoke.

'Oh really, is it? I didn't know.'

Noises could be heard coming from the rehearsal room above them, the sound of chairs scraping along the wooden floor, the rumble of a baritone, the occasional high piping, dissenting sound of a female voice, but not enough to disturb this curious encounter.

'So . . . what should we do?' She was surprised at how nervous she felt.

Tom took his time to answer her. 'Just stay here, I suppose.'

'Yes, I suppose.' She could feel her blood pumping through her veins. 'Or . . .' she continued, trying to appear matter-of-fact, 'you could walk back up the stairs and wait, or I could walk down the stairs and I could wait and then you could go back up . . .' Her words drifted. Tom moved his face a little closer to hers.

'I'll walk with you Katherine,' he said gently.

They did not pull away from each other, but stayed in the soft, dark nearness, his face moving even closer. Their breath was mingling in the perfumed heat that now existed between them. Doubt coursed through her veins in hot flux.

'So,' Tom whispered tenderly, and he waited.

Suddenly, the door of the rehearsal room above them opened and the sound of voices spilled down the stairwell toward them. Footsteps could be heard on the stairs. As though guilty of a crime, Katherine reacted by clumsily pushing up into Tom in an attempt to move past him. He made no effort to make the passage any easier for her. On the contrary, as though out of his solicitude, he took some furtive pleasure in witnessing the tight swell of panic he saw rising within her and he placed his leg squarely and firmly on the step above her, widening his stance to curtail her movement. She continued regardless with an inappropriate and edgy determination and attempted to squeeze her body through the tiny gap that remained between Tom and the balustrade, placing her two hands on his chest and pushing herself against him. She made her way up the stairs and didn't look back.

On the night of the second costume fitting for *Carmen*, Katherine watched as Tom placed his hands on the costume templates on the table as though picturing their final arrangement and then lifted his head to look at her. He held his gaze on her. Had he scanned her body with his eyes, she would have assumed that he was, in fact, imagining her wearing the finished costume, assessing it, criticising it. But his eyes rested only on her face. Just as it seemed he was about to say something to her, a junior tailor came into the room, loped straight over to the worktable and began inserting pins into the pieces of fabric.

The young tailor turned to Katherine and asked her to remove her jacket, which he then proceeded to hang on the coatrack by the door. He lifted the costume templates from the table and placed them over her blouse and across her upper body. He pinned two or three of the pieces together, which appeared to form the basque of the costume, and then, unfolding a larger piece of cotton, asked her to step into it and to pull it up to her waist. This was the section that would form the skirt. She slipped off her shoes and stepped into the mock-up, taking care not to loosen the tacking. The young tailor worked away pinning and adjusting the material around her body while Tom watched. Even with her head lowered, Katherine could sense his eyes burning into her.

When the mock-up costume had been fitted, albeit loosely, the young tailor stepped back to wait for the assessment from his senior.

A moment or two passed before Tom spoke. 'Now, the sleeves, Mr. Agnew. They mustn't be too tight, too restricting, so make sure that when they're attached that you leave room without losing the line.' Tom's voice was animated as he stepped toward her. 'The bodice needs reshaping just there for the skirt to flare out more at this point.' Here, Tom used his hands to indicate to Mr. Agnew exactly how and where the material should be gathered and contoured at Katherine's waist. Then Tom knelt down at Katherine's feet to examine the length of the skirt. 'Bring the hem of the skirt to mid-calf. We can get a proper sense of that later when we have the shoes, and' – he stood up again—'now the overskirt – the overskirt should fall no lower than here.' Again he indicated what he wanted to Mr. Agnew by placing his hands on the cotton material and pulling it close against Katherine's legs. Tom's hands brushed against her stockings and this time stayed awhile. Katherine felt a tender chill.

Mr. Agnew nodded silently.

Tom continued. 'I want the buttons down the centre and the trim around the hips to converge lower than where you have indicated here. The overskirt is not to conceal the buttons or the trim, but be brought underneath them, but still worked high at the back. See, see here.'

Tom stretched over to the worktable, brushing back some layers of material, and thumped an urgent finger on the costume designs, which were revealed underneath. 'See what I mean? I want the buttons echoed on the cuffs and the coat – do you have the rough cut of the coat?'

'Not yet, Mr. McKinley,' muttered Mr. Agnew.

'Why not?' asked Tom a little impatiently.

'I've work to do!' Mr. Agnew replied, lifting his head to give his senior a hard stare. The door clicked open and in walked the young woman Katherine had seen sitting on the ledgers in the outer room. The young woman still wore her blouse with the ivy pattern on it. She held a cup of tea precariously in her hand, as though she were carrying something unpleasant that had to be disposed of.

'Tea for the lady,' she said severely, hardly seeming to move a muscle on her face at all.

'Just put it there.' Tom pointed to the table by the window, 'away from the rolls of fabric.' The young woman put the tea down and then left the room.

Katherine cast her eyes over to Tom, who was now writing something in his black notebook. She felt excited by everything about him. The strong angle of his jaw. The broadness of his back and shoulders. The fairness of his skin, his hair, the soft expression in his eyes when he smiled. The large expanse of his palms when he touched her. The coarse strands of chest hair, which were now sticking out over the top of his shirt where he had pulled his tie loose a little and which she probably should not be seeing. Everything about him.

Tom indicated to Mr. Agnew to come over to the worktable and continued to issue instructions to him.

'The coat needs to fall lower than the dress, of course—'

'I'm busy, Mr. McKinley. I'll see what I can manage,' Mr. Agnew replied sharply, interrupting him.

However, Tom kept talking, as though Mr. Agnew had said nothing. '—have a mock-up of the coat for the next fitting and follow the designs exactly as I have laid out here. Understand?'

With that, Tom left Mr. Agnew reluctantly studying the designs at the table and walked toward Katherine. As she looked up at him, he kissed her full on the mouth and then, pulling away from her, he whispered to her quickly, 'Meet me at Corn Market on the corner of Arthur Street at seven.'

Then he turned back to Mr. Agnew and said, 'And help Miss Fallon out of the mock-up. We don't want her to stab herself on the pins – we'll leave that to Don José in the last act!'

Tom emerged from the crowd on Arthur Street precisely at seven, and Katherine felt herself shrink at the sight of him, as though she was pure heart and nothing else, her body a pulse.

'Am I late? I walked the town for a while and I lost track of time,' he said.

'No you're not late at all. You walked the town?' Her voice was light, surprised. 'How lovely.'

He smiled.

It tilted her world.

'And what would you say to a cup of tea?' he said.

The noise of the tearooms at the Café Royal appeared to exist independently of its makers. It hung like a weighty halo of sound. Like a clamorous, constant din no matter how the arrangement of people changed beneath it. Even had the tearooms emptied in a single rush, it felt as though the gabble would continue unabated – a vapourous, omnipresent tearoom music.

It was not just the excited voices of the customers that accumulated as a ringing canopy under the decorative ceiling; it was every sound that was made in that room. It was the screeching of chairs on the wooden floor as people marked their arrivals and departures, and the jittery creaking of adjustment as they positioned themselves comfortably in their chairs at the small tables covered in white tablecloths. It was the clanging of the cutlery on silver trays by the exasperated waitressess, who smelled of sweat and soap. Their clumsy, deliberate, unrepenting handling syncopated with what seemed like their thoughts of private vengeance. It was the clatter of delf by waiters too unimpressed by their own busyness to care. And it was the singular holler of orders being flung across the room like lone birds swept up in a wind-filled sky.

Wasn't it as though the light had created them? He and she and all life in the Café Royal? she thought. They glistened. Everything glistened. The Art Deco lamps suspended from the high ceiling were like large, glowing soup bowls dropping into the cloud of sound. Light ricocheted off the gilt-edged mirrors on the four walls, off the glass display cabinets, off the silvered glinting slices of knives, forks, and spoons, off the swinging glass doors that led into the kitchens, off the pearls and paste that hung around the porcelain necks of the fine ladies. Not even the plumes of smoke rising from the cigarettes of the customers diminished its radiance.

It was its own world.

The large doors leading into the tearooms from the foyer swung backward and forward as people bustled in and out. Nearby, a high-spirited couple chatted about a film they had just seen. Other people were looking out for the arrival of friends. Four young women sitting together chimed together like a carillon, their words ringing around them. One woman sat on her own just to the left of the doorway, every so often lifting her head to view those coming and going. She twisted her teacup on its saucer, occasionally tipping it to peruse its contents. As she lifted the cup to her mouth, small drops of tea fell onto the saucer like brown baby lemmings falling into a shiny white sea.

Never before had she seemed so aware of the detail of her surroundings. Never before so keenly as this.

Tom managed to order a pot of tea from a waitress who, as she arrived to take their order, was already leaving them. There was no point of stillness where the relationship between customer and waitress was acknowledged. The waitress's front teeth stuck out and her pen did not stop moving on her order pad. She was a dreary creature in this circus of glass and light. She kept writing and walking, creating for herself a novel of calories and libations. She wove her way through the tiny alleyways between tables without needing to look where she was going, her front teeth leading the way.

A huge pot of tea arrived almost immediately, deposited at their table en route as it were. The waitress was gone. Tom opened the lid of the teapot, his fingers protected by a paper napkin. Tea leaves floated in hot water; it had not yet become tea.

'How many have you pocketed?' Katherine said wryly. Tom looked puzzled and slightly taken aback. A moment passed. 'The sugar lumps. They've been disappearing into your pocket.' Her voice was coloured with mock accusation.

'Not exactly the worst habit in the world,' he replied defensively. Then his face relaxed. 'I'll eat them later, on the walk home. You don't miss a trick. Or here' – he changed tack—'you have them, then!'

With this, he plunged his hand into his pocket and dumped the small handful of off-white lumps across the table and into her lap. She yelped with delight at having caught him out, throwing her head back with laughter, her skirt now cradling his saccharine contraband. Quick as a flash, he lifted the teapot and made as if he was going to pour the hot, steamy contents over her sugared lap.

'Do you like tea with your sugar?'

He looked at her, his eyes smiling right at her. She grabbed at the teapot to stop him and felt the hot steel of the teapot burning her hand.

They sat in the café as the evening unfolded and Tom told her a little about his work, pulling occasionally on his cigarette, about what shows he had designed costumes for, about his night-walks along the riverside. As he spoke, his eyes seemed never to tire of her and his smile remained gentle and confident. It seemed the easiest thing in the world for her to listen to his voice, which reached her through the noise of the café like sweet perfume.

Not every night, but most evenings, he said, he followed the narrow dirt path along the Lagan's embankment until it brought him home. He remembered his father used to take him along the same path when he was a child, but only recently had he begun to walk it again. Occasionally, he would check the Albert Clock at the end of High Street as he left the tailors' rooms, to time his journey. Sometimes, particularly on moonless nights, he said, the shadows on the embankment merged so densely with one another that he could not tell where the path ended and where the water began – both a weave of ink black. On those nights, he had to test the ground as he moved to see whether hardened earth or yielding wet lay beneath his feet. He had to sniff the air to sense whether what lay before him was the thickness of clotted vegetation or the thin, cool envelope of the river's breeze. Not even the orange light that eased across the river from the heart of the city could guide his way.

'We'll walk the embankment together,' he said 'some night when the moon is full. I'll show you.'

Yes, yes, she would like that. She would like them to walk the embankment together, she said. She was enthralled by the way in which he seemed to draw joy from everything around him. Her world seemed wider.

When Tom walked her home through the city, people moved around them like eddies and currents before a squall. He sang to her along the upward slope of the Mountpottinger Road, past Cluan Place, across the junction at Beersbridge Road, past the Unitarian Church with its sign saying THE LORD GIVETH AND THE LORD TAKETH AWAY. His voice was so smooth, it had made her want to weep. He sang the 'Indian Love Call' and 'We'll Gather Lilacs in the Spring' as they walked past The Mount, past Paxton Street. He bought her an ice cream at Fuscos, near John Long's Corner, and then sang her a vanilla and raspberry serenade as they crossed Isoline Street. A dome of soft memory in the making, creamy white, trickled with sugar sweetness, berry-berry red. Their tongues tasted childhood and their lips chilled and they walked together, creating a song line through east Belfast.

They walked on down the final slope of the road until they reached the flat where Katherine lived. Popping the last of his ice cream into his mouth as though it were a tiny dunce's hat, he kissed her cheek, his lips cold white. As he walked away, she could hear him sing quietly to himself, his voice moving on a curl of night air.

She opened the street door with her key and made her way up the stairs to the flat where she lived above a chip shop. There was no effort to the climb; it was as though she were floating up the stairs. Never before had she felt this much alive.

Entering the flat, she was greeted by her mother in the hallway. Her mother held a side plate with the remains of a sandwich on it and was on her way out to the kitchen.

'Ah, Katherine' – her mother was unable to hide her disappointment—'George has been waiting all evening for you.' Katherine quickly looked at the clock in the hallway – it was now eleven o'clock – then back at her mother.

'What?' she replied with an immediate sense of alarm, and walked quickly into the parlour, where George was waiting. The 'good' cups and saucers were sitting on the table next to him, gold-rimmed and lady-thin. But George obviously had had more than enough tea, and the cups sat idle, like a rejected lot at an auction. They sat like George sat.

He has every right to be even a little frosty with me, Katherine was thinking, as she had obviously forgotten that they had made arrangements to meet up, but George rose immediately with a smile and offered her a chair.

'Sorry.' Her voice sounded strangely timorous now, after the laughing, after the singing, after the cold ice cream. She looked slightly confused. 'I forgot about tonight. I had a costume fitting . . . It took longer than I thought . . . I . . .'

'No, no.' George's voice soothed the rising ripples of apology. 'No, we didn't make any plans for tonight, Katherine. I just called by because I wanted to see you.'

She was stopped in her tracks.

'Oh,' she said.

'So,' George continued tenderly, 'you've just come from the costume fitting? That was a late one.'

Katherine looked at George, at his kind face and his gentle eyes, and heard herself say, 'Yes.'

She walked slowly over to the chair by the parlour table that George had offered her and sat down, absentmindedly brushing a thin sprinkle of sugar dust from the folds of her skirt onto the parquet floor of the parlour. The soles of her shoes slid across the tiny, glistening grains, as though the floor were slipping from under her.

Her mother, having returned from the kitchen, was wearing a slightly embarrassed smile and was twisting the beads of her necklace in polite agitation.

'What a long time you had to wait for this young lady, George!' Mrs. Fallon said, shaking her head. With a sudden impatience, she turned to Katherine. 'Katherine, do you want some tea?'

'No thanks, Mummy.'

'And you'll hardly want a sandwich this late.' Her mother was giving her the answer with the question.

'No, I'm fine, thank you.'

'Well, I'm hitting the hay now. Frank will be home in a minute. Vera has already gone to bed. George, give my regards to your mother and father.'

'I certainly will, Mrs. Fallon. Good night.' George remained standing.

'Good night, George.' Then quietly to Katherine: 'You shouldn't have kept that poor man waiting so long.'

Katherine lifted her head to her mother, hoping her face would not betray the confusion she was feeling inside.

'Good night, Mummy.'

'And say a decade of the Rosary as usual before you go to bed,' Mrs. Fallon offered quietly.

'Don't worry, Mummy, I will,' said Katherine.

Mrs. Fallon gave a series of small head nods, then closed the parlour door behind her with a gentle click.

George immediately moved over to Katherine and swept his hand against her hair, then kissed her on the forehead, taking in the smell of her skin and the unfamiliar odours that now perfumed her. He pulled his chair closer to her and sat down. He took her hand, beginning, absentmindedly, to stroke his fingers along the elongated soft hollows between her knuckles.

'You must be tired.'

'No,' she replied simply. She looked at George. His black hair was brushed back from his forehead in a smooth, soft wave, his deep brown eyes each ringed with a tired grey smudge. She removed her hand from George's gentle hold.

The silence between them hung heavily. She could not help feeling that she should not have told George a lie about why she had been late in getting home. The lie now sat like another presence in the room, expecting to be fed.

Then George smiled.

'Talk to me,' he said. She was being uncharacteristically quiet. She wanted to say so much to George, but her mind was strangely still. And something within her began to feel a little desperate. Familiarity defined her relationship with George. They had been together for two years and at this stage could almost predict each other's behaviour. George was a good man, considerate and thoughtful and a little afraid of passion. But when she had been with Tom that night, everything had felt buoyant and possible and vital.

She breathed deeply to blot out these thoughts of Tom and then opened her eyes wider to George; she did not want to exclude him. He reached and squeezed her hand, which was now resting on her lap. His touch warmed her; his tender confidence reassured her. If she ignored the lie, she told herself, if she chose not to feed it, it would go away.

'How did your fitting go?' George was rubbing the tips of his fingers across her nails.

'The fitting?' she said almost sharply. She could sense her heart beating faster. She had spoken too quickly, she realised. Her voice sounded too abrupt, her tone too shrill, too defensive.

'Yes. Your fitting.' George said slowly and emphatically. 'You said you were late because of a costume fitting.'

'The fitting went fine.' She was shaking her head as she spoke, as if to denote that there was nothing, no, nothing different or unusual to report. 'It's all just a mock-up at the moment. There's no real costume yet, but some adjustments to the sleeves need to be made, and to the length and to the waistband, and the neckline needed reshaping, and something at the back needs realigning; that was all.' She was shaking her head again.

'Not a lot needs changing, then?' George retorted wryly.

She looked at George, unable to respond to his irony. Her forehead creased a little. She could feel her mouth filling with saliva. She wanted to swallow.

'Seems like a lot of carry-on just for a show,' he continued.

'George . . . I've something to tell you,' she mumbled, unsure of how much she wanted to tell.

George swept his hand across her hair again.

'You look a little tired, Katherine.'

'I'm fine.'

'What is it?' George, although cautious, could not, however, hide the impatience in his voice. 'Is everything all right?'

'Fine.'

'Are you sure?'

'Yes.'

'You seem a little—'

'A little what?' She looked at George as she cut him short. Her tone was defiant now.

'You just seem a little annoyed at something, at me perhaps.'

'Why should I be annoyed at you?' She looked at George with such coldness that it took him aback. He felt himself automatically pulling away from her.

And everything seemed to be falling around her. The nicer George was being to her, the more difficult she was finding it to tell him what she wanted to tell him and the more hardened she grew. *Something has altered. Let me tell you. We are altered . . .*

From below them, they could hear the last customers leaving the fish and chip shop, muffled voices travelling down the street and then vanishing into the evening. The fug that had risen from the constant frying of fish and chips throughout the day and had hung between her and George as they sat in the parlour now settled heavily on the furniture, on the tablecloth, and on their clothes, with a spreading, greasy odour. George stood up from his chair and reached forward to lift the teacups from the table. He was suddenly feeling dispirited now and thought it best that he should go.

'I'll clear those away. Just leave them.' Katherine's voice was sharp.

'It's no trouble, Katherine.'

'No, please, leave them.' She was biting the air.

'Just what is it that has you so angry?'

Katherine fell silent for a few moments as she tried to gather her thoughts.

'I'm not angry – you're right, I'm tired, that's all.' She lifted her head to look at George.

'What do you want me to say, Katherine?' George could not disguise the chagrin in his voice.

'I don't know. Nothing. There's nothing to say.' For the first time that evening, her tone was imploratory.

George looked down at her hands, which were clenched into

fists on her lap. He lifted each hand in turn and pulled the fingers gently open.

She looked at George, the dark brown hues of his eyes deepening moment by moment.

'I'm sorry, I'm so sorry—' she said, feeling the sting of tears well up in her eyes.

'Not to worry. While I was waiting, your mother and I had a great conversation about the merits and demerits of the Mother's Union!'

'No, I don't mean that, I mean . . .' But she could not bring herself to say it. She could feel something closing within her. '. . . Yes . . . I'm sorry . . . I'm sorry I was so late.'

Her apology was all that George needed, it seemed, for he smiled widely at her.

'Katherine, I've something to show you,' he said eagerly, and then he put his hand in the pocket of his jacket, sat down beside her, and presented her with a small blue velvet box.

'This is why I wanted to see you tonight, Katherine, and *I'm* sorry, sorry that I couldn't wait until we had made plans to go out, but it was just that I put the final payment down today after I had finished work' – his nervousness and excitement was making him speak very quickly now—'and I was able to collect it from the jeweller's, and I know that I should have taken you out somewhere nice to give it to you, but, here we are, and I hope you really like it and that you'll say—'

He stopped talking suddenly, as though realising he was in the middle of a speech he had yet to write. Katherine had her head bent so that he could not see the expression of complete bewilderment on her face. Only a short while ago, climbing the steps to her flat and thinking of Tom, she had felt transformed, had felt something new opening up within her. But now, looking at George, she realised how little she knew about Tom. And she knew George; that was the truth of it. She knew his ways, trusted him, relied on him, knew that he loved her and would care for her. Here is a decent man. Here is George. What did she know of Tom? Her thoughts were collapsing now like a stack of cards. Trembling, she held the blue velvet box in her hand.

'I hope you like it, Katherine.'

She opened the box. The box was lined with indigo satin, a tiny piece of night sky. Out of this sky, the neat diamond of a ring shone like a lone star. Around it, the ring's gold band gleamed like a lick of yellow moon.

'Will you marry me, Katherine?'

Katherine slowly lifted her head and looked at George. In that moment, his sweet humility caught her. She knew, deep in her heart, that if she refused George, he would be devastated.

'Yes,' she said, still trembling, while on the wooden floor of the parlour, under the table, the lie still sat, its tongue coated with sugar, waiting for scraps.

Two days after George had asked her to marry him, Katherine slipped the dustcover over her accounting machine in the offices of the Ulster Bank and closed the block of files that had been resting on the wooden trolley by her table. There was a chorus of good-byes and 'Show us again' from her envious colleagues, who rubbed their hands up and down their thighs as they cooed with admiration at the engagement ring on her finger. She quickly left the building and turned right along Waring Street, crossing onto Rosemary Street and then cutting through Berry Street into Smithfield Market.

It was there that she spotted the small figurine sitting in the window of an antiques shop. The porcelain statuette of an old man with weathered skin, sitting cross-legged, a piece of cloth in one hand and a needle and thread in the other. When the proprietor informed her of its price – it was much more expensive than she had anticipated – she did not falter for a moment, but instead emptied her purse of its two shillings onto the counter. She then asked the proprietor if he would take something as security on the rest of the purchase so that she could take it with her, and then she slipped off her engagement ring and placed it on the counter beside her money. The proprietor made it clear to her that though it was not usual for him to agree to such an arrangement, he would agree nonetheless, for the value of the ring she had offered him was more than satisfactory. He wrapped the statuette in a double layer of brown paper, securing its edges with a long piece of string, and handed it to her.

She left the shop with a rising sense of exhilaration. An urgent breeze began to rise up in bursts from around the street corners, flapping the awnings above the shopfronts and rudely lifting the hem of her skirt. She held the brown paper parcel close to her chest, its paper crackling like a catching fire. As she arrived at the tailors' rooms, Mr. Boyne's grey-haired secretary was leaving, as was the young woman with the ivy-patterned blouse. The last of the junior tailors had laid out their work carefully in place, to be ready for the following morning, and were taking their jackets and caps hastily from the coat stand by the door before they headed home. Katherine walked past the tailors without glancing at them. She could see that the door to the anteroom was open. As she approached it, she could hear him singing quietly. She could feel his voice pulling her in. She entered the room and could see him standing at his worktable, his head slightly bowed. As he lifted his head, he smiled at her through his song. Then he walked to the door, his eyes never leaving her, and closed it behind them both.

Katherine and Tom lay still and awake on the rucks of cloth that he had spread out on the wooden floor. Crimson and gold. They lay curled into each other and fully dressed, her back against his chest, as though they were both waiting to be discovered in an empty house. Both concealed the true extent of their desire for each other, choosing instead a cautious foreplay of touch and conversation. Their senses were magnified by the uncertainty of decorum – its appropriateness or its waste of time – and so they hovered in a state of sexual suspense. The lamp on the worktable cast a hoopful of honeyed light across their bodies, while the cloth warmed under them and released the odour of its new thread. The statuette now sat on top of the work cabinet beside the boxes of buttons, its brown paper wrapping left like a discarded skin on the floor. Behind them, in the far corner of the room, the clock ticked, but neither of them wanted to shift from their position to look at it. So every so often, Katherine tapped Tom's pocket watch with her fingernail and he told her the time. If she was late getting home, her mother would worry. They lay quietly, losing the sense of time as time passed, drifting even into moments of drowsiness, their eyes opening to gleams of silk and brocade and then the *tap, tap, tap* of her fingernail against his pocket watch.

'Quarter past nine.'

Through her spine she could feel Tom's heartbeat. This distinct life resounding through her. This life she did not know. When she was a child, she would often place her ear against her father's chest and, as she listened, feel that she was attached to an ancient tree, the steady tempo of his kindness, the layer upon layer of compassion ringing its deep tones, the vibration filling her ears and her head and her body. Solace tapered from an ancient wood. Here, that same resound, that same sense of bliss, but instead she was a new bird in a new forest, in her nest of skin and bone and body heat, the ridge of an unfamiliar pulse threading its way through her. A slender, yielding wood surrounding her, protecting her, exciting her.

'You haven't told me yet.' Tom's voice was soft and unhurried.

'What have I not told you?' She turned her head a little toward him.

'What it is you do.'

She sighed and stretched her legs, her upper back pushing into him slightly. She smiled.

'Oh, it's all so boring, and predictable. I work in the Ulster Bank offices on Waring Street. I add up all the figures on my accounting machine, and when they don't add up, I find out why, because there's always a reason, because it's all mathematics, and then I fix that and I move on. And that's what I do, all day, that's it. I account for things.'

'You're an accountant?'

'An accounting clerk. There's a difference!'

'And where did an accounting clerk learn to sing so beautifully?'

'I'm very flattered you think so. But I'm not that good.'

'I can hear you above me as I work. I think *all* the tailors are in love with you.'

She shrugged off Tom's comment.

'No, I'm not that good at all. My father was a lovely singer, though. Not that he sang professionally or anything. He was a draftsman. Worked in the drawing office of the Belfast Corporation. But he was a larger-than-life character, should have been a performer himself. Would always sing to me when I was a child. And never had a bad word to say about anyone.'

'And does he still listen to you sing?'

'No, no,' she said gently. 'He died when I was nine.'

'I'm sorry.'

She moved her head to rest her cheek against Tom's arm.

'How did he die?' Tom's question surprised Katherine, so direct was its tone, so personal. But she embraced it nonetheless, felt the relief of responding to it.

'Well . . . I was told he died from an accident at work, but I'm not so sure. I think it may have been a heart attack or something. I don't know. It was never talked about. Never. And it was all so sudden. He just wasn't there anymore – how can a person be just not there anymore? I feel as though I spend every day waiting for him to come back,' she said. 'Isn't that strange?'

'No, not so strange.'

The clock behind them ticked.

Then her tone shifted quickly. 'So that explains it, then,' she said. 'He passed the singing on to me. You can blame him!'

Tom gently stroked the pale skin exposed along her forearm.

'And you're not such a bad singer yourself,' she continued.

They lay silently again. Then after a moment, she released a deep sigh. 'Why do people say that?'

'Say what?'

'Why do people say "I'm sorry" like that, as though they are responsible for the person dying?'

'It's just a formality.'

*Tap-tap-tap* went her fingernail on his pocket watch.

'Quarter to ten,' he said quietly.

'If only I could have done something so that he didn't die,' Katherine said quietly. 'I don't even know what I mean – I'm sure there's nothing I could have done – but if only it had happened when I was with him.'

'Katherine, you were only nine. There's nothing you could have done.'

'I know . . . but I can't make any sense of it.'

'Maybe stop trying.'

Suddenly, voices rose from the photographer's studio on the ground floor, where staff were locking up after working late. There was the bang of a door and then silence. From the lamp on the table Katherine could detect a limp fizzing sound. She turned her head to look. A moth had caught itself inside the shade and was trying to escape.

Tom adjusted his position on the cloth, resting his chin lightly on her hair.

'Thank you again for the present,' he said. 'I'm very impressed.'

'You're very welcome – again.'

'Is it supposed to be me?' he said, laughing a little as he spoke.

'No!' she protested, nudging him with her elbow. 'No, of course not.'

They drifted each into their own world for a few moments. All was quiet.

'How did a young man like you find himself as senior tailor anyway?'

'I'm not as young as you think.' Tom traced his finger across the back of her hand.

'You must be good at your job, then.'

'Well, my father originally owned this business; he and Mr. Boyne were partners. It had started off as a modest alterations service, but then during the First World War, it thrived, making uniforms.' Tom spread his hand over hers. 'Anyway, here's where I started when I was sixteen, and five years after that I volunteered for the army, as the whole mess had started up again. I was stationed in Sussex on administration duties – so I know just how boring accounting is' – he strokes her hair—'and I was never drafted out to fight. But just as the war ended and I returned home, my father died.'

'I'm sorry.' The response came automatically; then, realising what she had just said, she checked Tom's reaction.

'You see. Just a formality.' He smiled, then pressed his body a little more into hers.

'Well, two years on from that now and I find myself in my father's shoes.'

'But only Mr. Boyne's name is used for the business.' She was curious.

'It's a long story, but my father had signed nothing to secure any of his holdings on the business, so I'm an employee here, just like everyone else, nothing more.'

'And you live on your own?'

'No, at home with my mother and sister.'

They fell quiet. Their warm breath spread like a low smoke around them. She clicked her fingernail against Tom's pocket watch again.

'Forget the time, Katherine.'

'I can't.'

Tom glanced at his pocket watch.

'Nine fifty-five.'

'So you're an old bachelor, then.' She gave a short laugh, but she could feel her pulse begin to race. She swallowed hard.

'Oh, call me an old romantic . . . I've just been waiting for the right person to come along.'

His reply pained her like a soft burning in her stomach. She closed her eyes in an attempt to quell it.

'Don't you believe in love at first sight?' he asked her.

She didn't answer him. Instead, she shifted the conversation in a different direction. 'And where exactly do you live?' she asked him quickly.

'Why do you want to know – exactly?'

'You know where *I* live. You walked me there. You could find me anytime you wanted to.'

'Ravenhill Road.'

'And you walk home by the river?' She sounded incredulous. 'Hardly a shortcut.'

Tom paused. 'I know, you're right.'

Katherine breathed deeply, then wriggled her shoulders as a way to settle into him a little more. She was aware of how late it was getting, but there was something she had wanted to ask him. Her eyes lifted to a costume rail in the corner, which was covered in a large cotton sheet.

'Tom . . . the costume you've designed for me, for Carmen—'

'Yes.'

'It can't be as elabourate as you've been making out. Everything is still "make do and mend." So all those things you were saying to Mr. Agnew at the fitting about the material, and the beading, and the sateen lining – you're such a showman!'

The moth beat its wings against the shade in a furious pitter.

Pushing his body closer to her, Tom raised himself slightly on one arm and slipped the other around her waist. He placed his mouth close to her ear and said quietly, 'You won't believe how beautifully made it will be, Katherine. Wait until you see. Mr. Agnew wouldn't know where to start. *I'm* going to make it for you, Katherine. *I'm* going to make it. Let me tell you what I'm going to do . . .'

The furious pitter of the moth came to a sudden stop.

'First I'll run the tracing wheel along the paper pattern. The tiny tracing wheel will make no sound as it moves, obeying the gentle thrust of my arm around your shape.' He moved his hand down her shoulder and along the length of her arm. 'I'll cut the material, holding it flat by the weights I've placed across it. My shears will slice effortlessly through the salmon-coloured silk and its lining of lemon sateen, and through the mandarin-and-cherry-coloured bouclé wool, for the blades are obscenely sharp and the cloth will surrender easily.' He spread his fingers along her thigh to her knee. 'Then I'll drape the roughly assembled bodice of the costume around the tailor's dummy, pulling the waist of the garment tightly in toward the front.' He brought his hand up under her skirt and shifted her legs to open them a little. 'I'll bring the raw edges of the material together to pin them into a seam, snipping the armholes a little, if need be, as a surgeon might incise a flap of skin.' His hand moved upward along her inner thigh, rubbing against her stockings. 'Then I'll bind the seams with taffeta. When I press the seams under the hot iron, I'll take in the smell of the new cloth and imagine how your sweet body heat will perfume it.' Then slowly he released his hand from under her skirt to turn her fully around to him, pressing his body gently on top of her. 'Then I'll take some strips of whalebone and place them into a basin of warm water to soften them. I'll cut the corners off the bone with the blade of my pocketknife, making a little curve at each end.' He leaned his body more heavily onto her. 'And then I'll insert the bone through the aperture of the casing, sliding it firmly upward all the way to the top of the seam. I'll draw the bone back just a little, if I need to, so that it won't force the material. The spring of the bone must always be right.' He stroked her face and neck. 'I'll begin to insert another strip of whalebone into the casing. Then another. And another. And the garment will slowly take on your shape.' He put his face close to her to smell her skin. 'When I attach the panels of the skirt to the bodice, I'll roll the material between my thumb and forefinger to firm its position; then I'll fasten the rolls with thread as I go.' He kissed her face, his hand moving across her breast. 'Once all the sections of the skirt are in place, then I'll slip the garment onto the tailor's dummy again to check that the waistline sits well down into the curve of the figure.' His hand moved up under her skirt again. 'I'll sew twenty-two buttons down the front of the bodice, along its opening. Twenty-two buttons I've already handmade from silk.' His hand pulled at her underwear. 'For each buttonhole, I'll work with a cerise linen thread, taking my time to allow the purl to come to the edge of the slit.' He kissed her again and eased her legs farther apart.

She feels it is the strangest experience in the world, amid the perfumed heat, among the folds of warm cloth that wrap around them both in the crimson-edged light. A part of herself she has never known before, now discovered, now occupied, now made transparent.

# 3

*August 1969*

ISABEL ARRIVES IN ELSA'S BACK GARDEN wearing bright yellow hot pants. She stands with a bold composure and a slender hand on her hip beside the small three-legged table, which has been covered with a green checkered tea towel. There are three plates on the table and a handwritten card saying 'Home Baking.' Isabel is eyeing the roughly cut rectangles of boiled cake on the plate nearest Elsa, who is sitting politely on a little stool on the other side of the table. Elsa is looking at Isabel.

The Bedford girls have organised a summer fair in their back garden. Maureen and Elizabeth, in particular, had begun pestering their mother early that morning. Elsa's sunburn had tempered her enthusiasm a little – she was still feeling hot and sore – but when Katherine agreed, Elsa had immediately drawn a sign in purple crayon on a piece of cardboard saying SUMMER FAIR IN BACK GARDEN – ALL WELCOME and had hung it on their front gate. The money they would raise from this humble affair, the girls had decided, would go to the Black Babies of Africa. Katherine, however, had persuaded Elsa not to add this to the bottom of her sign, but just to put FOR CHARITY instead. The Black Babies was, after all, a Catholic charity, Katherine had patiently explained to her daughters, and so – as she had phrased it—'they had to be careful not to put their Protestant neighbours out a little.' Despite struggling to understand this, Elsa had nevertheless followed her mother's advice. Katherine had also suggested to Elsa that she change the prize for one of the games that was being planned for the fair at the far end of the garden. Elsa was intending to place three buckets upside down beside the apple tree. Whoever could hit all three of the buckets blindfolded with a rubber ball would win a holy picture of Saint Francis of Assisi. The picture, Katherine had suggested, should be replaced with a small bag of toffees. Elsa had understood this suggestion perfectly. Of course, she had thought, everybody in the world would *much* prefer to win a bag of toffees than win a picture of a solemn-looking saint.

Despite the beautiful day, Katherine feels tired and cold, as though still in shock since her encounter with the seal the day before. The cuts on her legs from the rocks are beginning to sting, perhaps because they're beginning to heal, she thinks. She wants to keep her mind on the summer fair. She wants to have a lovely day with her children.

Elsa is looking at Isabel. Isabel lives the next road up from Elsa, smokes Benson & Hedges in the back field on her way home from Sunday school, and once chased Elsa down the street, waving a pair of her father's underpants. Elsa had felt frightened of the underpants, as though they held some sinister secret of the grown-up world, and had then felt stupid for feeling frightened. Isabel's father was a dapper, fervently religious man who made lampstands out of seashells and empty wine bottles, disapproved of having a television in the house, and never cut his grass on a Sunday. But Elsa thought that underpants were underpants no matter whom they belonged to.

The boiled cake that had been made for the fair had not been boiled. It had been baked in the oven like any other cake. But its generous quantities of sultanas and raisins had been steamed gently so that they were plump and soft before being folded into the mixture of cinnamon, flour, eggs, and sugar. Katherine had made this cake with her mother when she was a child and now made it regularly with her own children. Elsa and Elizabeth, that morning, had slipped their girlish fingers around the insides of the deep ceramic bowl as Katherine was putting the cake into the oven and had lifted the remains of the fruity mixture to their mouths and licked their fingers clean.

Isabel knows how nice boiled cake tastes. She has tasted it before. There are eleven slices on the plate.

'Your hot pants are lovely,' Elsa says to Isabel, feeling somehow that only a compliment will be worthy of a reply.

'They're from my half cousin. She lives in Canada. She also sent me a purple pair. I could've worn them today, but I didn't want to.'

'They're lovely,' Elsa repeats meekly.

'I suppose so.'

Isabel looks at Elsa with a charged disdain. 'You know yous are the only Catholic family in this street.'

'Yes, I know.' Elsa lowers her head as though she has been found out.

'In this whole *area*.' Isabel says the word *area* as though she has just overheard it from a couple of whispering grown-ups. She tilts her chin skyward.

'Well, there's also Mr. and Mrs. McGovern—'

'Just sayin'.'

'And really we're half and half, 'cos Daddy was a Protestant and only turned Catholic when he married Mummy.' Elsa pushes her finger into a piece of boiled cake as she speaks.

'You go to a Catholic school, so yous are Catholics, so yous are.'

Elsa looks at Isabel and has nothing to say.

'I got caught smoking in the back field,' Isabel continues, suddenly impressed with herself. She nods her head slowly and widens her eyes at Elsa to denote just what serious trouble she is in.

'Did your mum catch you?'

'No, Mrs. MacAllister from our Sunday School did. She's a big pig! She should mind her own business. What was she doin' in the back field anyway? How much is the cake?'

'A penny a slice,' Elsa replies.

'And how much is that?' Isabel points at the one home-baked cherry iced bun that has survived since yesterday.

'A penny a bun.'

'There's only one bun.' Isabel adjusts the seat of her hot pants.

'It's a penny.'

'And how much are those?' Isabel fingers some custard creams that have been placed hastily onto a paper napkin.

'You get three for a penny.'

'How much did ye say the cake was?'

'A penny a slice.' Elsa begins to grow more and more nervous during this exchange, as if Isabel's haughty tone has the power to reveal Elsa as a liar.

'The cake looks r-e-a-l-l-y-n-i-c-e.' Isabel spreads her words like lemon curd on warm bread, a cue for ingratiation.

'My mummy made it.' Elsa wants to stay Isabel's friend.

'*My* mummy makes a chocolate and lime Victoria sponge cake for the Sunday School prayer meetings every third Sunday. The vicar always says it's the nicest cake he has ever tasted. He says that every time.'

The sun is now shining directly into Elsa's face, making it crinkle like paper.

'Your face is really red,' continues Isabel.

'I know.'

'And you got white patches of stuff on your chin.'

Elsa strokes her chin to see if she can feel the remains of the calamine lotion. 'I got sunburn.'

'But I've no money with me.' Isabel talks now in a strange, tiny voice, adjusting the seat of her hot pants again. Elsa wishes she did not feel a compulsion to placate Isabel. Despite herself, despite how Isabel makes her feel, Elsa finds herself picking out the biggest slice of boiled cake to give to Isabel.

'You can have this for nothing if you like.' Elsa is smiling on the outside.

Isabel curls her top lip away from her teeth and then quickly pokes the air with her index finger just in front of Elsa's face by way of a thank-you. Elsa feels unsettled by the gesture but finds herself smiling once again at Isabel. Isabel then sidles off to peruse what the fair has to offer her, nibbling superciliously at her slice of boiled cake.

One of the tables at the fair, a folding card table with a felt-covered top, displays some fragrant items, small bars of lavender soap, a bottle of shampoo, bubble bath in a snowman that has been sitting around since Christmas, and a miniature bottle of 4711 eau de cologne. Another of the tables, a box turned upside down and draped with a beige head scarf, displays an assortment of books – *The Lodger, The Reluctant Legionnaire* – and a few well-read copies of the *Reader's Digest*. There are also two children's books on the table, ones Maureen and Elizabeth had felt were too babyish for girls their age.

The table nearest the end of the garden is the white elephant stall, upon which they have arranged all sorts of oddments in various clusters: rubber balls, pieces of Lego, a doll's bed with one of its legs broken, some pencils, an eggcup with BUTLINS HOLIDAY CAMP printed on it, Twinkle comics, a skipping rope, and a small papier-mâché mountain with grass painted on its flanks and a long winding river of blue ribbon that Elizabeth had made.

Elsa had thought how strange the words *white elephant* were together as she had written them on a piece of paper with her green crayon. She still had no idea what this expression actually meant, even though Maureen had taken pains to explain it to her. 'Just things, different things together. Oddments. You know!' But the more Maureen had become impatient with Elsa, the less Elsa understood what Maureen was explaining.

Earlier that morning, Elsa had watched as Maureen had developed a plan for the afternoon. On the oddment table – before it had officially been entitled the white elephant stall – Maureen had found a blue glass ball, the size of a large orange, which was nestled in a straw-coloured lacy bag. When the light caught the glass ball, it shimmered aquamarine, sea green, and pinks. No one knew where the glass ball had come from. Katherine had suspected that it had been part of a promotional gift she had received when she had bought two pairs of nylons. But she couldn't quite remember.

Maureen had lifted the blue glass ball out of its lacy home and taken it with her to Katherine's bedroom. Elsa, curious to know what her big sister was up to, had followed her up the stairs and had sat quietly outside the room, watching through the half-opened doorway. Maureen had then selected her means of transformation by prospecting through her mother's wardrobe. She had tied a green paisley scarf around her head and a brown woollen scarf around her shoulders and had secured one of Katherine's skirts, a mushroom-coloured calf-length cotton one, around her waist with a soft leather belt. She had walked around the bedroom in majestic circles, her skirt swishing and swooshing as she did so. Then she had fingered the contents of the little cream ceramic dish that sat on Katherine's dressing table, and which held a few pieces of Katherine's jewellery. But not finding what she needed there, she had opened her mother's wooden jewellery box. The lid of the box was painted as if it had been embroidered with fine threads displaying little spots of cerise and sage upon a yielding black. The sudden movement of the box had set its tiny mechanics whirring and releasing the delicate *plink plink* of the opening notes of the theme from *The Third Man*. Maureen had found the looped earrings she had been looking for in the scented honey-coloured innards of the box and had clipped one on each ear. She had smeared the lids of her eyes with a deep green and had reddened her lips. Then, holding up the hem of her skirt and angling her head to one side, she had paraded up and down the floor of the bedroom in front of the oval mirror of the dressing table, admiring her daring transformation into Madam Maureen, fortune-teller extraordinaire.

The wooden clotheshorse, draped with sheets and blankets, provided the structure for the walls of Madam Maureen's fortune-telling tent. A pink cotton sheet, fastened to the sides with clothes pegs, was its low slung ceiling.

Maureen had stuck a sign saying A PENNY FOR YOUR FORTUNE on the front of the tent and had hung a pink silk scarf over its entrance.

Katherine had a little book of cloakroom tickets, which she said she would give out to people so that they would know what number they were in the queue. They could give Maureen the money before they left the tent. Maureen had begun to feel a little nervous as her mother was explaining this to her.

By the time Maureen had declared her tent officially open, Elizabeth and Elsa had just finished organising various games for the fair. They had a pin the tail on the donkey game. The donkey – drawn by Elizabeth with crumbling white chalk on an old freestanding blackboard they had found in the coal shed – had legs of different sizes, each of which disappeared off the bottom edge of the blackboard in search of a hoof. The tail had been cut out from paper and coloured with brown crayon, and a small lump of Plasticine had been placed where the tail should be attached to the donkey. They had a game of hoopla set up on a tea tray on the grass, with prizes of a little woollen doll, which Elizabeth had knit at school; a felt rabbit belonging to Maureen, which she said she had outgrown; and a small teddy with a pinched expression and tiny beads for eyes, which no one could remember owning. It was the setting up of the three upturned plastic buckets by the apple tree that Elsa and Elizabeth had found to be the most frustrating, as Stephen had kept picking up the buckets and taking them away to some other place in the garden and then filling them with stones, or carrots from the kitchen, or putting his socks in them.

Peter Barnsley had been the first to arrive at the fair, and indeed had been the only visitor for the first fifteen minutes or so. Elizabeth and Elsa had said nothing to him. Instead, they had watched him with a burning sense of disappointment as he paraded around the garden, his hands stuffed deep into his pockets, his nose dirty, sporting a wide proprietorial grin on his face. This had not been the opening to the fair that they had expected. Where was the excited rush of people?

Katherine had gone into the house to answer the telephone and to change Stephen's nappy. Maureen had been sitting in her fortune-telling tent all the while, quiet and expectant in the heat. It had seemed like a very long time before enough people had appeared to make it feel like the fair had indeed begun.

Next in line to arrive, after Peter Barnsley, had been the

Wilson children. All four enormous children had wandered awkwardly and aimlessly around the garden from one table to the next with blank expressions on their faces. Elsa had watched them and had thought of Mr. Wilson, their father, with his shiny accordion. Mr. Wilson was a tiny man who had eyes that were permanently half-closed – a condition he had been born with – so whenever he wanted to look up, he had to tilt his head right back until it nestled between his shoulder blades. An unfortunate combination, Elsa had thought, his height and his eyes. On bonfire nights Mr. Wilson always played 'She'll Be Coming 'Round the Mountain' and the Protestant loyalist anthem 'The Sash My Father Wore' with a feverish agility, always working up to a stirring rendition of 'Spanish Eyes.' Elsa often wondered if he thought of his own eyes when he played it.

Then Mrs. Hamilton had arrived with her incredibly noisy twin boys, Kenneth and Keith. One of the twins – Elsa thought it might have been Kenneth, but she had never been sure – had been recently expelled from school for setting fire to the caretaker's dog. Mrs. Hamilton had apparently just shrugged her shoulders in the principal's office when she had been called in to explain, saying in a watery tone of voice, 'Oh, boys will be boys.'

Katherine had come back out to the garden with Stephen in tow and had begun to offer tea to the parents and lemonade to the children. She had handed out some cloakroom tickets to those in the small queue that had already formed outside Madam Maureen's fortune-telling tent, announcing as she did that Madam Maureen was finally ready to receive customers.

And Isabel had arrived, a summery tune of blond and yellow, swinging her hips to her own music. Purple or yellow, purple or yellow? went the melody, all the way up the driveway of Elsa's house. Yellow or purple, yellow or . . . As soon as she had spotted Elsa at the home baking stall, she had made a beeline for her. Yellow or purple?

'They're lovely,' Elsa had said.

'I suppose so.'

Now, the summer light showers everything. Isabel wanders around the garden, perusing every table, adjusting her hot pants and eating her boiled cake. Elizabeth invites Isabel to play hit the bucket, but Isabel just shakes her blond curls and wanders off. Then Isabel pushes her way in front of the youngest Wilson girl, who is waiting patiently in the queue to have her fortune told by Madam Maureen – even though the Wilson girl has a cloakroom ticket and Isabel doesn't.

Elsa leaves her home baking stall and wanders over to the back of Madam Maureen's fortune-telling tent. She wants to see what is happening inside the tent and carefully pulls back one of the sheets. Madam Maureen is hard at work. She rubs her crystal ball. She is looking at Peter Barnsley's dirty nose. She tells Peter Barnsley that he is going to marry a Chinese woman and that he is going to make it big in the carpet business. She tells Mrs. Hamilton, who is next in line, that she is to make sure that she does the football pools this Saturday, because there are big winnings in store for her, and Mrs. Hamilton laughs a high little laugh, like a bird's trill, and shakes her head as though she feels sorry for Maureen as she leaves the tent. Maureen then tells Isabel that she is going to become very sick but that a man in a white coat will ask her to marry him. A doctor. He will save her life. And they will travel up the Amazon together and have lots of children and live in the jungle among lions and tigers and collect coconuts and bananas for breakfast. Isabel is, however, unimpressed and leaves without paying. Elsa watches as Isabel bends to exit the tent and sees that Isabel's gold hot pants are now stuck firmly between the cheeks of her arse. And Maureen tells the youngest and largest of the Wilson girls, who struggles for what seems like an interminably long time to get inside the tent, that she is going to live in America and have a huge house with a freezer and two televisions. The Wilson girl smiles. Now Maureen shakes her head as though she feels sorry for the Wilson girl.

Elsa pulls her head back out of the tent and sees that at the end of the queue Katherine has placed a very compliant Richard

Marr. Richard Marr lives right across the street and has straight brown hair that falls over his eyes. Maureen has had a crush on him since the beginning of the summer. She discreetly told only her best friend, Patricia, who, of course, told only her mother, who, of course, told only Katherine. Elsa pokes her head back into the tent and watches; she cannot wait until it's Richard Marr's turn to have his fortune told.

Maureen gives a jittery, stupid sort of laugh when Richard Marr ducks his head in under the entrance to the fortune-telling tent. Her cheeks streak crimson as she looks intently into her wondrous ball of the sea as though her thoughts are racing and chasing inside it like a shoal of frenzied sea fish, and she stammers out quickly that Richard Marr will win a competition and get a dog. It's all over so quickly. Richard Marr leaves the tent as quietly as he entered it. Maureen has a look on her face, as though she wants him to come back in again and then again she doesn't.

After Richard Marr, it is the turn of one of the Hamilton twins, who nearly knocks the whole fortune-telling tent over as he clambers into it and looks like his mother sent him in. Elsa is almost sure that it's Keith. Maureen becomes instantly agitated with him and tells him that one day he will go deaf and that he should learn sign language as soon as possible.

'Fuck off, wee doll,' he says leaving the tent abruptly and taking his penny with him.

As Elsa shifts her position, she accidentally stands on the sheet, tugging it a little. Maureen turns her head sharply to see who is there. Elsa quickly darts away from the tent and runs back to her home baking stall before Maureen finds her out. Elsa stands at her stall thinking of Richard Marr and can't help but feel sorry for Maureen. She watches now as her mother moves over to the fortune-telling tent.

Katherine enters the tent, bending in under the silky pink folds of its entrance and squeezing onto the small wooden toolbox that has been upended and that serves as a seat for each of Madam Maureen's customers. Katherine is holding Stephen, who is wriggling excitedly in her arms. As Katherine is settling herself and trying to position Stephen comfortably enough on her lap, she registers how Maureen appears taciturn and withdrawn.

The chatter of people outside only serves to enhance the sense of secretiveness and enveloping calm that this enclosure of sheets and scarves has created. Outside, Mrs. Carter, who has just arrived, can be heard talking animatedly to Mrs. Hamilton about her husband's angina. Some of the children are calling out to one another, laughing and squealing. Isabel can be heard in the midst of the babble, her confident, defiant syllables punctuating the summer air.

Inside the tent, Stephen has become quiet. He is staring cautiously at Maureen and holding on to his mother. Katherine's head is bowed slightly under the gentle droop of the cotton sheet that forms the roof of the tent, like a billowy inverted cupola. The sunlight is diffused through the sheets and scarves and it now bathes the inside of the tent in a mellow raspberry light.

Stephen breaks the calm by blurting out 'Marmar' and pointing at Maureen in sudden recognition and relief. This strange creature in the swathes of green and blue and with the solemn dark eyes is his big sister. He is delighted with himself and arches his back, pointing and laughing at Maureen.

Maureen is annoyed at her mother. Katherine senses this and immediately attempts to tease Maureen out of her sombre mood by leaning forward and talking in a deep staccatoed voice.

'Tell-me-my-fortune-Madam-Maureen-please.'

'Stop it, Mummy,' Maureen replies sourly. Stephen flaps his chubby hand up and down in the air. 'Marmar,' he calls out, squealing and laughing.

'What-can-you-see-in-your-crystal-ball?' Katherine insists.

'Mummy, p-l-e-a-s-e.' There is definite hurt.

Katherine looks at Maureen. The green curved shadows around Maureen's eyes and the slit-sharp red of her lips betray the emerging young woman she is becoming. There would have been a time when Katherine would have known exactly how to coax Maureen out of a bad mood. But more recently, within the past few months, those same moods had taken on a certain heat. Katherine would witness Maureen defiantly withdraw from her and realise that, so easily, she had said or done the 'wrong' thing. After trying all her usual ploys, Katherine would end up feeling out of her depth and ever so slightly foolish. Maureen now seems to have the capacity to judge her mother and her mother's methods, and Katherine is painfully aware of the scrutiny.

'Marmar dere.' Stephen begins kissing his palm, then flings out his hand in Maureen's direction.

'Oh, of course.' Katherine endeavours to lift Maureen's spirits with mock surprise. 'I've forgotten to give you a penny.'

Katherine produces a penny from her purse, her head still bowed in supplication under the swoop of the sheet above her. Stephen grabs Katherine's purse and begins banging the table in front of him, babbling and singing. Maureen quickly lifts the crystal ball, her ball of the sea, to save it from falling and breaking. The frenzied sea fish have dispersed; the crystal ball is empty.

'I don't want a penny.' Maureen's annoyance still pulses.

'Ah, love, what is it? Is it Richard Marr?' Katherine realises that she has arrived too quickly at the nub of the problem and consequently has given herself away.

'Nooo . . .' Maureen says the word slowly enough to let Katherine know that, in fact, it *is* Richard Marr.

'Mama look. Awh gon.' Stephen's two arms are now outstretched; his eyes are wide. He has dropped the purse at Katherine's feet. It has magically disappeared.

Katherine bends down to retrieve the purse.

'Take the purse out to Li-li, out to Li-li. Mummy will come in a minute.'

'Li-li,' repeats Stephen and, firmly gripping Katherine's purse, toddles purposefully out through the silky pink door of the tent to find Elizabeth, biting and licking it as it slides smoothly over his face.

'I'm sorry. Did you mind him coming in to get his fortune told?' Katherine is treading carefully.

'I don't see anything in the ball,' mumbles Maureen.

'Oh, have another look. Will I travel to faraway places? Will I build a spaceship in the back garden to take me to the moon?' Katherine, keenly aware of just how juvenile she might be sounding, is determined and tender. 'It was only for fun, pet; don't take it all so seriously. Anyway, I think Richard Marr was delighted; he's always wanted a dog.'

'He told you what I said!' Maureen's voice is urgent.

'Well . . .' Katherine is hesitating. 'I asked him and he was too polite not to tell.'

Silence. Maureen's fingers, still clutching the crystal ball, have white-hot edges to them. She raises her eyes to look at her mother. She is turning the crystal ball slowly in her hands, mulling something over and over in her head. Then after a gentle intake of breath, she says to Katherine, 'Mummy . . . what does love feel like?'

'Love?' Katherine echoes gently. A single silver-gilded fish darts back into the crystal ball of the sea.

'I mean . . . how do you know? How do you know when you're in love?'

'Well . . .' Katherine had not expected this. Maureen's directness takes Katherine by surprise. 'Well . . .'

'Is it supposed to make you feel rotten?' continues Maureen.

'Rotten? Not particularly, no, pet. Rotten in what way?'

'Rotten about yourself.'

Katherine looks tenderly at Maureen, trying to decipher exactly what her daughter's emotions are. Her own emotions are beginning to race.

'You just know,' Katherine continues softly.

'But *how* do you know?' Maureen's tone is anxious.

'Because . . . you feel . . . you feel yourself floating and burning at the same time.'

Katherine hears herself explaining it as if it is fact. As if she knows exactly what love is. Can decode it, clarify it, quantify it.

Floating and burning.

Maureen looks cautiously at her mother.

'And it makes you feel different from before.' Katherine smiles at Maureen, the corners of her mouth turning down with compassion.

Floating and burning and different from before. So these are the codes of love, glimpsed and now shared. And Katherine has explained it to her daughter as though she has understood it herself. As though she has understood how the experience of love preoccupies and claims its space. As though she has understood how the experience of love has preoccupied and claimed her.

Stephen comes toddling back into the tent, the silky pink scarf sliding over him slickly in one rapid movement, revealing him suddenly as if he were part of an illusionist's magic trick. The lack of space curtails him immediately.

'Li-li ky-ing,' he shouts excitedly. 'Ky-ing.' He presses his two hands into Katherine's lap, looking up at her intently.

'What's wrong with Elizabeth?' Katherine is distracted a moment from her conversation with Maureen.

'Awh gon.' Stephen turns and heads out of the tent again, assuming that his mother is right behind him.

'Don't worry, my love.' Katherine strokes Maureen's face. Then shifting slightly on the wooden toolbox, she continues: 'I should go out and see what's going on with Elizabeth.'

Maureen sighs deeply, then straightens her body. She looks at her mother. There is a brief pause.

'I'm going to change out of these clothes.' Maureen says.

'Good idea, pet.' Katherine still talks quietly and tenderly. 'Let's see what's happening outside.'

'Oh, wait a minute.' Maureen looks down into her crystal ball 'A friend is going to visit you very soon and bring you something.' Maureen looks at her mother and seems a little less upset.

'Oh, thank you, love – something nice, I hope.' Katherine smiles at her daughter, placing her penny on the table. 'Come on, let's go outside.'

Maureen puts the crystal ball down. There are now two black pennies on the tabletop, two dark eyes staring at her. She pulls the scarf briskly from her head and makes her way out of the tent to follow her mother, stooping gracelessly through the exit and leaving the vapours of confession behind. Outside, the sunlight blasts them both.

In the dusky raspberry light of the fortune-telling tent, the crystal ball lies on the table, like a glass heart in which the sun has set. The two dark eyes look into it. And shards of tiny silvery fish have now returned. They swim and dart in the mellow hues. Among the fish now there are words floating, drifting. And as the words turn and twist, they catch the muted rays of light and flicker as though they are burning.

Floating and burning.

The words among the silvery fish: 'What . . . does . . . love . . . feel . . . like.'

Katherine finds Elizabeth crying. Stephen, as instructed by his mother, had given the purse to Elizabeth. But Elizabeth, too busy orchestrating blindfolds and buckets and hoops and prizes, had hurriedly put the purse down in the longer grass by the edge of the swing and then could not find it. Katherine now wipes Elizabeth's eyes with a cotton handkerchief and reassures her that they will find the purse. And they do. They find it on the white elephant stall beside the bottle of 4711 eau de cologne – as easily as that. Someone had spotted it in the grass and had placed it there for safekeeping.

The sun continues shining, warming the heads and backs and arms of everyone at the fair. Katherine is chatting to Mrs. Carter. Isabel is showing Peter Barnsley that she *can* climb a tree in hot pants and is settling herself on a slender branch of the apple tree to prove it, looking like a glinting golden fruit. Maureen, now out of her Madam Maureen costume, is helping Elsa sell off the last bits and pieces on the tables. Elizabeth is sitting on the grass, making a long, long daisy chain for Stephen, who is clapping his hands in delight. And Richard Marr, who had been the one who had pinned the tail closest to the donkey's rear, is sitting on the garden wall with a small glass of white lemonade, looking at Maureen.

Surprisingly, no one has managed to hit the upturned buckets beside the apple tree. A small bag of toffees sits in the grass in the summer sun, growing soft.

It is evening and the girls are getting ready for bed. As they brush their teeth, they take turns singing hymns through the gentle white foam in their mouths. In the bathroom, crowded around the washhand basin, they elbow one another as they sing. Their spittals of praise make them giggle and swallow too quickly and choke and giggle all the more. They brush the holy words around their mouths until their teeth are as clean as their souls ought to be. They sputter into the washhand basin and watch their venial sins, their cross words, their white lies, their small unkindnesses, all the little bits and pieces of themselves that make them them, swirl down the plughole. They are sanctified in a skittish kind of way and their tongues are sweet and minty.

Katherine stands at the bedroom door watching them, but she is preoccupied. The question that Maureen had asked her earlier inside the fortune-telling tent keeps repeating in her mind like the words of a song she cannot loose. Over and over. An incantation to the fantasy of his return: *What does love feel like? What does love feel like? Floating and burning: just like when he holds her with that polite formality yet his forehead presses a little too heavily against her temple as they move. Just like when the hazy coppery light is splintered by intense, triumphant bursts of gold and crimson. Like when she can feel his weight against her, his breath a pulse upon her neck and the faint scent of almonds from his mouth. Surely she will hear what he says to her no matter how quietly he speaks. What if they do not look at each other? What if, in fact, their eyes are closed and their mouths have fallen slightly open, as though they are astonished at each other? Her green chiffon dress has fallen low at the back, so that her shoulder blades are illuminated in the soft gleam. The yellow light behind them is like an evening sky that defines their silhouette. The broad slab of his palm has moved across the hollow of her back and guides her to the floating rhythms of the music. The sleeve of his grey suit has ruffled back a little, revealing a length of wrist. They sway easily. But the pressure of his forehead on her temple is increasing, as though it is giving him away, for he cannot hide his lust for her. It feels like he is back with her again . . .*

Suddenly, the three girls spill past Katherine into their bedroom, laughing and collapsing like whirling skittles on the floor. Katherine rouses herself (what's gotten into her?). She speaks quietly but firmly. 'Easy now, girls. You'll wake Stephen. C'mon, into bed.'

The girls' bedroom is, for the most part, a hand-me-down from the previous occupants, the turnip planters. The delicately floral wallpaper print has faded gradually with each season passing, but the cornflower blue of the carpet has remained resolutely cornflower blue despite the fact that, in parts, it is now threadbare and worn and shows the straw-coloured weave of its underside. On the wall opposite to the door stands a tall wardrobe with a light, grainy veneer; its door closes with a slight wobble and a quick click. Its key has been removed so as to avoid accidental incarceration. George and Katherine have added to the room as and when they can afford to. Tangerine curtains have recently been hung to brighten the room, the new paper roller blind they put up has since been punctured here and there by fingers idle or curious, and, on the floor in the centre of the room, there is a rug the colour of gentle lime. The rug's edges now curl up like a fortune fish.

Alongside the tall wardrobe, there is a built-in cupboard whose white sheeny doors conceal a modest collection of toys, dolls, books, Lego blocks, skipping ropes, balls, board games, and a whole model village of Applewood Green and its inhabitants, apart from Dr. Broom, who has slipped down through a tiny hole where the plaster skims the skirting board (when Elsa shines a flashlight down into the tiny cavern, she can just make out the top of his black hat), and so whenever they play with the model village, Dr. Broom always has to be away on an emergency call.

The three single beds have been arranged at one end of their bedroom around its neat chimney breast. The bed that lies across the breast is Elsa's, the other two, Maureen's on the right and Elizabeth's on the left, fit snugly into the recesses on either side.

The girls, in their excitement, are now crawling on their hands and knees from one bed to another like escapees through a maze of tunnels, continually turning this way and that, as if no one can find the way out. Katherine, tired after their busy day organising the fair, is hopeful that they will settle down.

'Socks off, pyjamas on,' she orders, noticing the first notch of impatience in her voice.

'No, Mummy. Play chicken shadows,' pipes Elsa.

'It's too late, love, and it's been a long day.'

Maureen and Elizabeth now join in. 'Please, Mummy.'

'Just one game.' Elsa's tone of voice is all leverage to win her mother around. Elsa's palms are pressed together and her eyes are wide in mock prayer.

'Ple-e-e-ase.'

Katherine is feeling tiredness like a soft white pain. She looks at her three daughters, expectant, imploring, and needy. They are shuffling awkwardly into their nightclothes, hurriedly stuffing two legs into one pyjama leg, like giddy mermaids. Katherine feels the weight of Elsa's manipulation as though a drowning man is pulling her under the surface of the sea. If she yields, is easy in herself, her own lightness will save them. If she resists, the children will become saturated with her irritation, slipping away from her into a dismal and unnecessary fretful sleep, while she will return to the kitchen, her lungs full to their saltwater brim with a nagging and futile remorse. But after a day doing every little and last thing for them, she now longs to close the door on motherhood, just for a brief while, and be whoever she is without them. If that possibility exists. Through her haze of fatigue she hears herself say, 'Okay, then, just one game,' and immediately she comes afloat with the drowning man.

The girls excitedly turn out the central light in the bedroom, leaving only one bedside light on. They squiggle in beside one another on Elsa's bed, leaving room for Katherine. Katherine lifts Elsa's socks, which have been left on the floor, and, easing off her slippers, pulls one of the socks over her toes. The sock flops like a gnome's soft hat.

Katherine now surrenders gladly to the gentle massage of her own laughter and the closeness of her daughters. Their limbs are like the limbs of foals, playful and gauche. Katherine is squawking and clucking and creating voices to go with the shapes her floppy-socked toes are making, becoming farmer and fowl. Her yielding to her children has brought bounties once again, as it always does. The girls are laughing hysterically.

'That looks like Maureen and Richard Marr,' says Elsa.

'What do you mean?' Maureen asks.

'When *that* sock' – Elsa points—'flops over *that* one, it's like you and Richard Marr in the tent – kissing in the tent – look!'

'We were not kissing!' Maureen thumps Elsa.

Katherine jumps in. 'That's unkind, Elsa. Say sorry to Maureen. Easy, Maureen. Don't hit Elsa.'

'What *were* you doing, then?' asks Elizabeth.

'Not *you* as well!' says Maureen.

'What's wrong with kissing somebody?' asks Katherine, trying her best to defend Maureen.

The three girls stop and stare at their mother.

'It's yuck!' says Elsa. 'And the nuns said that if you ever kiss someone, then that means you have to marry them, because nobody else will want you if you've already kissed somebody else.'

Maureen and Elizabeth are nodding in agreement.

'Oh really – is that what they told you?' Katherine frowns.

'Yes, Mummy. That's what the nuns said. Didn't you know that?' says Elizabeth with a serious expression on her face.

Katherine looks at the three girls. For a moment, she is lost for words. Then she pipes up, 'Okay, I think the game is over, girls – time to sleep!'

Still chatting and arguing, the girls, nevertheless, climb obediently into their respective beds. Eventually, their babble calms and a sudden, still atmosphere descends on the room as they fall asleep.

When Katherine now checks on them, she quietly moves to each of their beds in turn. Elsa's mouth is open slightly, and if Katherine looks closely enough, she can determine Elsa's lower lip twitching with a tiny pulse. One of Elsa's arms is stretched out underneath her head, her hand firmly grasping the wooden bars of the bedstead as though she is trying to save herself from falling off the world or floating away from it. Katherine knows only too well Elsa's anxieties in falling asleep and thinks to herself now what a trusting child she is to ride this fear of nighttime again and again.

Katherine then brushes back a few strands of brown-black hair that have fallen softly over Maureen's face, unveiling a young woman, not a child. The contours of Maureen's face have been altering continuously through these summer weeks, so that now it is all future. And on the other side of Elsa lies Elizabeth, hidden under the blankets, so that only tufts of light brown hair stick out.

Katherine leaves the girls' bedroom like a lioness reluctantly leaving her cubs, and before she goes downstairs, she pushes her own bedroom door back a little so she can get another quick glance of Stephen. He lies sprawled in his cot like a basket of spilled fruit, arms splayed alongside his head and open to the world, legs stretched over the little mountain he has made of his blankets, head settled into the downy hollow of his pillow. Katherine pulls his blankets up over his legs and chest. She can't resist kissing him.

As Katherine makes her way to the kitchen, she looks out the window. It is as though there are two skies in one. Where the sun has set, on the far side of Cave Hill, the sky is an intense ball of golden light, bleeding beads of orange and fiery pink. The rest of the sky is a cool blue, peppered only here and there with dots of purple cloud.

Looking at the garden under this indecisive sky, she can see how overgrown it has become. Somehow during the resilient ring of daylight, she had not been so aware of this, as though growth checked itself under surveillance and issued forth only when the eye was averted. For now in the pearly streams of evening light, she can see how much the ivy has spread itself over every wall of the garden into the uneven flower beds, seething, it seems, right in front of her as it grows, and stretching its viny fingers down and under the honest chins of the nearby shrubs. What started as a tender touch has tightened and overtaken like an eager, parasitic love. A porraceous palette she sees through her kitchen window. There, the faint silvery white of the dead nettle. And there, the flat, delicate umbels of the ground elder. And there, in the midst of the falling dark, the ghostly outline of Madam Maureen's fortune-telling tent, its sides now drooping with the settling weight of the moist evening air. How on earth did she not notice, when she was playing with the girls earlier, that their beds were still missing some sheets and blankets?

Out of the silence, the telephone rings. Katherine moves quickly from the kitchen out into the hallway to answer it. It is George, calling from the station.

'Katherine, I'm sorry, I was called into the station straight from work and I'm going to be home much later than I thought. Okay, love?' His voice sounds agitated.

'I was wondering, George. Everything all right?'

'Ach, reports of petrol-bomb attacks are coming in thick and fast and there've been arson attacks across the city, so it could be all hours before I'm back. Don't wait up.'

'I'm sorry I didn't realise things were that bad. Are the police out, too?'

'Yes – yes – listen, Katherine, I have to go.'

'George?'

'Yes?'

'I didn't get a chance this morning to say sorry about yesterday, about shouting . . . when you were leaving . . . and the statuette . . . I didn't mean . . .' Katherine's voice is shaking.

'I don't want to talk about it, Katherine.'

'I don't know what's wrong with me.'

'I have to go.'

'I'm tired. That's all it is, I'm sure.'

'*Katherine.*'

'All right, George, all right. Be careful, won't you.'

'Yeah.'

'Oh, George, you missed a great day. We had a fair in the back garden and—'

But George has already hung up.

On her way back to the kitchen, Katherine finds the remnants of Madam Maureen's costume – the green paisley scarf, the mushroom-coloured skirt, the soft leather belt – stuffed into a corner under the stairs. She picks them up and throws them over the end of the banister to be put away properly in the morning. She is too tired to do it now. She turns off the lights downstairs, leaving on only the outside light by the front door for George's return home. She turns off the lights upstairs, in the girl's bedroom and on the landing, and welcomes night into the house. She climbs into bed, but she does not sleep.

Floating and burning at the same time – Isn't that how she had explained what love felt like to her daughter?

*Floating and burning.*

*Back with her again. To hold him. To smell his skin. To kiss him . . .*

# 4

*September 1949*

A ROUTINE HAD DEVELOPED. Against her better judgment, she knew, for routines served only to consolidate things and then make them feel normal. Yes, she knew that. But she could not help herself. Tom had a hold on her that she could not deny. And there was – if she was to be totally honest with herself – the thrill of this secret world.

The excuse she gave to her mother, to her colleagues at work if they, perhaps, asked her to join them on an evening out, and to George was always the same: She was rehearsing *Carmen*. And although no one ever questioned her, the lie had its way of niggling at her nonetheless. She'd sense the crimson streaks of guilt along her neck and then the buds of tightness underneath her skin as she tidied up her work and made her way from the Ulster Bank offices onto High Street. But by the time she reached Boyne & Son, Men's Tailors and Outfitters, all thoughts of her deceitfulness would have evapourated into thin air and she would feel as though she had just burst from a cocoon.

As Katherine would arrive at the tailors' rooms, the last of the junior tailors would be leaving, having cleared their tables, stacked their rolls of cloth against the back wall, and set their sewing tools in orderly fashion ready for the following day's work. Only Ivy would remain. That's what Katherine liked to call her – the girl with the ivy-patterned blouse. Her real name, she had learned from Tom, was Miss Beacham, Miss Celia Beacham, but 'Ivy' had become a private joke between herself and Tom and so the nickname had stuck. As Katherine walked toward the anteroom, where Tom was waiting for her, Ivy would be sitting on her roost of ledger books, her back to the room. No hellos were exchanged, so busy was Ivy at her desk, but Katherine was convinced as she walked past her that Ivy's eyes and ears were taking everything in.

Katherine was content to sit and watch Tom work, there in the coppery light of the room, curled up on a wooden chair, her heels drawn in underneath her, her arms gently wrapped around her knees. And he appeared content just to have her near him. They would chat, as he worked, about music or the weather or about what new film was showing at the Imperial Picture House or at the Classic. She would lift his cigarette from the ashtray on his worktable and take a drag from it, leaving traces of her orange-red lipstick along its length. Or sometimes she would sing snippets from *Carmen*, but so quietly, it was as though her voice were coming into him from a different room. Tom sat at his worktable, his shoulders hunched forward, sometimes overcasting the braided edges of a blazer or adjusting the buttonholes in a waistcoat. Or sometimes pressing a recently finished evening tailcoat under a hot iron; then the room would fill with the intoxicating smell of new cloth. Like the splintery smell of powdered stone, she thought. Sometimes she would wander around the room as he worked, picking out buttons from their boxes, inspecting paper patterns, half dreamily playing with the spools of dark thread. Some would have found the quietness austere, unsettling even, but Katherine felt protected by it, as though nothing else in the world existed. It was only when she heard the click of the glass panelled door from the main room as Ivy left to go home did she feel the small bite of adrenaline in the pit of her stomach.

The waiting over.

Her hair falling from its soft coil. His hands loosening it. The movement filling the pores of her scalp. She cannot take enough of him in. A brushstroke of cloud in the evening sky. The ticking of the clock. A bruise now on her left hip.

One evening when Katherine arrived at the tailors' rooms, Tom was not there. Ivy, as usual, was sitting at her desk. Her blouse this time had tight red roses on it. Her slender white fingers moved like bleached bones across the yellowing pages of her ledger book. Her mouse brown hair was so neatly pinned back on either side of her head, it seemed as though her lily-pale ears had just bloomed out of it. She smelled of tea and lavender. Katherine stood by the open doorway of the anteroom. Ivy lifted her head from her work. When she spoke, she revealed a row of tiny teeth.

'If you're looking for *him*, he's gone!' Her tone was almost triumphant.

'Mr. McKinley, he's gone?' I have never seen a mouth so small as hers, thought Katherine.

'Yes, gone. But he'll be back. Said he'd be half an hour.'

'Oh, right, thank you.'

'Though I reckon he'll be ages if Mr. Boyne has his way.'

'Mr. Boyne?'

'Mr. McKinley has important business with him, if you know what I mean.' Ivy's mouth was a tiny, bitter slit.

'No, I'm afraid I don't.'

'Money issues.' Ivy raised her eyebrows and then gave a slow and precise nod to Katherine as though to denote that she would be saying no more on the matter. But barely a moment passed before she continued. 'Thought you'd heard. Nothing that a few whiskies between them in the Orpheus won't solve, I suppose.' Ivy looked gratified. 'But we all know that Mr. Boyne is not a patient man.'

'Sorry – Miss Beacham, isn't it?' Ivy narrowed her eyes in confirmation. 'Miss Beacham, I really have no idea what you're talking about.'

'You see, I was just as surprised as everyone else – I never thought Mr. McKinley would be the gambling type.' Ivy shook her head slowly from side to side.

'Gambling type?'

'They say it was only a mere flutter here and there – the dogs on a Saturday, the occasional horse race – but last month Mr. McKinley lost a whole week's wages following a tip-off from a man he hardly knew who works in the pub just across the road there – apparently!' Ivy swiveled on her ledger books, pointing out the window located on her right to indicate the pub in question. 'And then, in a panic, he borrowed money from Mr. Boyne's business in order to get himself back on track – unbeknownst to Mr. Boyne, *of course* – but Mr. McKinley lost that, as well. Terrible, isn't it? They say all he needed was one win, just one to sort it all out, and now it's all one big mess. Mr. Boyne – apparently – wants to proceed with—'

Katherine cut across Ivy. 'They say? Who say?'

'Oh, people – you know.' Ivy toyed with the tiny pearl buttons on her rose-covered blouse.

'No, I don't know, and I really don't think it's anybody's business what Mr. McKinley—'

'Doesn't matter anyway. I've done my job. I've passed on the message about his being half an hour late for your *fitting*.' Ivy's mouth snapped closed like a trap, but her eyes held on Katherine. It was as though Ivy was waiting to see what Katherine would do now that she had received this information about Mr. McKinley.

Katherine stared back at Ivy with a cheeky defiance.What a nasty piece of work, she thought, walking slowly into the anteroom and closing the door behind her.

Despite this little display of arrogance, Katherine felt uneasy. What could Ivy have meant? Was Tom in some kind of trouble? Was he hiding something from her? Her conscience prodded her, urging her to find the one fault that would bring her back to her senses; willing her to find the solid reason that would prove that her relationship with Tom was all wrong. See? her conscience was trying to say. It wasn't meant to be. You know nothing about him. You don't know what he could be hiding. You should be with George. What has possessed you?

Katherine paced the room, unable to sit easy in the wooden chair, frequently glancing out of the window to see if she could catch a glimpse of Tom making his way back along High Street, pulling absentmindedly at this piece of material and that.

Above her on top of the work cabinet, the porcelain statuette of the tailor, which Katherine had given to Tom as a present, still stood; she had placed it there the first night they had stayed together in the tailors' rooms; a sentry to their lovemaking. As she flicked through scraps of paper on Tom's desk, Katherine felt as though its eyes were watching her, two tiny infinities, sequinned black, following her every move. Judging her perhaps. Katherine reached up and turned the statuette around so that it faced the wall.

Twenty minutes later, Katherine heard the familiar ring of Tom's voice from the main room, then the high-pitched trill of Ivy's voice in reply, but plaintive not chirpy. Katherine opened the door of the anteroom. Tom was leaning over Ivy as she sat at her desk. There was a serious look on his face. Ivy had her back to Katherine and her head bowed, as though she was working fastidiously at the figures in her ledger book, but the tip of each lily pale ear was now ridged with pink. Tom lifted his head and quickly turned to Katherine. 'Just checking that Miss Beacham had passed on my message, Miss Fallon,' he said with a smile. 'Sorry to keep you waiting.'

'No, it's fine . . . really.' Katherine was immediately warmed by his polite pretence. 'Yes, Miss Beacham informed me you'd be late.' She played along with him, holding her position at the doorway.

'This shouldn't take long, Miss Fallon. I've only some adjustments to make on the bolero, that's all.' Tom straightened himself and walked toward Katherine.

Ivy sniffled loudly as he left her side.

Once inside the anteroom, Katherine's words rushed at Tom, 'Where were you?'

'Sorry, Katherine, I had a few things to sort out.' He seemed calm, good-humoured. Then, taking her hand, he said casually, 'Would you like to walk the embankment tonight?'

'Is everything all right?' Katherine kept her voice quiet.

'Yes, everything's fine. Why do you ask?'

The outer door clicked shut. Ivy was gone. Katherine's mind was racing now.

'What were the things you had to sort out, Tom?' Katherine could see plainly that Tom was a little taken aback by the seriousness of her tone.

'I had a meeting with Mr. Boyne,' he said slowly, 'I'm trying to reclaim some of the assets that had originally belonged to my father. The legalities are complicated, but I think I can find a way of getting around that. I have to play my cards right with Mr. Boyne, though; he's no dozer, so it might take a bit of time.'

As Katherine stood before Tom, there was nothing in his manner to suggest to her that he was hiding anything from her. Maybe best just to forget what Ivy said, Katherine thought. What a story for her to spin. All that stuff about gambling. What was she thinking? Tom wouldn't lie. Best put no stock in it. She looked into Tom's eyes; they were soft and clear and direct. She felt her breath catch a little. 'That's fine . . .' she replied gently. 'I was just wondering where you were . . . that's all.'

'Let me take you for a walk,' he said.

Only a crease of light reached them from the other side of the river, so that she could hardly see her feet in front of her. Her walk with him across the uneven ground sent a shudder through her bones with each misjudged step. Lifting her foot higher than necessary or not high enough. Scuffing her shoes against embedded stones. Catching the pocket of her coat on the hollow tubes of broken reeds. Hidden brambles plucking at her sleeve and calling her back. Knowing that the water was only feet away from her, only inches away at times. She could feel the coldness of it waiting.

He moved with ease. For him, just another walk home by the river.

They had set off from the corner of High Street, across the Albert Bridge, passing by the McConnell's Weir, where a steel girder had broken away from one of the abutments and had lodged itself in the water. In the dark, she could hear the girder confusing the current. They continued along the Ormeau Embankment, where suddenly the light just seemed to fall away from them in pieces. Eventually, they found a sitting stone just a little downstream of the Ormeau Bridge, a flat hunk of rock where the narrow path broadened a little on the embankment. The river below them was the colour of metal.

She felt as though the sharp night air was skinning and deseeding her senses. Why? She could not explain it to herself. Something to do with the murky blackness, perhaps. Something to do with Tom's playful disregard for her: Taking her for a walk along the embankment with no moon to guide them. Something to do with what Ivy had said about him. It was all playing on her mind. She felt a shiver through her spine.

Then out of the dark he took a box of matches and his tailor's notebook from his pocket. He opened the book and tore a page from its centre. He twisted the paper and set it alight with a match. Their faces were illuminated for a few seconds in its glow. Then he gently threw the twist of paper into the river. He tore another page and set it alight and then another, and another. Tiny bombs of light fell into the black. Blossomed on the water like fire lilies. They held their light in the wet dark for a few moments and floated in a cluster with the current, then went out. She breathed the night air in. She watched the display. She listened to the sound of the water against the stones. She sighed. She began to feel warmer as they sat together. Her eyes adjusted to the dark. She looked out over the river. The reeds were brushed flat like long, wet hair against the bank from the last fall of heavy rain. She lifted her head. The night was beautiful. The sky so full of night clouds, it was as though it wasn't there at all. Seen through his eyes, her city was transforming itself in front of her, and she realised that it wasn't what surrounded her that was affecting her as much as his interpretation of it. Her city was rounding itself out of darkness and into light. Like a new world being bidden. She looked at him as he put a match to another twist of paper and a tiny arc of light streaked his face. He brings wonder out of the ordinary, she thought. That is his talent. His gift to me. There is no need for me to be unsure. He held the twist of paper up to her face. Show me, he said. She smiled at him. She knew what he wanted. She opened her handbag and took out her mirror and her lipstick and, as the paper burned close to her face, she eased orange-red across her lips. Then she took out her music sheet and, folding it in half, she pushed it against her mouth to take the excess. He watched her. I do this every time before I sing, she said to him. Every time it's a signal that I will nurture my dreams until they come true. What dreams, Katherine? he asked. To sing, she said. To sing all over the world, to travel and see what the world has to offer. To go to America. She laughed. You don't think it's stupid or mad to think like that, to want to do that? No, he said, far from it. I'll follow you, he said, and I'll dress you in silks. I'll make all your costumes big enough so that I can hide under your skirts. She laughed again. He took her music sheet in his hand. You know what the words mean? He asked her. No, she said, she didn't, well not exactly. Not all of them. You should be ashamed of yourself, Carmen. Here, take this. He handed her another twist of paper. He ignited it. It burned in her hand. Then, he read aloud, *'Si tu ne m'aimes pas, Si tu ne m'aimes pas, je t'aime; Mais si je t'aime, si je t'aime prends garde a toi!'* So, this is what you are saying to José, he said. And then, he wrote out his translation for her at the bottom of her music sheet: 'Love you not me, love you not me, then I love you; But if I love you, if I love you, beware of me!' How do you know these things? she asked him.

The paper light went out and the river lilies faded. He and she disappeared together into the black of the world. But when he kissed her, she was all the colour of orange-red.

You don't think I'm mad to have dreams like that, do you? she asked him.

No, he said, I don't.

You don't?

She alighted the number thirty-one trolley bus into town. The conductor pulled on the bell rope. As the trolley bus pulled away from the curb, she reached for the rounded grab handles on the ends of the seats and carefully made her way down to the front of the lower saloon. She tucked her pearl grey woollen coat under her and sat down on the princess blue leather seat. She sat, appalled at herself.

Her menstrual period had been only one week late, but this was so unusual for her, for her cycle had always been regular. So regular, in fact, that, month by month, she could predict when she would start almost to the very hour.

In her pocket she carried a set of her mother's rosary beads. It wasn't in her nature to pray, even though her mother had always insisted on the family saying the Rosary every evening for as long as she could remember, even though they never missed Mass on a Sunday, even though the nuns at school had driven Catholicism into her with a devout and steely determination. But she needed to turn to something. She needed providence, intervention; she needed her luck to change. She slipped her hand into her coat pocket to touch the rosary beads and whispered a prayer.

The conductor came to collect her fare, tapping impatiently on his ticket machine. She handed the conductor twopence for the short journey she was taking, only three stops from her flat on the Castlereagh Road to the corner of Templemore Avenue. She would walk the rest of the way from there. The conductor punched a hole in a mustard-coloured ticket and handed it to her. She held the ticket in one hand and with the other she wiped the misted window beside her and looked out through the finger-width slices of clear glass as the streetlights moved past her in long, crystal streams.

Only one week late.

And for that week, she had never felt so much confusion. Her emotions had swung, like a pendulum, from one absolute to another. One moment, she would picture that everything was as it once had been. Tom had somehow suddenly melted away in her mind and she and George were a devoted couple again. The next moment, her heart would seize with panic at the very thought that she might never see Tom again. Over and over again she brushed against, then swept past the unthinkable: She was one week late.

She rubbed her finger anxiously where, for a brief time, she had worn her engagement ring. It would be weeks before she would be able to pay the remaining money due on the statuette and retrieve her ring. What had she been thinking? George had believed her when she had told him that she had thought it best to put the ring away safely until after *Carmen* had finished. She could not wear it as the character Carmen, she explained to him, and she could not possibly run the risk of taking the ring off in the rehearsal room or in the church hall – where they would perform the following week – as so many things went missing. And George had thought it prudent of her. He had not questioned her decision for a moment. She had taken advantage of his kindness, she knew. She had betrayed him. She was appalled at herself.

Over the past few weeks she had seen very little of George. He had been helping to organise a ceremony in honor of the members of the Fire Service who had helped in raising money for the rebuilding of the Ulster Hospital for Women & Children. George himself was to receive a commendation at the ceremony for his contribution as a retained fireman, and, sitting on the number thirty-one trolley bus, she was on her way to join him.

Appalled at herself. Appalled at where her own desires had brought her. Not quite comprehending how she was allowing herself to behave so irresponsibly. Sinfully, perhaps? Appalled at how she was resisting nothing. Most of all, appalled at how she had betrayed George. How could she ever forgive herself?

There was one thing she would have to do to redeem herself. She would have to bring it all out into the open. She would have to be brave enough to face the consequences. She would have to tell George what had happened and that it was over between them.

She touched the rosary beads in her pocket again. She gazed at her reflection in the misted window. She was a phantom silver shape in her pearl grey coat against the princess blue leather of the seat.

The trolley bus reached the corner of Templemore Avenue and, as she stood up from her seat, the conductor pulled once on the bell rope. She disembarked at McMordie's Hardware shop and, crossing Castlereagh Street, she reached her destination within a matter of minutes.

It was a modest ceremony; a group of perhaps fifty people had gathered in the main holding area of the station. Among them were George's mother, Anna, his father, William, and his older twin sisters. Four fire engines sat two behind two, each machine primed for manoeuvre at a moment's notice. The firemen stood on one side of the vehicles, their families and friends on the other.

George's mother and father greeted Katherine with wide smiles. She stood beside them and listened as the deputy chief fire officer opened the proceedings, informing guests that a short display would be presented by the firemen after Mr. Balmer, senior consultant of the Ulster Hospital, had said a few words, and that some of the doctors, working in the restored wing of the hospital, would introduce themselves, and that there would be refreshments – tea, coffees, sandwiches – kindly provided by the women parishioners of the local Church of Ireland, at the end of the evening.

Katherine caught the look of pride on Anna Bedford's face and the seriousness of William Bedford's expression, which immediately had softened into the round face of a beaming boy when his son had smiled at him. She saw George's twin sisters, Heather and Susan, giggling and whispering comments about the young firemen who flanked the four glistening fire engines, suddenly respectfully hold their composure as Mr. Balmer stepped forward to make his address. She heard the singular, dry, nervous cough she knew to be George's as his name was called out in special acknowledgment of his exceptional contribution in raising money for the funds. She watched as George walked past her to shake Mr. Balmer's hand. How smart in his uniform, how handsome humility made him, how gentle and loving his smile as he turned to her, how proud she felt, how wretched she felt, how she felt her body and mind disintegrating where she stood, feeling she was falling away in pieces, crumbling like old, dried skin. She must tell him. She must tell him about Tom. Words echoing, ringing in this cavern of light and steel in which she now felt captive. The heat of the room in her pearl grey woollen coat. The glare of the lights on the high ceiling. Her stomach hot. The flash of gleaming red from the fire engines. Her head tight. The heat in her woollen coat. Her legs unstable. And her body collapsing like a door blown shut.

In the last moments of consciousness, she could hear George calling to her, and a slack, embarrassed laugh from the crowd who had gathered around her as someone asked, 'Is there a doctor in the house?'

George had taken Katherine home after the Fire Service ceremony and had urged her to rest the following day, but she had gone into work regardless, informing her mother over breakfast that she felt better and only a little tired. All day at work, she battled with herself. Blaming herself for not telling George about Tom, hating the fact that she had lost her nerve. Next time I see George, I promise I'll end it, she said to herself. Next time.

At five o'clock, Morna McFarlane from the Arrears Department at the Ulster Bank offices asked Katherine to join her and a few of the cashiers for a drink at Sherries. But too eager to meet up with Tom again, Katherine declined with her usual excuse.

'You're terrible, you are. You and your singin'.' If I didn't know any better, Katherine Fallon, I'd have said you had a wee fancy man hidden away there somewhere!' Morna pushed her round chin into the air and pressed her plump hands against her ample chest. 'Wait till I tell George.' She laughed loudly, then pulled on her heavy wool coat.

Katherine smiled nervously.

'Don't look so shocked – unless, of course, you *do* have a wee fancy man!' Morna fastened four big brass buttons. 'Well, come here to me – next time you're going out, you're going out with *me* – right!'

Katherine nodded.

'It's just them two new cashiers – Helen and Sheila – they're no fun. All they talk about is illnesses and operations and who's died and who didn't die but nearly died. Like two old crows.' Morna busily fixed the straps of her leather handbag over her arm as she spoke. 'Right,' she said, shaking her head in resignation, 'I'm off. I'll see ye tomorrow, then!' Then just before she disappeared around the corner of the corridor, Morna turned her head and shouted back to Katherine, 'And don't forget to say hello to your wee fancy man for me!'

As Katherine approached the tailors' rooms that evening, the door swung open as though it was being wrenched off its hinges and Ivy rushed out past her with tears streaming down her face. By the time Katherine turned to her to ask her what was wrong, Ivy had disappeared down the stairs and was gone. Katherine found Tom in the anteroom, sitting quietly at his worktable. He lifted his head and smiled at her as she entered the room.

'What's wrong with Ivy – with Miss Beacham?' said Katherine, perplexed.

'Oh, nothing . . . nothing.'

Katherine stared hard at Tom. 'Nothing? Didn't you see she was in floods of tears?'

'She's upset.'

Katherine couldn't hide her concern. 'I can see she's upset! But *why* is she upset? What happened?'

'I think it's unrequited love,' Tom said casually, and went back to his work.

Katherine felt pricked by his nonchalance. 'That's a bit cold-hearted. What if she needs someone to talk to?'

'I'm sure she'll be fine.'

'She told me you had "money issues" with Mr. Boyne,' Katherine said abruptly.

'She told you what?' Tom lifted his head.

'She told me you were gambling and that you'd lost a lot of money. What did she mean, Tom? Are you in trouble?'

'Nothing of the sort.'

'Please, Tom, you can tell me anything.'

'There's nothing to tell. Don't mind what Miss Beacham says – she's prone to hysterics at the best of times. Really, Katherine, everything is fine.'

'But why would she say such a thing if it wasn't true?'

'It *isn't* true, Katherine, I promise you. Miss Beacham has a very active imagination – and has all day to sit and feed it! Don't pay any attention to her. Come here to me.' He held his arms out to her. She embraced him, but as he held her, she felt a chill rinse over her skin.

It was Wednesday night, the opening night of *Carmen*. From where she stood in her shadowy corner behind the scenery flats of the church hall, Katherine watched Charlie Copeland rocking to and fro on a little wooden stool. The stool sat to the side of an array of street sellers' baskets and wooden wheelbarrows, which were to be brought on after the overture. It wasn't the first time she had witnessed this self-imposed incarceration of Charlie's, from which, this time, it seemed to her, he could not release himself. She watched his strained yet muted expression and knew it to be merely a faint extenuation of the whole fevered scenario going on inside his head. Charlie's glasses slipped down the bridge of his nose, which was moist with sweat. He nervously pushed them back. Charlie had only ever sung onstage before as part of the chorus and now, as Zuniga, he had lines to say – had lines to 'deliver,' as the director had put it. With very little time to go before 'curtain up,' he had the demeanour of a man preparing not for his first performance, but for his own execution.

Right beside him, squashed into a tiny section of the backstage area that was free of props and stage furniture, the Cigarette Factory Girls practiced their choreographed routine for the first extract they were to perform, their smooth, white, young faces all wearing the same kind of forced smile. Their conical felt hats, which were perched precariously on the sides of their heads, shook violently as they danced. Katherine could see clearly that they were only adding to Charlie's agitation. They were jumping and fussing and becoming overly excited, thumping on the floor as they moved, insisting they rehearse the same piece again and again. Whenever they stopped to draw breath, she could hear Charlie muttering loudly enough so that the girls would hear him say, 'What in God's name are they at, these lumps of girls? Why can't they rehearse somewhere else? Why are they so damn eager?'

Her gaze lifted from Charlie and across to James McCauley, who was standing behind the street sellers' baskets, wearing too-generous earrings as Escamillo. The earrings looped like two large, glinting dog's ears to grace his shoulders. He kept making small movements with his head, testing out their weighty sway, a little unsure as to whether or not they made him look foolish, so that his heavily made-up eyebrows seemed to be signalling pathos even before he had begun to perform.

Then beside her, Rosemary Wylie appeared, talking to the air and insisting on leaving her wristwatch on. It had been a present from her fiancé and she was refusing to part with it. No one would notice that it wasn't in period, she was saying – what was the period anyway, did anybody know? Rosemary Wylie was playing the part of Micaela, but from the very first day of rehearsal, it had been obvious that she would much rather have been playing the part of Carmen – it was the way in which Rosemary Wylie had smiled at everyone when the cast list was announced, as though she were smelling something dreadfully unpleasant. Now, she was not happy with the three enormous gold leaves that had been sewn across the bodice of her costume. They were unflattering, she thought; they interfered with the shape of her bosom. Much better the décolletage that had featured in the original costume designs. Why had it been changed? The stage manager, a plump, short-haired woman named Cissie McGee, whispered loudly from the prompt corner that there would be no time to discuss costumes. Most of the cast had seen their costumes for the first time tonight. Some of the costumes were not even finished – that's just the way it had turned out – and so everyone just needed to get on with the job at hand, check their props and be ready for the performance. Curtain would be up in ten minutes. Rosemary Wylie's features sank slowly back into her face, as though they were flotsam on quicksand, as she listened to Cissie McGee, her nostrils flaring in a last but vainglorious attempt to save herself.

Hugh Drummond – Don José – suddenly arrived and rushed into the backstage area, tucking his ruffled shirt into the waistband of his pantaloons and swinging his costume jacket high above his head and around his shoulders. Urgency always made Hugh feel important. He slapped Charlie Copeland on his back as he passed behind him, nearly knocking Charlie off his little wooden stool.

'Charlie, my good man, just made it. And how's the lumbago this evening!'

Charlie made strenuous efforts to regain his composure before replying sourly, 'Never better, Hugh, never better.'

'Oh, hello there, girls!' Hugh watched the Cigarette Factory Girls skip and hop as he tucked in the last ruffle of his shirt.

'Hugh Drummond, where have you *been*?' Cissie McGee's whisper was a razor blade.

'I told you – I have rugby training Wednesdays!'

'Rugby training! But this – is – it's the opening night!'

'It'll be great – don't worry.' Hugh rushed off to check that all his props were in place. Cissie McGee sighed loudly with exasperation.

Katherine stood quietly, watching everything, hardly visible to anyone in the dim light. She needed to focus on what was happening. She needed to watch Charlie Copeland and James McCauley and Rosemary Wylie and Hugh Drummond and the Cigarette Factory Girls and Cissie McGee in order to keep her mind from splitting. She needed to pay attention to every detail around her in order to distract her from what she knew she had to do. And as she ran her hand along the front of her costume, she could feel where some of the buttons would not close properly, as though her abdomen had swollen a little since the costume fittings. Glancing through a gap in the scenery flats, she could just about make out Mrs. Davenport, Miss Robinson, Mr. Creaney, and Miss McGrath taking their places at piano, violin, flute, and percussion, respectively, in the tiny orchestra pit at the front of the stage. They were smiling and nodding to one another as they organised their music sheets on the stands. Those in the audience were settling themselves. It had been decided that Katherine's mother, her sister, Vera, and her brother, Frank, would come to see Katherine perform *Carmen* on Friday, the second-to-last night of the show, as George would be off duty from the Fire Service then and could accompany them. Tonight, however, he would be working and would call on Katherine at home after the show.

Katherine felt a rising pressure in her chest. She knew things could no longer remain as they were. She knew what she had to do. She had to tell George that it was over between them. And tonight she would tell him. Tonight she knew she would not see Tom, as he was taking his mother and sister out to the Grand Central Hotel for his mother's birthday. So she would go straight home and she would have time to talk to George. But the more this thought took position in her mind, the more she felt her body tightening with a sickening dread.

Cissie McGee began issuing orders from the prompt corner again. Immediately, Katherine turned her head to listen to Cissie, who said if anyone, for any reason, did not have a costume check before the performance, they would, unfortunately, have to wait until after the show and approach Miss Harper then. Cissie McGee stroked her thorax apprehensively as she spoke. It was Miss Harper who was to take over all the costume requirements now that the show was up and running. Well, almost up and running, Cissie added, giving a short, nervous laugh.

Katherine looked at Miss Harper, who now stood beside Cissie McGee. Miss Harper's dark brown hair fell softly onto her shoulders, highlighting the sweet cherub curve of her face, and in her hands she held a small black notebook. It was Tom's. The one he had used to record Katherine's measurements. The one whose pages he had made the fire lilies from. Oh, Tom. Katherine's thoughts began to race. She felt her blood was jangling in her veins, her heart tight and heavy, her breath lost to her. Everything as it once was, she said to herself. No – now everything was not as it once was and never could be, no matter how badly she wanted it to be. Now everything had changed.

'I was hoping to find you here.'

She was suddenly startled by Tom's voice. She turned to him, her breath catching in her throat.

'Tom – you're here?' She felt the blood drain from her face.

'You like the costume?'

'What are you doing here, Tom? Why are you here?' Katherine's tone was slightly desperate now. 'You told me you wouldn't be here tonight!'

'Plans fell through,' he said with a composure that pricked her a little. 'Mother wasn't feeling well. Anyway, tell me what you think of the costume.'

Katherine stared at Tom.

'It's lovely,' she said eventually, a slow chill seeping through her veins.

'That's it? That's all you can say?' He feigned disappointment to humour her. 'And after all the time I spent!' He laughed quietly. She said nothing. He looked at her. In the half-light, he could see the growing concern on her face. He reached out and lifted up her chin a little.

'Katherine, are you all right?'

She did not answer him.

'Don't worry, Katherine – all the material and the beads and the – they were from an old stockpile of my father's stuff I discovered in the storeroom. It cost me nothing. Don't look so worried.' He stroked her hair, attempting to reassure her. 'And I know you don't exactly look "make do and mend" but what the – I wanted to make it for you.'

She felt her body as a leaden weight. She could not deny to herself how her heart had opened like a glorious flower at seeing him. But now there was a darker edge to everything. Now as she looked at Tom, she felt the overwhelming weight of her intentions. In admitting to herself what she would lose, she wasn't so sure that she wanted to lose it anymore. Or, perhaps in truth, she wasn't so sure that she could deal with the consequences. She could feel her courage slipping, as though the floor itself had tilted and she had nothing to hang on to. The courage she had fought so hard to find. The courage she knew she needed in order to tell George. She couldn't hold on to it.

Tom took Katherine's hand and pressed something small into her palm.

'Take Mr. Agnew's keys to the tailors' rooms. Meet me there after the performance tonight.'

The tender pains of reasoning shook her; the pulses of shame and desire shuddered through her. And then, while her mind and heart were arrested by and flooded with this sweet confusion, he kissed her. But this time, she pulled away.

'I can't, Tom. I won't,' she heard herself saying.

A loud, tense voice came from the stage; it was Cissie McGee calling out to the cast. 'Five minutes to "curtain up," everyone!'

For the first time, she saw Tom's expression take on a gravity that almost frightened her, so deep was its measure. 'You will,' he said, looking directly into her eyes.

She could not contain her distress.

'Tom – I can't. This was all an awful mistake. All of it. All an awful mistake. I can't.' She felt her stomach lurch. 'It's just not possible!'

'An awful mistake? What are you talking about?' he asked, putting his hands on her waist as though to hold her steady. 'And why is it not possible?' He took her face in his hands. 'Katherine, we were meant to be together.'

Suddenly, the music started. Miss McGrath, a dark-haired, heavily built girl of about seventeen, hit the cymbal so loudly that three elderly ladies in the front row jumped in unison out of their seats, covering their chests with their hands as they did so, as though to hold their hearts in.

Katherine took a deep breath. She was shaking. She found herself taking the keys from Tom and slipping them into the pocket of her costume.

Tom smiled at her as he left.

She turned her head to catch Rosemary Wylie strutting confidently toward the downstage entrance, her high heels giving her the extra height she did not need. Charlie stood beside Cissie McGee, fidgeting with his cravat. He kept talking to her. It was all too ambitious, he was saying, all too ambitious. They had never tackled more than a medley of popular opera arias before and now here they were staging *Carmen* and there was just too much to remember. Charlie pushed his glasses back into position on the bridge of his nose.

The Cigarette Factory Girls bustled onto the stage and shook their felt hats to the tambourine.

And then it was her turn to step out of the shadows and enter as Carmen. As soon as she stepped into the light and onto the stage, there arose, all at once, a unanimous swell of 'Oooohhh' from the auditorium as the audience saw her costume.

It was how the bubbling stage conversations amid the cast members had all slowly wound down to a halt and how the orchestra, section by section, seemed to fall to sleep – first the strings, then the wind, then the lonely percussionist, all droning to a final stop. Rosemary Wylie had been the last to turn her head, and a low groan emitted from her throat like wind from a corpse.

It was only now they all saw Katherine's costume clearly for the first time. While every other character in the production had had costumes adapted from hand-me-downs and any possible pieces of material – curtain, upholstery, industrial fabric – any pieces that could be reshaped and refitted to suit their parts – uniforms for the soldiers, shawls for the street hawkers, Don José's pantaloons, Escamillo's waistcoat, Micaela's gold leaves – anything 'make do and mend' – Katherine's costume had been so beautifully tailored, so exquisitely and meticulously assembled, so expertly decorated that it drew from the cast not the reaction of appreciation but the embarrassment of inappropriateness.

Her costume was everything that Tom had said it would be the evening they had lain together in the tailors' rooms. Ottoman silk and soft bouclé wool, the colours of salmon, mandarin, coral, and cherry. The bodice fully boned and lined with lemon sateen. Tiny silk buttons. Beaded embroidery and silk-thread tassles along the edges of the bolero. An intricate arrangement of pleats and gores along the skirt. A silk vermilion braid trimming the hem in a long, scandalous line.

Charlie Copeland was the only one who broke the silence. 'How lovely you look,' he whispered loudly to her, his head poking out from the downstage entrance.

She could not begin singing until the excited murmurings from the crowd had settled.

A woman in the front row, wearing a flat turquoise hat, began frantically scanning the program page she was holding in her hand to find out who had designed such a magnificent piece of couture, and then she turned to her companion.

'A dream tailor, don't you think?' the woman said, her eyes wide with admiration.

# 5

*August 1969*

IT IS THE EARLY HOURS OF THE MORNING and George returns home exhausted and unsettled. Katherine is in bed but still awake and she hears him slip off his boots in the hall and hang up his jacket on the hook just under the stairs. She hears him give that singular, unproductive cough he gives whenever he feels anxious or worried or defeated, and even from up in the bedroom she can already smell the burned air and smoke that has followed him home. George moves up the stairs, stepping cautiously so as not to wake Katherine, yet he is relieved when she lifts her head from the pillow to look at him.

George lies beside Katherine on the bed, not getting into it, but lying on top of the blankets, stretching out on his side, his legs straight, his toes curled slightly. The night's events still surround him with all their confusion and uncertainty. He looks at Katherine, then casts his eyes down like a dog waiting for instruction. He squeezes his eyes tight, as though he is blocking something out or as though there is some griping pain gnawing at him. When Katherine lifts her hand to touch his cheek, his world immediately loosens. He begins shaking his head and talking in rapid, whispering bursts like a man possessed.

'It was totally unprofessional of me – I should have stayed out where the other men could find me – but – I just acted on impulse – I didn't check myself – I don't know why—'

'George, what is it? Slow down. What happened?'

'It was – we didn't have the manpower – there was so much trouble everywhere last night, we were overstretched – we were called to a house fire – Willowfield – had nothing to do with the mess that was going on in the city – the petrol-bomb attacks

– nothing. And it was only because I knew the layout of the house—'

'George,' Katherine says gently, 'slow down, love.'

George takes a deep breath, then continues.

'Those houses in Willowfield, I know the layout, that's why, I know the layout like the back of my hand.' It is as though he is trying to rationalise his behaviour to himself as he explains the evening's events to Katherine.

'But I didn't even tell any of the men I was going in. For some reason, I just grabbed a breathing set and headed straight for the kitchen at the back, why I don't know, some gut feeling, I just headed straight for it, through the living room, past the stairs' – he is reliving the geography as he speaks—'and I could see nothing, not a damn thing, I was as blind as a bat, the house was so thick with smoke, not a damn thing. And the heat was so fucking intense. But the kitchen sink, it was so cold, so icy cold in that heat. And I brushed against the cloth hanging beneath the sink and I just knew. There, in among the pots and pans, her soft leg, then her sock and her shoe.'

George stops talking for a moment, his eyes staring into the distance, and then resumes as though there has been no hiatus.

'She was hiding there . . . underneath the sink. And I guessed when I lifted her out that she was probably no more than three years of age.'

He smiles now.

'I was so pleased to have found her. So pleased. I had been no more than two, three minutes in getting to her. I could hear muffled shouts coming from outside – two firemen had been ordered to go in by the back lane. And I carried her on through the house. Blind. Careful not to hit her head or her arms against the walls. I wanted to talk to her. I wanted to tell her that everything was okay.'

George's pace grinds down. Katherine raises her body a little, moving in toward him.

'The paramedics were ready outside to take her. And it was

only when I pulled off my mask I could see her properly, see her long brown curls and her little mouth and her cheeks all dirty.'

George lifts his head to look at Katherine.

'But her dress was spotlessly clean.' He looks pained now, bewildered. Then, almost in an instant, his recollection is flushed with an intense anger. His voice rises.

'And that fucking idiot just standing there gaping at me when I came out of the house, that young Barton fella, couldn't put out a fucking fire to save his own life, never mind anyone else's – standing there with that cartoon face of his, delighted with himself, banging his lips together like a fucking ventriloquist's dummy! I couldn't bear to look at him!'

'George, stop. Everyone was doing their best, just like you were. That's unkind. James Barton's a good lad. He was only pleased that you'd rescued her. And the thing is, you had rescued her – that's wonderful!' Katherine reasons with him.

George looks at her with a quiet despair. 'She was dead, Katherine. I knew it as soon as I'd touched her.'

'Oh.'

'And the child's mother screaming into my face as though it was my fault that she'd left the child alone in the house. Christ!' George shakes his head. 'But I shouldn't have gone in on my own without an order. Why did I do that? I shouldn't have gone in. I could have put other lives in danger. I could've . . . It's just not the way it works.'

'Oh my God, George.' Katherine slowly rises onto her knees on the bed and puts her arms around George to comfort him. 'Oh my God.'

They hold each other in the dark.

'Who, or what, do I think I am? I'm only a damned retained fireman for God's sake.'

'You reacted to the situation, George, that's all. You did your best.' Katherine speaks quietly as they embrace.

'Well, my best wasn't good enough.' He whispers it, as though he feels the fall of an ordered world.

'And you're tired,' Katherine says gently.

George rubs his brow with his hand. 'The station will call again shortly; I'm sure of it. There've been baton charges with the RUC in Cupar Street. The Arkle Bar has been petrol-bombed. There are buses and cars burning everywhere. The city's gone to hell.'

'Oh my God, George,' she says. She kisses him affectionately. 'Try to sleep, even for a little bit, in case they call you back in. We'll talk this through in the morning. This is a terrible thing that happened, George, but you're not to blame yourself, because you did your best. C'mon, love, try to get some rest.'

She pulls the blankets over them both, George still in his uniform shirt and trousers, and as they embrace, they feel the unalterable, durable presence of each other.

'Try to sleep,' Katherine repeats softly to George. They curl into each other and attempt to settle. George gives another unproductive cough, then another, though he still cannot seem to clear his throat.

The air in their room hangs silently, although it is as if, at any moment, the sounds of the unsettled city, on whose rim they lie, will drift into their ears and line the insides of their skulls with brittle pictures. The relief that dawn may bring will be a little while yet.

'George, do you think everything is going to be okay?'

Out of the stillness, George is a distant voice. 'With us?'

Katherine inhales quickly, slightly taken aback by George's words, and lifts her head to him. 'No, George – I meant – the violence in the city – I meant everything that's going on in the city.'

'Katherine,' George says quietly in the dark.

Katherine shuffles in the bed, edgy now. 'Yes.'

'Do you remember the Milk Bar in Lombard Street?'

Katherine's response is flat, confused. 'What?'

'The Milk Bar in Lombard Street.'

Katherine turns away from him. 'George, what are you talking about? It's late. Go to sleep.'

'The night I asked you to marry me, we went there.'

Katherine turns around to him again, 'No, George, we didn't go anywhere that night,' she says with assurance. 'And what has this got to do with anything? You need to rest. You've been through enough tonight. What has you thinking?'

'No, that night, I remember, I showed you the ring and you put it on and then we went out together. We walked into town and went to the Milk Bar, and do you not remember how giddy we got? And you sat on the high stool at the end of the counter, clinking your nails against your glass of tonic water and swinging your legs like a schoolgirl. And we laughed. Remember? We laughed at nothing.' George's voice is now strangely light.

Katherine feels her pulse lift. 'No, George, I was late getting home that night and we didn't go anywhere. Remember? You waited for ages. Talking to my mother.'

George continues, as though Katherine has said nothing. 'I remember feeling so happy. Thought I would go mad with happiness. Just sitting beside you. And everything right with the world. And I started reading the menu on the wooden panelling in front of us. Someone had written up the menu with a spelling mistake. "Tea, coffee, milk shakes, hot soaps, sandwiches." And the more times I said it, the more you laughed.'

'No, George, I don't remember that. That must have been a different night.' Katherine's voice carries a gravity with it now. She is aware that George's memory of the evening is very different from hers. As though he is only selecting the bits of memory he wants and reassembling them to invent moments that never happened. There is a disconnected quality to his voice, which is making her feel uncomfortable.

'And the waitress kept looking at us, and her cheeks were getting redder and redder, and you said—'

Katherine interrupts him. 'I think you should get some sleep, George.'

'It's just that – if it wasn't that night – whatever night that happened – we were happy together, Katherine. Happy. That night did happen. I remember it as clearly as though it were yesterday.' George turns his body fully around to Katherine.

'We're still happy.' Katherine has turned her face into the pillow.

'Are we? This was different.' George speaks slowly. 'Then, we were only prepared to see the good in each other.'

Katherine moves her arm out from under the blankets and lets it fall outstretched above her head. It is a lick of white skin in the darkness and George reaches out to stroke it with his fingerstips. Her skin is soft and warm and yielding under his touch.

'But there you were. And you kept giving me such a beautiful smile, Katherine, that I was the happiest man in the world.' George reaches out his hand now to stroke Katherine's hair. 'I'm trying my best, Katherine, but . . . it never seems enough. Please let it go, Katherine.'

Katherine feels as though she is shrinking in the darkness, pulling down into herself like a small creature sensing the approach of something ominous; her voice now comes from a faraway cave.

'That wasn't the night you asked me to marry you, George. I don't know what night you're talking about.'

'Please let it go, Katherine. Please.' He is begging her now.

'You're tired, George. Sleep. You need to sleep.'

'Do you love me, Katherine?' George says from the lightening dark.

Is he crying?

'Yes, George, I love you.'

And then on their honeymoon, the most anger George had ever felt. She was able to provide that for him. The most anger ever. An anger that had pushed him out of his words. He had had no language with which to describe it. He had had no name for it.

Katherine is holding something in her hand. It is a folded piece of paper. She opens it. It is a grocery list. *Sliced pan, custard powder, two onions* . . . She looks at the piece of paper in her hand. It is folded again. She opens it again, but somehow the paper remains folded. Each time she opens the piece of paper, she finds it folded. She opens the piece of paper many times. Twenty, thirty times – she is losing count. She never sees the paper folding back in upon itself, but it is always folded when she looks at it. Then suddenly, it is open in her hand, although she has not tried to open it. She sees the words '*Si tu ne m'aimes pas, je t'aime!*' handwritten in blue ink and the imprints of her lips skirting the edges of the paper.

A swarm of orange-red insects.

One of the mouths trembles slightly and softly parts. A sweet sound issues from its white centre. A breathy almost imperceptible 'Aah,' but a definite note, not a sigh. It melts on the air. The mouth opens again and this time the breath lengthens and releases itself in a curved line of sound. This happens three, maybe four times before another mouth opens on the page, then another, and another, until all the mouths – hundreds of them now – are opening and closing, the sound building and building in intensity until it becomes a seraphic rhapsody. Katherine opens her own mouth just a little, mimicking the undulations of the paper mouths to sing along with them. But suddenly, the mouths shut with an abrupt *snap!* The song is now left hanging in the air, pulsing, but disembodied from its source. Violently then, the song rushes at high speed in through her half-open mouth like a tornado being sucked into her. It fills her up. She feels her limbs begin to vibrate uncontrollably as they swell and grow longer and wider. The cuffs of her blouse split as her arms and hands become huge; the buttons fly off the front of her blouse; her throat and shoulders rip through her collar. Her feet force themselves out through the ends of her shoes and socks. She is a swollen, fatted pupa prematurely rupturing through her larval skin. Floating now in water. Floating like a swollen carcass, her flesh weeping and skinless from the scald of the sea. There is something beside her in the water. Something huge, but she cannot see it. Something dark and wide. It is getting closer to her. Closer and closer. It rises up out of the sea. It is a huge head with a huge mouth and it is coming to swallow her. The terrifying lips open to take her.

Katherine gives a sharp gasp and sits bolt upright in the bed. The room is dark except for the spoon of light that bends in under the bedroom door from the landing. Stephen is crying. Katherine turns to George in the bed beside her. He is an imageless shape, a smooth, silent mound of sleep. Katherine tries to gather herself for a moment. She feels that her body is tingling all over, as though she has pins and needles that have caught fire. Glowing sparks of brittle, fizzing light through her. But though her limbs feel weightless, her head feels heavy. She gives a dry cough and then climbs out of bed to attend to Stephen. Stephen is already calling her name, his arms outstretched to her approaching shape.

'Mama.'

'Sssssh, darling, everything's all right.'

His fretting makes his voice judder in his throat like a frightened bird, as though he is attempting to decipher where the large animals that have been chasing him have gone.

'It's okay, my pet,' Katherine says, soothing him. 'It's only a dream.'

Katherine lifts him out of his cot. Once he is in her arms, his body sinks immediately into her chest, his head tucking into the curve of her shoulder. His weight speaks slumber once again. Katherine rocks him to and fro, kissing his head, caressing his soft, downy curls with her lips, breathing in his skin smell of daisies and milk.

'My beautiful boy,' she whispers, 'my beautiful boy,' and she becomes a lullaby. After some minutes holding and swaying him, Katherine carefully tilts her body and, keeping her motion as smooth as possible, places Stephen back in his cot and covers him with his blanket. She reaches across to lift up her cotton underslip from the back of the chair, where she left it the night before as she undressed, and, rolling it into a loose, soft bundle, she squeezes it in under the blanket beside Stephen. The smell of mother for him to feed off.

As Katherine stands beside Stephen's cot, she feels exhausted, the tingling in her body having given way to a thick grogginess in her limbs and in her back. Her head still pulses heavily. She leaves the bedroom quietly so as not to disturb George or Stephen and makes her way down the stairs to the kitchen. She walks to the counter beside the sink, the linoleum feeling chill against the soles of her feet, and fills the kettle with water. In the back room beside the kitchen, where the fibres of love and life are woven together, Katherine now stands and waits for the kettle to boil.

More than she can handle. That's what it feels like. But it's just that they're both exhausted. Tiredness like a shock in her bones. And her dream has shaken her. At least the station did not call him back and he sleeps still. Katherine knows how deeply George will now wrestle with a sense of failure at not having rescued the child alive, at not having arrived at the fire more quickly, or taken the appropriate orders from his superiors. She knows how difficult it will be for him to accept the fact that there was nothing he could have done to save her. She knows how desperate he would have felt as he made his way back through the house, carrying the girl in his arms, and she knows deep down that, in a sense, he will always carry her.

The kettle begins to screech, and Katherine lifts it off the burner. She pours the hot water onto the tea leaves in the teapot, giving the hot water a quick stir with a spoon before putting on the lid. She still feels exhausted.

She hears a noise behind her. She turns around, to see Elsa standing at the kitchen door, a pale ghost of a child in her white nightdress, her hair dishevelled.

'What are you doing up, Elsa?'

'I heard Stephen crying. What time is it, Mummy?'

'It's early, or it's late, Elsa, I don't know. What does it matter, love? Go back to bed.'

'I can't sleep. Can I have a drink please, Mummy?'

Katherine, although knowing she should show her disapproval

at Elsa being up out of bed at this unearthly hour, cannot help but feel relieved that her daughter has now joined her.

Katherine pours Elsa a glass of milk and then a cup of tea for herself. They both stand in the kitchen without switching on the overhead electric light, so reflective are the steely shards of morning as they fall in around them through the window.

Katherine looks out to check the sky.

'I'd say it's maybe four o'clock.'

'Isabel didn't think the fair was very good, Mummy.'

'Really? Well, she's wrong, don't you think?'

Elsa shrugs her shoulders. Katherine turns her head to look out the window again.

'Look. Madam Maureen's tent is still standing.' Katherine puts down her cup of tea and pulls back the curtain that hangs by the kitchen door, taking the key from a little hook on the wall behind it. When she opens the back door, both she and Elsa stand together on the back steps.

The fortune-teller's tent looms in the cool, transparent haze of the garden in front of them like the last surviving pavilion of a lost crusade, tilting on its axis, a rickety vestige of defeat, its lank flaps subdued further with light droplets of morning rain.

'Get the cover from the sofa, Elsa. We'll sit out awhile.'

Elsa brings out the grey woollen throw with its mint green edges and gives it to her mother. Katherine wraps it around them both, and they sit on the back step, huddled together. Elsa drinks her milk in tiny sups. Katherine strokes Elsa's hair for a moment and then turns to look around her.

'Wasn't this Elizabeth's nightdress?' Elsa asks.

'What, my love?' Katherine drinks her tea.

'This nightdress I'm wearing, did it belong to Elizabeth or to someone else?'

'I think it was Maureen's.' Katherine lifts the cuff of the garment back a little to examine it.

'Yes, it was Maureen's. Look, she embroidered a tiny blue *m,* just here.' Katherine shows it to Elsa.

'Does that mean that it's still hers?'

'No, love, it was Maureen's, then it was Elizabeth's, and now it's yours.'

Elsa laughs. 'Then it'll be Stephen's, and he'll look like a girl!'

Despite her tiredness, Katherine smiles at how her daughter finds humour in Stephen's getting his sisters' hand-me-downs. As she watches Elsa now, she marvels at the inconsequentiality of time. In an instant, Katherine can look at her daughter, as she is, the contours of her young face elongating and changing with each slight shift in her understanding of the world, and also see her, at one and the same time, as a baby, all rounded flesh and soft bones and wisps of fluffy hair. Two images of the same child completely at one, completely preserved and still living, still breathing, still available to her at any moment.

'Mummy?'

'Yes, Elsa?'

'Isabel said she felt sorry for me because I was a Catholic.'

'Really?' Katherine looks at Elsa. 'And why did she say that?'

'She said because Catholics are dirty and stupid and poor.'

'Isabel said that, did she?' Katherine cannot hide the concern in her voice.

'And she said that lots of people hate Catholics and so they'll hate me, too.'

'Isabel should watch her tongue. And what else did the little blurt say?'

'Just that she'll still be my friend because she needs someone to get sweets for her in Mr. McGovern's shop because she doesn't like going into the shop because Mr. McGovern's a Catholic, too.'

'That child needs a good talking-to.' Katherine shakes her head.

'Mummy?'

'Yes, Elsa?'

'Why does it matter if you're a Catholic or a Protestant?'

'It doesn't – unless you're Isabel, of course!'

'But it does, Mummy, 'cos sometimes I get frightened coming home from school in case I get stopped, 'cos that happened to Mary Feely and she got beaten up and she had to move to a different school.'

'Well – that's not going to happen to you, Elsa. Don't worry, love.' Katherine can feel her throat tighten. She feels anxious now, forlorn even.

Elsa pulls the grey woollen throw around her shoulders and drinks her milk. 'Anyway, I feel sorry for Isabel.'

'Do you now, love, and why's that?' asks Katherine quietly.

'Because she has a webbed toe and that needs an operation to put it right.'

'I think it's more than her webbed toe needs operating on,' Katherine mutters to herself; then she turns to Elsa and pulls her close. 'We are what we are, pet, and that's all right, don't you think?'

Elsa nods in agreement.

Night falls back as the morning sky slowly opens like a huge door. Shafts of apricot light appear behind the silhouettes of the gardens shrubs, which splay their long leaves as though they are giant black insects stretching their long legs.

Katherine and Elsa sit like two pilgrims on the steps of a new day.

'I could catch ghost moths in this nightdress,' Elsa whispers.

'You could.'

'Where did you hear the story about them being the souls of dead people again?'

'My father told me.'

'Granda Jack?'

'Yes, Granda Jack.'

'And where did he hear the story?'

'I suppose he always knew the story without knowing where he had heard it or where it came from. Like lots of stories.'

'I like those kind of stories that you don't know where they came from. They're not so scary.'

'Why's that?'

'Because they mightn't of even happened yet; they might have just been dreamed. And that means that there's a chance that they'll never happen, if you don't want them to.'

'And what if you want them to happen?'

'You have to keep dreaming them.'

With morning's inevitable growth, Katherine and Elsa become less like spectres and more like themselves.

'And if they were the souls of dead people,' Elsa continued, 'and you caught them, would you have to hold on to them forever, or could you just let them go when you wanted to?'

'I don't know, Elsa.'

'Because you might get to like them too much; you might get too used to them, like pets. Moths could be pets, couldn't they, Mummy? And then you wouldn't be able to let them go.'

'Perhaps.'

'Could we get a pet, Mummy, a hamster or something? I'd love a hamster.'

Katherine is becoming more and more soothed by Elsa's company, carried by her daughter's unconscious grace to feel the eloquence of ordinary things. There is no other sound on earth like it, the voice of a child who sees the world as God's safe harbour.

Katherine gives Elsa an affirmative pat on her knee.

'Let's get two hamsters!'

'Really?' Elsa is amazed.

'Yes, why not. I'll talk to your father about it, shall I?'

'Yes, please.' Elsa beams at her mother, then looks out into the garden, the huge smile remaining on her face.

'I wish I had met Granda Jack. Do you miss him, Mummy?'

'Yes, I miss him. Every day I miss him.'

'He looks funny in the photograph on the mantelpiece.'

'I know, but he was carrying on to make me laugh.'

'Why's he holding you up with one hand?'

'It was a trick for the camera. My mother took the photograph in Tollymore Forest. I was actually sitting up on a wooden post, but it looks like he's holding me straight up in the air with one hand.'

Sunlight tongues of pinky apricot now lick the edges of the garden shrubs, giving them back the dimension that the night-time shadows had stolen. The day looks nearly ready.

'Elsa, I think it's time to go in now; I'm feeling a bit tired.' Katherine pats Elsa on the head. 'We'll leave Madam Maureen's tent until later, shall we?'

Elsa smiles at her mother and nods her head, fixing the grey woollen throw around her.

'Let's go,' says Katherine.

As they rise from the back steps, Katherine lifts her head. She notices a line of dirty orange light across the city, like the glow of a distant furnace, and feels the heavy fall of her heart.

# 6

*September 1949*

HOW HEAVILY IT RAINED. It was as though the weather could not stop itself. Rain fell from a liquid sky like pellets of broken silver, battering against the buildings and the pavements, falling so suddenly and heavily that the earth did not have time to drink it in. Water spilled off the streets and the gardens, running in long and furious ropes into the rivers and the sea. As Katherine closed the door of the church hall behind her, the rain hammered on it as though it wanted to get in.

It was Friday. Tonight, George and her family would come to the church hall to see her perform *Carmen*. All day at work, Katherine had not been able to concentrate on her accounting duties. A large portion of her day was spent checking and rechecking the entries in her ledger. A colleague had kindly pointed out three mistakes that she had made within the first hour of starting work. But even as she brought her mind to follow the figures in her ledger with as much rigour as she could muster, she still found herself pressing the wrong keys on her accounting machine. By half past five, she was exhausted. She had left the Ulster Bank offices and had run the short distance to St. Anne's church hall in the pouring rain. The cheese and pickle sandwich that she had made for herself that morning to have before the show, she had thrown in the bin as she entered the hall; the thought of eating it had made her feel queasy.

She made her way to the small dressing room upstairs, towel-dried and pinned up her hair, and changed into her costume. Twenty minutes later, she was ready to join the rest of the cast backstage, all of whom were warming up for the performance that evening. Charlie Copeland was rocking back and forth as usual on his wooden stool, Rosemary Wylie was complaining to the Cigarette Factory Girls as they practiced their dance routine about the ugly, tight shoes she had been given, and Hugh Drummond could be overheard telling James McCauley a joke. 'So *he* says to her, "Drinkin' makes you look very bonnie," and *she* says, "But I haven't been drinkin'," and *he* says, "No, but *I* have . . . !"'

Just before 'curtain up,' Cissie McGee swung around to Katherine from her prompt table.

'I can see your mother and sister in the fourth row, Katherine. Is that George with them?' Katherine looked out through a gap in the curtain.

'No, that's my brother, Frank. I wonder where George is?'

'Who's George?'

Katherine pulled back from the curtain and turned around. It was Tom. Hearing him say George's name like that shocked her to the core.

Tom kissed Katherine. But this time, she pulled away. Cissie McGee gave an embarrassed cough.

And then it happened. Katherine heard herself saying flatly to Tom, 'George is my fiancé.'

Tom started laughing. 'George is what – who?'

'My fiancé,' she continued. 'I'm engaged to be married.'

Tom's face froze. 'I don't understand, he said slowly. 'I don't understand, Katherine.'

Katherine could not bear to return Tom's gaze. She continued with her head bowed. 'I didn't know that we would – I had no idea that we – I didn't mean this to happen.' She stopped, then lifting her head she said solemnly, 'Oh my God, Tom. I'm so sorry.'

'No, Katherine,' Tom was shaking his head, trying to reason this through. 'No, no, no – if we need to talk about this, Katherine, we can.'

Katherine raised her eyes. Her voice became charged as she suddenly ripped through Tom's words. 'No we can't! We can't talk about anything! There's nothing to talk about! I'm engaged to be married to someone else! And I have been since the first time I met you! It's not right! Do you hear me? It's just not right!'

The Cigarette Factory Girls stopped dancing and Charlie Copeland stopped rocking back and forth on his little wooden stool. They all turned to look at Katherine and Tom. In the awkward silence, the rumble of rain on the roof grew more intense.

Tom shook his head again. 'No, Katherine, no, please don't do this to me. I love you.' He stood staring at Katherine. She could see the boy in him again, innocent, pure, just like on the night she had first met him, the night when she had woken him from his sleep in the tailors' rooms.

Cissie McGee broke the silence by calling out a verbal 'Stand by' to the performers waiting stage right, waved furiously to indicate the same to those stage left, and then cast a nervous look toward Katherine and Tom.

Katherine and Tom stood motionless in the dark.

At that moment, Katherine realised how she had not calculated anything. How these dreams of hers had blinded her. How she had rashly and foolishly ignored the obvious until now. She had blatantly refused to consider who would be betrayed and how long afterward guilt might remain. And, instead of facing the consequence of the situation, she had buckled like a frightened child and had clung instead to what she knew, or at least clung to what she thought she knew.

'I think you should leave now. Go,' Katherine said abruptly, her eyes filling with tears.

Tom's eyes held on hers. 'No Katherine, no, please, I beg you, don't do this, please don't do this.' The sincerity in his voice chilled her to her core. He looked at her, his eyes deep as chasms, frightened, desperate. 'Why did you keep that from me? Why did you not tell me?'

Katherine looked at Tom. She was speechless. Then she dropped her head and covered her face with her hands, as though to make herself disappear in the darkness. As though to hide in her shame.

Time seemed to stand still.

Then, through her fingers she said softly, 'We have nothing more to say to each other. It's over, don't you understand? Go. I never want to see you again.'

'I can't live without you, Katherine.'

Katherine dropped her hands from her face and looked straight into Tom's eyes. 'Go,' she said.

Is it just the way she remembers it or did she really see the light leave his eyes, dark though it was behind the scenery flats? Did she really see something extinguish within him? Is that how it happened? Is that what she did to him? A slipping away, at once awful and unremarkable.

She stood in the dark, her cold blood coursing through her veins. She tried to make out Tom's shape in the dark as he moved away. Then he was gone. She wanted to change her mind. She wanted to call him back.

'This letter was just delivered to the stage door.' Cissie McGee was in a state of panic.

'Sorry?' Katherine lifted her head.

'This letter just arrived for you. Just handed in. But we're almost ready to start! You'll have to read it later.' With that, Cissie McGee barrelled at high speed back to the prompt corner.

In a daze, Katherine slowly opened the letter and by the faint light on the prop table beside her began to read it. Her hands were shaking. 'Katherine. Can't make it to the performance tonight. Called out unexpectedly on duty. I'm sorry I'm going to miss your performance. Will telephone tomorrow. Good luck. George.'

She stood at the side of the stage, behind the scenery flats, waiting for the performance to begin. She folded George's letter in two and pushed it against her mouth to take the excess of lipstick. Then she slipped it into the pocket of her costume, smoothing the fabric with her hand, taking a deep breath to calm herself in the midst of all the commotion happening around her backstage. She stood like a strange, gormless creature, as though on the brink of extinction.

# 7

*August 1969*

KATHERINE RISES LATER THAT MORNING, after a short, disrupted sleep, feeling as though she has not slept at all. Even getting dressed feels such an effort for her. She is comforted somewhat by the promise of a hot day when she opens the back door. Wafts of honeysuckle scent float on the balmy air and mingle with the slightly sour odour from the half-open dustbin beside the coal shed. But as Katherine turns her head to look over the city, her brow furrows in disbelief. Hanging in the sky is a huge pall of grey smoke like a wide, flat cigar, incongruous against the morning blue directly above it. The smoke's curling, dissolute plumes move listlessly outward before folding back in upon themselves, twisting around a dense grey centre.

This stretch of grey cloud is confirmation of the trouble George had talked about in the early hours of the morning, at which Katherine had shaken her head in disbelief. Now, it is there for her to see, ominous, foreboding, and undeniable. What in God's name is happening? She wonders. Riots in the streets, petrol bombs, cars and buses burning?

Katherine calls George, who is inside the house, cleaning the dried dirt off his black boots from the night before. He arrives in his socks, a boot in one hand, a damp cloth in the other.

'Look, George, look at the smoke.'

George follows Katherine's gaze. 'I know. I expected it. I got a call from the station this morning when you were still in bed.'

'Yes, I heard the telephone.' Katherine's voice is barely audible.

George speaks with a heavy and sober tone. 'A nine-year-old boy was shot dead last night, Katherine. Shot dead as he was sleeping. Half the side of his head gone. Indiscriminate fire, they say.'

'Dear God.' Katherine is stunned.

'There were clashes between crowds and the RUC all night.' George shakes his head. 'I've no idea how long I'll be needed, Katherine. It all depends on how difficult our access will be.' He kisses her on the cheek. 'I'll pass a message to the station to get one of the boys to telephone you if I'm going to be very late. Don't worry, it'll be fine.'

'And you've cleared this with the council? They've given you more time off work?'

'Yeah – they understand the seriousness of the situation.'

Katherine reaches out her hand to his face. 'How will I know that you'll be safe, George?'

'Don't worry, love, I'll be fine.'

'Okay.' Katherine stares into George's eyes. There is something urgent, something pressing in his expression. George lifts his arms – still holding his boot in one hand and the cloth in the other – and folds them around Katherine. He presses his head against hers. He holds her tenderly. He holds her for what seems like an age. 'I love you,' he says to her. Then, pulling gently back from his embrace, he kisses her on the lips.

*George.*

Katherine gathers herself. 'I've made sandwiches,' she says, visibly warmed by his display of affection. 'They're on the table.' She smiles at George. 'I love you, too,' she says, and then moves swiftly into the house.

With George gone now, Katherine sets about preparing breakfast for the children. She can hear the *thump-thump* of Maureen, Elizabeth, and Elsa upstairs as they jump heavily onto the floor from their beds, and above that she can hear Stephen squealing from the cot. She walks to the bottom of the stairs and calls up to the girls.

'Take it easy. Someone's going to get hurt. Maureen! Maureen!' The rumpus stops immediately, followed by an unearthly silence.

Then: 'Yes, Mummy?' Maureen's voice sounds hoarse.

'Lift Stephen out of his cot and come down for something to eat.' There is barely an acknowledgment from Maureen before the noise begins again.

After a lazy breakfast, Katherine rallies the girls to help tidy up the kitchen. She is now feeling exceptionally tired, although it is only late morning. She tries to shake off her worry over George, but it clings like an unsettling dream.

'We need to bring in the sheets and blankets and things from the garden,' she informs the girls with a forced briskness.

'I can't believe the summer holidays are nearly over,' Maureen moans as she scrapes off the remaining flakes of cereal from a bowl into the kitchen bin.

'There's ages left,' Elizabeth says.

'Well, there's not *ages* left,' Elsa says, correcting Elizabeth as she checks her upside-down face in her spoon; 'there's *two weeks* left.'

'You know what I mean,' mutters Elizabeth.

'Smarty-pants,' says Maureen, taunting Elsa.

'Big smelly pants!' replies Elsa.

Katherine gives Elsa a quick slap on her behind as she passes her by. 'Manners, Elsa!'

Stephen has been looking intently at Elsa from his high chair and is now peering into his own spoon. Then he throws the spoon on the floor, laughing loudly to himself. Maureen picks it up and gives it back to Stephen. Stephen throws the spoon back onto the floor again.

'All right, girls,' Katherine says, putting away the last of the dishes, 'let's sort out the garden.'

They dismantle Madam Maureen's fortune-telling tent as though they are a circus leaving town, imbued with the inevitable contemplation that transience brings and with the growing sense that somehow their world is changing. Katherine removes the clothes pegs, then pulls the sheets and blankets slowly from the clotheshorse and bunches them in her arms for washing. Maureen collapses the clotheshorse. Elizabeth gathers the cushions and lifts the little wooden table that had been used to hold Madam Maureen's crystal ball to put it away. Elsa becomes prospector of her own garden, sweeping her leg like a metal detector through the blades of grass to search for forgotten things. With her toes, she discovers the Butlin's Holiday Camp eggcup in the grass by the garden wall, the HOME BAKING sign crumpled and sodden with dew under the hedge, and the bag of toffees in the long clump of weeds by the apple tree. The toffees have melted into a sticky clump. They all work silently, lifting their heads a little now and then to check on Stephen, who plays beside them in the grass, and to sense how the morning swings on a light, warm breeze, on the piping voices from a neighbouring garden, on the solitary coarse bark of a dog chasing its tail.

Katherine, holding the roll of sheets and blankets, looks up at the sky.

Here and there is the blue promise of a hot day, but where is the sun? Grey smoke still hangs over the city. 'Dear God, keep George safe,' she whispers.

She gives each of the girls a penny for all their work setting up the fair and for raising money for charity and for helping with the tidying up. They will give the proceeds of the fair to Father Daly after Mass on Sunday. Maureen and Elizabeth both put their pennies away for saving. But Elsa wants to buy sweets from McGovern's shop. She runs down the crazy-paved driveway of her house, holding the penny in her hand. As she makes her way down the road, she can see the city spread out below her and she can blot it out with just one hand if she wants to.

The footpaths on either side of Elsa's road are edged by rectangular patches of grass. During these summer months, the men from the Belfast Corporation came as usual with their giant whirring machines and leveled the growth, tossing the freshly cut grass into the air. The children who live on the road played with it, creating ancient city walls that snaked the surface of their new world while unleashing smells of grassy sap and dog shit. Once these games were over and conquests had been lost and won countless times, the grass cities became deserted like abandoned archaeological digs, left to the mercy of the wind and the feet of passersby. Now Elsa kicks clumps of walls here and there as she runs, scattering the grass about the street and over the curbs, which are painted red, white, and blue.

Elsa reaches the bottom of the hill, where it broadens and becomes flat. There is a bigger, open area of grass where the remnants of this year's twelfth of July bonfire lie. The recent spell of hot weather has made the large circle of burned grass, left after the fire, seem blacker. Bits of charred wood and the twisted springs from a sofa lie scattered within the scorched ring. As is usual for bonfire nights, potatoes had been thrown onto the edges of the fire to cook slowly as people danced and drank in the spiky heat. The tiny Mr. Wilson had played his shiny accordion like a heavily pregnant woman fingering an ivory stomach. Heads and limbs had twitched to the beat of the Protestant loyalist anthems while lemonade and crisps had been divided among the children. Elsa liked the crisps and lemonade on those nights, but never the potatoes – they always had hard bits in the middle.

Elsa likes McGovern's shop. But there is a sweet shop at the top of the road that she does not like. This sweet shop is inside a house where an elderly brother and sister live together. In the small kitchen at the back of the house, the elderly sister has a Formica countertop on which stand a few jars of sweets and a shoe box of loose change. Her blind brother sits by the roaring fire in the parlour and frightens the children with his stillness and his white eyes. To get to the counter of sweets at the back means having to cross the wide red ochre tiles of the parlour floor, where the blind man sits. Elsa does not like that sweet shop because the blind man frightens her. The blind man sitting, fat and piggish, in his parlour, burning his visions by the fire, his eyelids like twists of newspaper, the front door of his house always open. Once Big Adam, a boy from Glenhill Road, had said that the blind man was cooking himself, slowly, day after day, cooking himself by the fire. The blind man's pink and stubbled skin sizzling and sweating and roasting and frightening her.

Now Elsa is inside McGovern's shop and the image of the blind man disappears as her eyes scan the dark cherrywood shelves that stretch from the floor to the ceiling. The shelves are divided like boxes displaying trophies – one packet of Bisto gravy, two tins of Fray Bentos meatballs, one packet of strawberry Angel Delight, two boxes of Brillo pads. Similar objects are displayed in the front window amid cardboard ads for Andrews liver salts and packets of 'Sahara brown' tights and 'nigger brown' shoe polish. The front counter is lined with jars upon jars of sweets and chocolates. As Elsa stands in the shop, the sugar perfume envelopes her and bathes her in vanilla aromas of comfort and delight.

Mr. McGovern is a polished man, eager to smile. Mrs. McGovern, on the other hand, is plump and non-plussed. They run their shop like they run their marriage, each purveyor of his and her own silently acknowledged territory in the bigger scheme of things. Mr. McGovern deals with the groceries, haphazard and indiscriminate as they are, while Mrs. McGovern parades as lollipop lady amid the traffic of sweets.

'All on your own today, sweetheart?' says Mr. McGovern absentmindedly, rubbing the breast pocket of his white nylon shop coat.

Elsa nods.

Mrs. McGovern, whose mouth is constantly set in a pucker of dissatisfaction, is filling an empty sweet jar with Black Jacks.

'What can I get you, love?' The pucker unpuckers itself for a moment.

Elsa's eyes scan the selection of sweets – bonbons, butterscotch, caramels, lollipops, Jujubes, Raspberry Ruffles, Sugarmines – the smell ambrosial and satisfying. Elsa points at the jar of flying saucers.

'Four of these, please, Mrs. McGovern.'

'Right-e-o.' Mrs. McGovern, laughing tightly to herself, as though she had been playing a game in her own head of predicting Elsa's choice, plunges her hand deep into the jar of flying saucers and then pulls out two pale pink ones and two pale blue ones. She puts them into a little paper bag.

Elsa hands Mrs. McGovern her penny and then, bejewelled with her saucer ships, she leaves the shop. The smell outside the shop sharpens almost immediately to a stink, as the chimneys of the plastics factory, along the adjacent dual carriageway, have begun to belch their fumes. The taste of plastic hits the back of Elsa's tongue. Elsa hears the flat click of the sign against the glass of the door as Mr. McGovern turns it to CLOSED and she catches Mr. McGovern blessing himself behind the glass. How stupid, she thinks, to do that, to give yourself away like that, to give yourself away as a Catholic in a Protestant neighbourhood where everyone can see you – that's something she knows never to do.

As Elsa makes her way home, the wail of the siren from the local fire station suddenly rises and begins to fill the sky. For a moment, Elsa imagines she walks the streets of a war-torn city just like the ones she has read about in her books from the library. She is an orphaned waif now in search of an air raid shelter or a nurse running to give aid to the injured. She is a spy who knows exactly where to find the prisoners and free them from the camp or the girl who risks her life on the dangerous streets to bring her family supplies. She slips a flying saucer into her mouth, always amazed that such lightness contains such sweetness. The fizziness inside the flying saucer delights her tongue as it melts, and with that, her fantasies slip away.

She knows the reality to be a far duller thing. She knows what the siren means. It means that her father will be late coming home. It means that her father won't be there tonight to read to her when it's time to go to bed.

Just as Elsa arrives back from McGovern's shop, Katherine, Maureen, and Elizabeth are bringing the last bits and pieces from the garden into the house. Stephen is pretending to be a rabbit and is hopping around in the grass.

Isabel arrives in a blue gingham dress. 'Are yous coming out?' she asks Elsa.

'Okay,' Elsa replies. 'Where to?'

'Up to the blackberry bushes. Julie Driver and Karen Kirby's goin'.'

Katherine catches sight of Isabel from the kitchen window and, remembering what the child had said to Elsa about Catholics being dirty and stupid and poor, comes bristling back out to the garden. Katherine is surprised at how angry she feels at the child.

'Isabel Stewart, what are you doing here?' Katherine says sharply.

'Just calling for Elsa, Mrs. Bedford.' Isabel smiles sweetly.

'Can I go up to the blackberry bushes with Isabel, Mummy? Please.' Elsa is smiling, too.

Katherine checks herself. Elsa appears to be harbouring no dislike for Isabel. On the contrary, she seems delighted that Isabel has called for her. Katherine takes a deep breath, gently reminding herself that, of course, children are children and talk about things they don't even understand. She shouldn't judge Isabel too harshly. There's obviously no harm done. Katherine nods to Elsa that she can go with Isabel. The blackberry bushes are close enough to home, hemming the corner of a neighbouring street and signalling a sort of suburban cusp, so Elsa will be safe enough. After that, there are only fields.

'And go no farther than the blackberry bushes, do you hear?' Despite Katherine's reasoning to herself, there is still effort in her voice.

'I won't,' promises Elsa, slipping the last flying saucer into her mouth. She walks with Isabel up the road.

At the blackberry bushes, Elsa is told by Isabel, Julie Driver, and Karen Kirby to stay put, to *'stay put,'* for they had something to talk about together that wasn't for her ears. Stay put and don't move and they will be back in a minute, they say.

So Elsa sits and waits among the blackberry bushes. She looks through the small gap in the growth that is intertwined with woody hawthorn. She watches the little river that runs through the blackberry bushes and on to – somewhere. On the other side of the river, the ground opens out into a grassy meadow where flowers grow – some nicotiana, some night-scented stock. In the river's bed, soft-mossed boulders sit, their surfaces scarred where fallen twigs and small stones have swirled over them. Other boulders, out of the river's reach, have been etched into by pilgrim lovers who, while swiftly carving a heart or the curve of an initial, have been discovered and have then fled, leaving behind them their lovers' stone chapter. An empty glass bottle hugs the farther bank, its insides stained with a skin of algae. A plastic bag, knotted and bloated, is caught in the river on a fallen branch.

Elsa wonders where Isabel, Julie Driver, and Karen Kirby have gone. For a few moments, she indulges in her favourite daydream, where she can go into McGovern's shop and take as many sweets as she wants to, all for free.

Above her head, blackberries, like clusters of swollen bruises, hang from the angular, fibrous stems of the brambles. The stems are streaked with an inflamed red and pulse deep pink at the point where their sharp thorns sprout. Dust has settled on the fruit, stirred up by a steady, if modest, flow of traffic from the adjacent main road, and has covered the druplets in an unappetising grainy film.

The bush shudders and a loose blackberry falls on Elsa's head like a tiny baptism. So the girls have come back – Isabel, Julie Driver, and Karen Kirby. They have come back with thin smiles on their faces. They're going to play a dare game, they say, and Elsa says okay. Karen can go first, Isabel says. 'Karen, we dare you to call your mummy a bitch.' They huddle under the blackberry bushes together and Karen Kirby calls her mummy a bitch, and Isabel and Julie Driver laugh. Elsa laughs, too, even though she doesn't really want to, because that isn't a very nice thing to say. And then it's Julie Driver's turn and Isabel says that Julie Driver is to throw a stone at a passing car. And Elsa asks, 'Isn't that dangerous?' and Isabel says, 'Well . . .' And Julie Driver scoots out from under the blackberry bushes and quick as anything goes to the edge of the road and lifts a stone.

Isabel, Karen Kirby, and Elsa watch from the bushes. Then a car comes along and Julie Driver throws her stone and it hits the wheel of the car, but nobody in the car seems to notice. Isabel says that it's her turn, and Karen Kirby and Julie Driver start to laugh and Julie Driver says, 'Isabel, you have to show your knickers to a passing car,' and Isabel has a strange look on her face, as though she is surprised and, then again, not surprised. So when the next car comes along Isabel, lifts her blue gingham dress and shows her knickers, but the woman on the passenger side of the car just looks at Isabel and looks away again, and the expression on her face doesn't change at all, as if she doesn't really care one way or the other if Isabel lifts up her blue gingham dress and shows her knickers. And then the car is gone and all three of the girls, Isabel, Julie Driver, and Karen Kirby, turn to Elsa and say that it is her turn. And they all have those thin smiles on their faces again. And Isabel says, 'I dare you to go over to the house across the road and show your knickers to the blind man.' And Elsa can feel her throat get tight almost immediately and she says, 'No, I won't.' And Julie Driver says, 'You have to; we all did our dare.' And Elsa says again, 'No, I won't,' and Isabel and Julie Driver and Karen Kirby all look at one another and smile. Elsa says that their dares were easy and to give her one of their dares, and Karen says that Elsa has to do the one she is given and she has to hurry up, or else they will have to punish her. And Elsa can feel her face getting hot and a heat rising up in her stomach, as if there is a red knot there, and yet she is shaking as though she is cold. And she doesn't know if she is hot or cold and she feels as though she is going to cry and can feel the huge wet beads well up in her eyes and she needs to swallow, and she says, 'Please,' but very quietly this time, because the thought of the blind man frightens Elsa, frightens her so much. Elsa is sure that if she walks through the always-open front door of his house and walks as quietly as she possibly can to stand in front of him and show him her knickers, the blind man will see her and choose her and grab her and push her head into the fire. The blind man waiting for her and somehow seeing her and somehow seeing her knickers and grabbing her head and pushing it into the fire.

Just then, Isabel and Julie Driver and Karen Kirby move toward Elsa and say that they are going to catch her and hold her and drag her over to the blind man, because they all did their dares and Elsa has to, and they seem to be still laughing, even though they are serious. And Elsa can feel her heart beating hard and her head tight and the hotness in her getting hotter and she wants to cry really loudly and she just can't stop herself from saying it. She says, 'Let me call my mummy a bitch instead, because she is,' and so she says it, says, 'My mummy's a bitch,' and then she turns and runs. She runs straight into the blackberry bushes and the wild hawthorn and she pushes her way through them, even though the curved thorns scratch and hurt her. She raises her arms to cover her face and keeps going, keeps pushing through the bushes, and she feels the thorns scraping off her skin, but she can't stop. And she can hear Isabel and Julie Driver and Karen Kirby calling after her 'dirty Fenian Catholic' and laughing their hard laughs. Because she must look silly. It must look all so stupid. The hot panic making Elsa run and her getting caught in the brambles and the whole bush of brambles shaking like something alive and terrified, and Elsa pushing her way, all the way through the blackberry and hawthorn, and not taking one of the little paths that are right there, right beside her, because the thought of the blind man has frightened her so much. And then she gets through the bushes onto the road on the other side, somehow. And she doesn't even look to see if a car is coming on the road, she just runs onto the road, and a car *is* coming, and the man in the car blows the horn so loudly, it makes Elsa feel sick, it is so sharp and sudden, and she is shaking and running. She runs all the way to the top of her street. She wants her daddy to come home. She wants her daddy to be home when she gets there. She runs home feeling frightened and sick and feeling stupid for feeling frightened and feeling ashamed of herself.

# 8

*October 1949*

THE RAIN HAD FALLEN IN RELENTLESS SHEETS on the Friday night of *Carmen*, but by morning the air had cleared and the sun had appeared like a large egg in an empty sky. As though rinsed clean, the new day had lived to belie the storm. Only the rushing sounds of the swollen rivers persisted to fill the air.

The events of the previous evening had left Katherine distraught, but what else could she have done? As much as she felt crushed by her rejection of Tom, she realised on reflection that it had been the right thing to do. Everything else could be forgotten now, everything else, as her father used to say, was water under the bridge. She would apologize to Tom wholeheartedly when she next saw him; she would talk it through with him. It had been wrong of her in her panic to hurt him so badly. She would do whatever it took to make amends, to heal the hurt she had caused him. And she vowed to herself, as she walked, to make every effort to redeem, on her own part, her relationship with George. She would take on any extra work she possibly could in order to pay back the money on the statuette and retrieve her engagement ring. She would rectify her rash decisions. She would bring her life back around to the way it had been. And there was something at least to be grateful for, the fact that George, throughout the whole affair, had been blessedly blind to it. At least there was that. He had remained unaware of how her passions had run amuck, of how she had been foolishly caught up in her own flights of fancy, of how she had been careless. She swallowed hard at this last thought, for her period was still late.

No, nothing would come of that; everything would be fine, she reassured herself.

There was no one in the church hall when she arrived. The onstage curtains were closed. The wooden chairs that had been set out for the audience had yet to be straightened back into their rows and the floor had yet to be swept for the performance that evening. She was suddenly calmed by the quiet atmosphere of the hall and by its familiar dusty smell. She stood for a moment to allow her thoughts to settle, lifting her eyes to take in the details around her. A single sheet of music had been left on one of the stands in the tiny orchestra pit, some of the fabric flowers from the street sellers' baskets had fallen onto the floor of the hall, and a handkerchief had been left behind on a chair. Feeling a little more at ease with herself, she walked to the door at the side of the stage and slowly climbed the small staircase that led to two narrow dressing rooms on the upper floor.

The muted strains of conversation, which she became aware of as she approached the ladies' dressing room, came to a sudden halt as she opened the door. Inside the room, a small group sat huddled together in near darkness. Cissie McGee, three of the Cigarette Factory Girls, Miss Harper, and Rosemary Wylie all lifted their heads and simultaneously turned to Katherine as she stood in the doorway. There was a ring of tension in the air. Rosemary Wylie swung around on her chair and began busily applying blusher to her cheeks, despite only being able to catch a shadowy image of herself in the mirror. Cissie McGee smiled broadly at Katherine but said nothing. The Cigarette Factory Girls stared blankly at one another biting their lips, and Miss Harper stood up briskly, as though she had just thought of something elsewhere in the building that needed her urgent attention.

'How can you ladies see in here, it's so dark?' Katherine said, switching on the overhead light. The sudden illumination of the room startled the women. Katherine threw her coat over the back of her chair and placed her handbag beside the little box of makeup on her designated area of the table.

'All ready for tonight, then?' Cissie McGee said in a rush to her.

'Well, I will be,' Katherine said.

'Any alterations needed?' Miss Harper's voice rose to a tiny squeak.

'No, I don't think so,' Katherine said, looking from one face to another.

'Right, then,' continued Miss Harper, moving toward the door, 'I'll be off to check on the gentlemen.'

Katherine sat down in front of her wall mirror to apply her makeup. The other women remained silent. She pulled her hair back from her face and tied it neatly with a ribbon. The women were staring at her.

'Is there anything wrong?' she said finally, perplexed at their behaviour.

Rita, one of the Cigarette Factory Girls, was the first to speak.

'You haven't heard, then?' Rita asked warily.

'Heard what?' she replied. There was a moment's silence only, for Rosemary Wylie could not stop herself.

'They say it was an accident, but that tailor fella, Mr. McKinley – his body was found in the Lagan this morning.' She delivered the news with a keen, rehearsed despair in her voice, but her eyes betrayed a simmering, voyeuristic expectation. Rosemary Wylie stared at Katherine and waited, as though waiting for a sign, any sign at all, to confirm the suspicions that Katherine and Mr. McKinley had been having a liaison. The frantic distraction with which Rosemary Wylie had applied her blusher had given her one big red cheek.

'Isn't it shockin'?' Cissie McGee shook her head.

'I heard it from Miss Harper, who had heard it from Mr. Boyne, who had heard it from the police no less when they banged on his front door in the early hours of this morning! I'm sure the poor man nearly had a heart attack being woken up like that.' Rosemary Wylie was in full flight. 'Someone said there was going to be a criminal inquiry – but that means that there must have been foul play of some sort. Why *else* have a criminal inquiry?'

'Who told you there was going to be a criminal inquiry, I never heard that,' said Cissie McGee.

'Why? What did *you* hear?' said Rosemary Wylie, turning sharply to Cissie McGee.

'Well, *I* heard that it was an accident and that he'd slipped off the bank and the Rescue Services found him.'

'Yes, the Rescue Services *did* find him, but—' Rosemary Wylie was cut off mid-sentence by Bella, the smallest and youngest of the Cigarette Factory Girls, who opened her mouth for the first time that evening.

'Is it true that somebody said that they saw him jumping into the river?'

'Really?' Rosemary Wylie swung around in her chair to face Bella.

Rita joined in, her eyes widening. 'That would mean suicide, then.'

'I thought someone had heard a distress call from the river, so why would there have been a distress call if it was suicide?' Margaret, the third Cigarette Factory Girl, chipped in.

'I never heard that,' said Rosemary Wylie, miffed that Margaret might have heard something she hadn't.

'I still don't think it was foul play,' said Cissie McGee.

'But no one saw it happen, so how can you be sure?' said Rita.

'And why would anyone do something to someone like him?' said Margaret sadly.

'Well, when the Rescue Services found him, he was already dead, so he couldn't tell them anything,' added Bella.

They all looked at Bella.

Then a knock came at the dressing room door.

'Yes?' Rosemary Wylie lifted her voice proprietorially.

The door opened and Charlie Copeland poked his head in. 'Any of yous ladies have an eye pencil I could borrow?'

Rosemary Wylie tutted as though she were addressing a naughty child. 'Charlie, you'll have to get one of your own.' She handed him her eyebrow pencil. 'And bring it back straight away!'

Charlie hovered at the doorway. 'I heard the news about Tom McKinley. Isn't it awful?'

'Yes, it's awful,' drawled Rita.

'But what I can't understand is why was he walking by the river last night when the weather was so bad?' Cissie McGee checked her watch as she spoke.

'There's lots of things I can't understand,' muttered Rosemary Wylie, throwing a glance over Katherine's costume, which still hung on the rail.

Both Rita and Bella caught Rosemary Wylie's expression but said nothing.

'Treacherous,' said Charlie Copeland, 'I never saw rain like it, and that river must have been freezing – you wouldn't have stood a chance – and that wind was howling like a song.'

Cissie McGee rose from her chair. 'That's coming up to the half hour, ladies. I'd better get organised. Everyone into costume, and don't forget to check your props.'

'And who would have thought that could happen to a nice man like that, eh?' Charlie Copeland settled himself against the door frame.

'Charlie!' Cissie McGee tapped Charlie Copeland on the shoulder as she passed him. 'The ladies have to get dressed now.'

'Oh, of course. Apologies, ladies.' Charlie Copeland straightened up. 'Thanks for the pencil. I'll drop it back later.' He saluted a stiff-faced Rosemary Wylie, then said before he left, 'And no doubts about it, you'll make heads turn in that costume again tonight, Katherine.'

Katherine didn't respond.

Rosemary Wylie's nostrils flared ever so slightly.

As Charlie Copeland and Cissie McGee left the ladies' dressing room, they continued talking. 'Well, I heard from James McCauley that there was a mud slide on the riverbank near the foundry.' . . . 'Really? Are you sure?' . . . 'Well, I think so . . . Hugh Drummond said that they didn't know how long he'd been in the water for . . . said that he could have been there for ages.' . . . 'no, really? . . .' And the voices disappeared.

Miss Harper was at the door. 'There's a policeman downstairs. He's waiting in the kitchen at the back of the hall. Says he wants to have a quick word with everybody before the show starts!'

Mr. Charles Boyne could be heard clearly through the closed door of the little back kitchen of the church hall as Katherine waited outside it. Directly opposite her sat Ivy, dripping flowers and tears. Katherine felt the need to say something to Ivy, the girl appeared so distraught, but could only think of asking her if she was next in the queue.

Ivy lifted her tidy head. Her eyes were red as rubies. 'I don't want to go in. I'll only make a complete fool of myself. I know I will.' She wiped her tears away with her cotton handkerchief.

'No,' said Katherine softly, 'I'm sure you won't.'

'You go in next,' she said, looking at Katherine, her tears flowing again as she spoke.

'Me?'

'Yes.'

'Are you sure?'

'Yes.'

'Thank you, Miss Beacham.'

'You're welcome, Miss Fallon.'

They sat together in silence, the politeness of their interaction startling them both.

'Too sensitive for his own good,' Mr. Boyne could be heard saying through the flimsy kitchen door. 'His father was the same. Never rested easy with the fact he had made his money out of the war. Uniforms, parachutes, that kind of thing.'

Ivy blew her nose, sobbed, blew her nose again then cleared her throat.

'All those things I said to you about him . . . ' She lifted her head. 'I'm so sorry I said those things . . . about the money issues, about the gambling . . . None of it was true.' The two ruby eyes stared directly at Katherine. 'I was just jealous . . . of you both . . .' She continued, bowing her head. 'He was kind to me – that was all,' Ivy said earnestly. 'But that was enough to make me . . . want him.'

The handle of the kitchen door turned and the two women froze.

'I couldn't deny the McKinley boy is' – here Mr. Boyne stopped for a moment—'was . . . a good employee. Like his father, a man of impeccable character. Always worked hard, too hard, if you ask me . . . Yes, a good lad.' The other voice in the room was less distinct, but Katherine could make out the words, 'Thank you for coming over, Mr. Boyne.'

Katherine turned her head quickly from the door as it opened. She could feel a flush of intense heat hit her cheeks. Boyne stood in the doorway, looking back into the room.

'Thought too much, that McKinley boy,' said Boyne as he tapped his forehead with the wet end of his cigar and screwed up his thick lips as a means to illustrate the perils of an elegant mind. Then he turned and moved solemnly past Katherine and was gone.

Katherine stood up from her chair. She wanted to acknowledge Ivy's candour in this awful situation, knowing that it couldn't have been easy for her to say what she had said. Katherine turned to Ivy. 'Thank you, Ivy, thank you,' she said to her kindly.

Ivy straightened her back. 'My name's Celia,' she said slowly to Katherine with a look that could kill.

When it was her turn to talk to the young policeman, Katherine found him sitting at Miss Harper's improvised sewing table, playing with a sewing-repair kit.

He arranged a straight line of buttons across the table, making minor adjustments to them as he talked to her. The buttons clacked a little against his fingernails.

'Do you know, I've never seen an opera.' He seemed almost proud of this fact as he revealed it to her. 'Never been to plays much, either, but I love a good film.' A button moved slowly and smoothly under the pressure of his finger, coming toward her like a planchette on a Ouija board, as though the button could provide for him a currency of prescience, could divine the truth and identify the lies from whatever she said. She was silent. The button moved back into place.

'You must be a good singer.' The young policeman had a large face. His manner had an element of laziness about it, as though he had been assigned to a job that he knew didn't need doing.

'And how long have you been at this' – he hesitated slightly – 'this opera singing, then?'

'Not long. About two years.'

'Long enough.' He sounded impressed. 'Very good. Very good.' He began to space the buttons farther apart. 'Now, my mother loves music.' He rubbed the bridge of his nose briefly with his large fingers. 'Loves Beniamino Gigli. Can't get enough of Gigli. Thinks he's very romantic, so she does.' The young policeman lifted his gaze from the worktable to look at her. 'Very popular with the ladies, don't you think?'

'I don't know,' Katherine replied.

The young policeman shot one arm up in the air, a way of freeing his wrist from the tightness of his shirt cuff, and bent his arm sharply to scratch the back of his neck. He inhaled deeply in an effort to swell his own importance a little.

'How well did you know Mr. McKinley?'

'Not very,' she said to the young policeman, trying to disguise the shakiness in her voice and conscious that Ivy – Miss Celia Beacham – was waiting outside the kitchen and could hear her every word. 'I hardly knew him at all.'

'Can you tell me, Miss Fallon, when you last saw Mr. McKinley?'

'Last night,' she said.

'And did you see him leave the hall?'

'Yes.'

'And what time would that have been?'

'Just before eight o'clock.'

'Right.' The young policeman remained still. He was waiting

for more information. When none was offered, he continued. 'And do you know where he was going after that?'

'No.'

The young policeman drew his lips into a tight pucker, his eyebrows pulling together. Then he shifted his position in the chair.

'And that was definitely the last time you saw him?'

'Yes.'

The young policeman smiled at her.

'That's fine, Miss Fallon. I won't keep you any longer. Sorry to hold you back from getting ready for the show tonight, but much appreciated. And who knows, I may just catch your performance tonight. That's quite a costume you're wearing!' He looked at her, leaning his body forward a little. 'We're simply trying to work out what time it happened. No reason to suspect foul play – it appears to have been an accident, a sudden fall; he was probably unconscious when he hit the water – but . . . thank you, Miss Fallon.'

The young policeman began to rearrange the buttons on the worktable once again, then looked solemnly at her.

'Are you all right, Miss Fallon? You look a little pale.'

'I feel I might get sick.'

'Oh, the old stage fright, eh?' said the young policeman, smiling to himself. He began to rearrange the buttons on the worktable once again.

Katherine rose slowly from her chair. As she stood, the lemon sateen lining of her costume caught on a rough edge along one of the chair's legs. She reached over to untangle the threads, which were tightly hooked around a splinter of wood. Her fingers were trembling. Unable to release the threads, she tugged forcibly at her costume, tearing the lemon sateen lining and leaving a gaping hole.

After the performance of *Carmen* that night, Katherine put on her pearl grey woollen coat and walked from St. Anne's church hall toward High Street. In her hand, she held Mr. Agnew's keys to the tailors' rooms. When she reached Mr. Boyne's premises, she could see her distorted outline on the dark, glossy sheen of the street door. She was a broken prism of light, shards of herself oscillating around a black centre.

She felt a sudden rushing pressure in her stomach. Her face and head became tight. She instinctively moved a pace over to the corner of the building, turning her body into the wall. Seconds later, she got sick on the pavement – fast and violent retching, which left her cold and weak. She stood for a few moments to gather herself, conscious that some passerby may have seen her, hoping that no one had. She pulled a cotton handkerchief from out of her handbag and wiped her mouth, then gently brushed away the line of perspiration from her forehead with the back of her hand. She turned slowly from the wall. Her pearl grey woollen coat was now flecked with spots of vomit across its collar and breast. A man walked briskly along the other side of the street but did not appear to have noticed Katherine. Embarrassed, nonetheless, Katherine steadied herself. She looked down at the mess she had made on the pavement, at the spots of vomit that covered her shoes. She wiped her shoes with the cotton handkerchief and tucked it into the pocket of her pearl grey woollen coat. She put the key in the door of Mr. Boyne's premises, went inside, and climbed the stairs to the third floor.

She stood in the tailors' room, where Tom had worked, lit only by the streetlamp, which cast its light into the room from outside. Everything in its rightful place, everything undisturbed. Stacked on the far table were the rolls of new cloth; above them on the shelf were boxes of tiny glass beads and cloth buttons. There on the worktable lay his measuring tape in its little tan leather case. She took off her coat and placed it over his chair.

She noticed his black notebook under his desk lamp. It was the notebook from which he had made tiny bombs of floating fire on the night of their river walk together. She reached out and lifted it, then opened it. Inside were notes on tailoring, on materials ordered, on buttons and threads recently stocked, on the cost of suits. She could see where Tom had torn pages from its seams. Farther on there were names and addresses of clients. 'Two-piece suit in striped wool: Mr. Napier'; '3 x button-down soft-collar shirts: Mr. Harris.' Katherine turned the pages, scanning their contents quickly. Near the back of the notebook and written in large soft letters was her name, together with the measurements of her chest, her hips, her waist, and her neck. Beside her name was written *Carmen* and the date of the opening night. But it was the writing at the bottom of the page that jangled her very bones. Written in pencil, in tiny letters, were six lines of a poem:

'*. . . yet still stedfast, still unchangeable,*
*Pillow'd upon my fair love's ripening breast,*
*To feel for ever its soft fall and swell,*
*Awake for ever in a sweet unrest,*
*Still, still to hear her tender-taken breath,*
*And so live ever – or else swoon to death.*'

And underneath the poem were the words 'I have fallen head over heels in love – isn't that what they say head over heels, as though I have tumbled, fallen into a dream. Which I have. I can hardly describe the feeling she gives me. Everything in my life feels new again. Everything has lifted from the shadows. I have never felt this way about anyone before. K. is my salvation. I need her so much that my heart hurts.'

And there, sitting on top of the cabinet, was the statuette. Katherine lifted it and held it carefully in her hands. She sat down on a bundle of white cotton that had been left on the seat of his chair. She felt that everything in the room was waiting. Waiting for him to come back. Perhaps if she sat quietly and still enough, she could draw him back to her. Perhaps all she had to do was wait, wait like every other object in the room was waiting. Wait until the morning was a net of silver threads that would pull him in. Pull him back to her. How could he be just not there anymore? The incoherence of it all. *Wait, wait, he will come, he will come!* She sat awhile longer.

Time tired of itself.

Maybe she could come back tomorrow and the night after and the night after that. As long as it took.

She knew how foolish she was being, for why would he come back after she had banished him?

She looked at the statuette in her hand. She would wrap it up in cloth to protect it and she would put it in her bag and take it home. She pulled a piece of white cotton from the seat beneath her. She looked at the cloth. It was spotted with her menstrual blood from where she had been sitting.

# 9

*August 1969*

KATHERINE STANDS AT THE KITCHEN SINK. She pushes the white cotton sheets, which had been used for Madam Maureen's tent, under the warm, sudsy water. Pockets of sheet puff up indiscriminately here and there under the force of her hand, like water lilies blooming. While the day is warm and dry, she would do well to get the sheets and blankets washed, dried, and aired.

A flat tiredness governs her every move now. It is a plain, numbing tiredness, like the tiredness that follows shock. Perhaps tonight, she thinks to herself. Perhaps tonight I will sleep more soundly and feel better for it.

She leaves the sheets to soak and, drying her hands, moves to the box radio, which sits on the floor in the corner of the back room underneath the television set. Turning the dial at the front, she watches the tiny yellow lights appear on its copper grid and a voice fades in.

'. . . has today speculated on the deployment of British troops into the city of Belfast after last night's violence, acting on the request made by the commissioner of police, Harold Wolseley. Mr. Callaghan has said that . . .'

She goes to the back door to check on Stephen. Elizabeth and Stephen are gathering stones together in the yard. The few stones they have found have been placed in a little rough heap by the coal shed. Stephen waddles slowly back and forth from the stones to a corner of the yard as though he is a mother duck building a nest. Elizabeth is praising his every effort with a 'Good boy!' Maureen sits on the garden wall, absentmindedly hammering her heels against it. Richard Marr has called and stands stiffly beside Maureen, his eyes to the ground, as though he is searching for a dropped penny.

Katherine, satisfied for the moment that her children are fine, goes back inside. She lifts the sheets from the sink, twisting them to squeeze out the excess water, and feeds them through the mangle, which stands by the kitchen table.

She stops turning the handle on the mangle and piles the sheets onto one arm to carry them outside to the clothes line. Into the crook of her other arm she places a small basket of clothes pegs.

When Katherine goes back outside, she finds that Richard Marr has gone and Stephen is crying because Maureen has kicked flat his little pile of stones.

'Ah, Maureen, why did you do that, love?' Katherine throws the sheets over the clothes line, puts the basket of pegs on the ground, and picks Stephen up.

'She's in a bad mood,' Elizabeth says, rolling her eyes as she builds up the pile of stones again for Stephen.

Maureen trundles past them all and disappears into the house.

Katherine kisses Stephen and puts him at her feet while she sorts out the sheets on the clothes line. She lifts up the basket of pegs, then she places a line of pegs along the sheets.

'Elizabeth,' Katherine says quietly, 'I need to go to McGovern's to get some things. Look out for Elsa coming back, will you? I'll take Stephen with me.'

'Okay.'

Katherine walks back into the kitchen holding Stephen. She notices water on the kitchen floor and assumes she has been careless ringing out the sheets. But looking more closely, she sees a steady trickle of water running from under the sink from one of the pipes. She will need to find someone to fix the leak. Harry Grey might be able to help her out, if she can find his telephone number. His work is always reasonably priced. Putting Stephen down, she reaches for the mop from under the stairs. The telephone rings. It is George, calling her not from the station but from a public telephone. Katherine cannot quite make out what he is saying, the noise around him is so intense.

She says little in response to him when he tells her he does not know when he'll be home. She replaces the receiver and then takes the mop into the kitchen. The newsreader's voice continues from the radio.

'In last night's shootings in Belfast at least eighteen people have been reported wounded and four dead, one a nine-year-old boy. In a statement, Anthony Peacocke, the inspector general of the RUC, commented that it was of the utmost importance that the public should be aware that the police . . .'

She finishes mopping up the water, but more of it is appearing on the floor. She goes to the kitchen drawer to search for the small address book that contains Harry Grey's telephone number. She cannot find the book because the drawer is so full of rubbish. She stops looking for the book. She takes the blankets she has yet to wash and stuffs them in underneath the sink to stop the leak. She feels sodden with tiredness.

She switches off the radio. Lifting Stephen into his pram, she walks down the road to McGovern's shop. The cloud of grey city smoke has broken into rills, which run across the sky. She leaves Stephen in his pram on the pavement outside the shop and goes in to buy her groceries.

Mr. McGovern is on his own. He is polishing the new glass fronts that have just been fitted on some of the shelves behind the counter. He is very impressed with how the glass fronts give a modern look to the shop. 'It is worth the money,' he is saying to Katherine; 'it is definitely worth the money.'

'And now, Mrs. Bedford, what can I do for you?'

'I don't need much today, Mr. McGovern.' Katherine's voice sounds almost monotone. 'I need some butter, please, Mr. McGovern, marmalade, a small bag of potatoes, and . . . eh . . . what green vegetable do you have?'

'I have a lovely ruby ball cabbage for you, just in. And it'll be lovely with that bit of butter, so it will.'

'That'll do fine, Mr. McGovern.'

'You've heard the news?' Mr. McGovern seems suddenly grave. His eyes widen as he looks at Katherine.

'Yes, some of it.' Katherine knows immediately that he is referring to the civil unrest in the city.

'Word has it, Mrs. Bedford, that soldiers are to be drafted into Belfast this afternoon, *this afternoon,* onto the streets.' Mr. McGovern keeps his voice low. 'If you ask me, that's very serious.'

Katherine's head begins to fill again with the words George had whispered to her in the dark, early hours of that morning.

'This afternoon?'

'Yes, as far as I know, Mrs. Bedford. There were riots all over the west of the city, spilling out in all directions. Crowds gathering on the streets, baton charges, families burned out of their homes. Reports of shootings, bombs. If you ask me, it's very serious.' Mr. McGovern shakes his head. 'They can put a man on the moon, but what good is that to us, Mrs. Bedford?'

'And the boy. There was a boy shot dead?' Katherine looks for confirmation.

'Yes,' Mr. McGovern replies solemnly. 'They say it was an accident, but—'

Just then, another customer comes into the shop.

'Ah, Mrs. Forsythe.' In an instant, Mr. McGovern's smile is back. 'I'll be with you in just one minute.' Then he turns to Katherine, 'The *Belfast Telegraph* – it'll be in shortly. I'll put one aside for you, Mrs. Bedford?'

'Yes, Mr. McGovern, I can send Maureen down for it later.'

Mr. McGovern hands Katherine her little net bag of groceries.

The climb back up the road from the shops exhausts Katherine, more than she can ever remember before. She can hardly get a breath. And there is really no shopping to speak of, nothing inordinately heavy. Something is draining her.

By the time she gets back home from McGovern's, the weather has changed. Whatever warmth there was is gone. Spats of dirty grey rain fall impatiently out of the sky. Katherine hauls Stephen's pram up the back steps of the house and into the back room, Stephen cooing happily and clapping his hands at her efforts. Katherine lifts Stephen out of the pram and, after putting him on the floor with the little net bag full of groceries to play with, pushes the pram out into the hallway. Coming back into the kitchen, she sees how the blankets under the sink are sopping wet. She searches for the address book with Harry Grey's number again, rifling through the household receipts, the information leaflets, the embroidery thread, the bills, the fat bundles of seed packets caught up with bits of string, the kitchen scissors, the shoelaces, which pack the kitchen drawer. She cannot find the address book. Rain hits more insistently against the windowpane.

She remembers the sheets on the clothes line and moves quickly to save them. She pulls the white cotton sheets off the line and throws them over her shoulder, leaving the pegs on the line. She rushes indoors. The heavens open. Suddenly appearing behind her is Elsa, soaking wet, her arms and legs bleeding.

'Oh my God, Elsa! What happened to you?'

'I fell into the blackberry bushes.' Elsa's tone is sullen. Elsa looks at her mother. She wants to tell her mother what happened at the blackberry bushes, but something is stopping her, as though she feels there is something dirty about it.

'You fell into the blackberry bushes?' Katherine sounds incredulous. 'But your arms . . . your legs, ach, Elsa . . . the side of your face! Are you all right?'

Katherine moves instinctively forward to touch Elsa, but Elsa shrinks back from her mother and lowers her head. 'I'm fine,' she mumbles.

'Those scratches'll need washing.'

'I'll do it myself.'

'It looks so sore, Elsa.'

'It's not.'

'It needs tending.'

'I'll do it myself!'

'You'll need plasters.'

'No, I won't! I'm all right!'

Maureen stomps into the kitchen. She pulls the cupboard door open and thumps a glass down on the table. She grabs the milk bottle that has been sitting on the kitchen counter and lashes milk from it into the glass. Milk spills off the lip of the glass and spreads over the kitchen table. Maureen takes a quick mouthful of milk from the glass and then dumps it on the table and turns to go.

'You're not leaving that mess for me to clean up, Maureen!'

'I'll do it later, Mum.'

'You'll do it now!'

'What happened you?' Maureen grunts at Elsa.

'Get a cloth and wipe it up, Maureen,' Katherine insists.

'What happened *you*?' Elsa snaps at Maureen.

Elizabeth bursts into the kitchen.

'Mum! Maureen's ripped my library book. She just got a pen and ripped it through the pages. The book's ruined!'

'It was only one page!' Maureen snarls.

'It was not.'

'You weren't reading it anyway!'

'I was so!'

'You were not!'

'Just because Richard Marr said no when you asked him to go out with you.'

'I never even asked him, so there. You just—'

Katherine cuts Maureen off.

'I don't want to hear how it happened, or why it happened. Just sort it out between you!' Katherine's voice is sharp.

'And what happened *you*?' Elizabeth turns to Elsa.

'You shut up!' growls Elsa.

'Maureen,' Katherine adds quickly 'wipe up that mess and change Stephen, will you?'

'Ma-ma,' Stephen calls.

'What?' Maureen's tone is gruff.

'I said, change him,' Katherine says with deliberation, feeling her temperature rising at Maureen's insolence.

'But I did that yesterday *and* the day before—'

Katherine's head swings abruptly around toward Maureen. 'CHANGE HIM!' she screams at Maureen. She screams more loudly than she has ever screamed before. All three girls stare at their mother. They have never heard their mother scream as loudly as this. They all stand frozen to the spot. All three of them stand as strange separate pieces. A moment more, and then Maureen suddenly grabs Stephen and rushes out of the kitchen. Elizabeth follows quickly behind them. Elsa stays for a moment longer, her eyes filling up with tears, before she leaves.

Katherine falls to her knees. Her skin goes cold and her body starts to shake. She feels disorientated and altered. She is folded over like a woman fearing an intruder or an abusive husband, immobilized and yet charged. A white heat is coursing through her. The unfamiliar sound of that voice, her voice, coming up through her, the vicious pitch of it. Like how a car crashing has its own singular, awful, distinct sound, separate from the damage done. The metal in her voice. She holds in that stiff rage and feels the surge of her ridiculous anger cleanse her body and clarify her mind.

Katherine acknowledges it now, her body a curve of pure energy, how she has compromised her life with George. How her betrayal of him has continued. How, throughout her married life, she has held on to the fantasy of Tom's return.

Had he not died, would he have haunted her so?

Had he not died.

*To hold him. To smell his skin. To kiss him . . .*

In the back room, where the fibres of love and life are woven together, the air now rings soundless.

There is something bright beside her. Bright, and luminous. She turns her head to look. She can see her own reflection on the blank television screen in the corner of the room. With the white cotton sheets falling across her shoulder and down her back, she is a giant ghost moth in a square of endless black, the earth's edges closing around her in the tilting dark.

'That is not my face,' she says to herself.

# 10

*November 1969*

THE SUMMER IS OVER. AUTUMN, TOO. Now the early winter-morning sun casts long, low shadows, as though it is already evening. At night, the chill air freezes the moon and the sky settles still and black.

Back at school Maureen, Elizabeth, and Elsa have been sitting in their respective classrooms, watching their breath mist up in the cold air. In the dim grey light, the pale faces of the stern nuns look as though they have been poached in milk. At break time, when the children will run outside, the blades of crisp grass that border the school yard will snap underfoot.

The city streets have become empty black lines that lead nowhere, sealed by a biting frost. Surprisingly, as the frost gathers, intent is held in check for a time and the city is locked quiet. Reflection is an utter possibility. Anger and provocation yield under each glacial veil that falls and the city for a time becomes a beautiful white lie. How easily life slips across the surface now, as ordinary as it comes. People going about their business with only the winters' vapours tingling through their bones, shopping and paying bills with stiffened notes, making icy trails to work and back, stoking laughter in half-heated foyers, scraping off the thin slush from their boots before they cross a neighbour's threshold for a cup of tea. Christmas is a little way off and the violent summer seems a distant made-up past. For now, the murk of riot has hardened to a halt. For now a kind of peace has returned. But when the thaw comes after this winter there will still be ice. Thick and black and solid and immovable. After this melting, the city will still be held under an endless winter.

And who would have imagined it? Who would have imagined the beautiful white lie melting to a brutal black?

Katherine has the collar of her navy winter coat pulled up across her face to shield her from the piercing wind. Elsa and Isabel have each buttoned their coats right up to the top button and wear woollen hats and gloves and thick woollen tights. Only Isabel wears boots. The fur lining of Isabel's boots splay untidily at their tops, where two fluffy toggles hang to assist the zipping. The soles, Isabel insists, are slip-proof.

'They're very nice boots, Isabel,' says Katherine as she walks with the two girls through Belfast's city centre.

They have come to see *Hansel and Gretel* at the Grove Theatre. Katherine has recently felt a renewed sense of confidence about going into the city. George has felt it too. He has been home more in recent evenings and over the past couple of months was called out to only a few house fires, one factory fire, and one fire at a farm near Comber, where an overheated sow had escaped and had stubbornly chased him through a scant-grassed, muddy field. Although soldiers had been a visible presence on the streets of Belfast since the summer, in terms of political unrest nothing much had been happening. So Katherine had suggested taking Elsa, Elizabeth, and Maureen as a treat to *Hansel and Gretel* (she also wanted to shake off this constant cold malaise that seemed to be hounding her). Neither Maureen nor Elizabeth, however, had shown any interest in going to the show, so Katherine had then suggested that Elsa bring Isabel.

'Do I have to bring her?' Elsa had asked sourly.

'No,' Katherine had replied, 'but you're either friends with Isabel or you're not – which is it?'

'I bet she'll be wearing something new sp-ee-cial-ly for the occasion,' Elsa said imitating Isabel's pretend-squeaky-clean voice. 'I bet she'll get bought something brand-new.'

'Which is it to be?'

'Okay, then,' said Elsa finally.

Out of the cold now and sitting in the noisy theatre, Elsa holds a bar of toffee in her hand and feels as though her fingers have become enormous in the welcome heat. She cannot bite the toffee bar, it is so hard against her teeth. She can only leave small indentations on the brown slab. Her mouth and lips are sticky. Isabel sits between Elsa and Katherine and does not speak, but instead sucks on a boiled sweet. She twists a strand of her blond hair around her finger with a look of self-satisfied contempt on her face.

Elsa cannot decide which is making her feel most uncomfortable, the unruly behaviour of the children around her, who are shouting and firing scrunched-up balls of paper at one another, the cloying smell of the musty velvet seats and the flaky, splintery odour of old cigarettes, or the fact that Isabel is sitting beside her. Having Isabel beside her makes Elsa feel as though she has been wrapped in a cold, damp blanket.

Elsa had been right. Not only are Isabel's boots brand-new but she also wears a brand-new dress bought 'sp-ee-cial-ly' for the occasion. Katherine had reacted in stiff surprise when Isabel's mother had informed her of the purchase, suddenly feeling concerned about whether the afternoon's experience at the show would match up to the *broderie anglaise* and the ruffled pleats that Isabel was proudly displaying in front of her.

The roar of the heaters that line the walls of the auditorium suddenly stop and the lights go down. The excited yapping of the children instantly explodes into cheering and squealing. Elsa and Isabel remain silent.

'It's about to start now,' Katherine says to Elsa, smiling at her. Elsa looks at her mother in the shadowy dark and feels warmed by her smile.

'Do you want some toffee, Mummy?'

'No thanks, pet.'

The show is a strange hybrid. A retelling of the fairy tale with some songs and some comic routines, but it isn't a pantomime, nor is it a musical, nor is it a play. The program and the poster describe it as 'A Magical Extravaganza for All the Family.' But the children in the audience are not settling to take it in and do not seem to care what kind of show it is.

The character of the wicked old woman who owns the gingerbread house is played by a man. He is trying out a high voice, but every now and then his confidence wanes and his baritone notes slip through. His movements are wiry and mechanical. He is dressed like a pantomime dame with a large unstable wig that he cannot leave alone and a wide skirt, on the hem of which he keeps trampling. He tugs at his costume to free it, and then he tramples on it again.

Isabel turns to Katherine. 'I need to go to the toilet, Mrs. Bedford,' she says in a dull voice.

'Em . . .' Katherine looks around her and then says to Isabel, 'There they are just over to the right.' She points to the side of the auditorium and Isabel slips out of her seat. 'Are you all right going on your own?'

'Yes, Mrs. Bedford. And I think I've got toffee in my hair.'

'Oh dear. Careful of your dress, Isabel.' Katherine cannot help but be a little concerned about Isabel's new attire. 'You'll find us again easily enough?'

'Yes, Mrs. Bedford,' replies Isabel flatly, and pushes past Elsa.

Elsa immediately moves into the seat vacated by Isabel so that she is now beside her mother. Katherine reaches over to Elsa and gives her a warm, tight hug and kisses her on the top of the head. Elsa looks up at her mother.

'What d'ye think, Mummy? Do you like it – the show?' Elsa is animated now, smiling and raising her eyebrows in anticipation of her mother's response.

'Oh – I think it's' – Katherine quietly struggles to find some appropriate words, 'it's colourful and it's rather entertaining, don't you?'

Elsa's eyes widen.

They both turn their heads to look up at the stage. A dwarf dressed as a wood elf has now come onstage and is skipping in little circles as he casts some spell or other on two children who are standing under a tree. He appears angry and waves his arms impatiently. The two children are distracted by the noise in the auditorium and they speak so quietly on the stage that they cannot be heard. The wicked old woman applauds the dwarf and cackles and then her wig slips sideways and she tries to fix it as she makes a face. She asks the children in the audience a question, her voice croaking with the effort, but no one replies over the general noise.

Katherine leans into her daughter.

'Don't you think it's rather entertaining?' Katherine starts to laugh a little. Elsa looks at her mother and then she starts to laugh, as well. She knows now that her mother thinks the show is not very good but doesn't want to say it. They are both trying to stifle the laughter they feel rising inside them, their shoulders shaking. Katherine's hand is now covering her mouth. Elsa's face is broad and beaming. They know that they should not be laughing, and this makes them laugh all the more. Katherine has a stitch now and holds her stomach. Elsa is imitating her mother's movements and wraps her arms around her middle and bends her head forward and then throws it back. Elsa's face is bright from watching her mother, watching everything about her. Katherine wipes away the tears of laughter that have now welled up in her eyes. Elsa copies her mother, even though her own eyes are dry. Katherine cannot help it and starts to laugh loudly. Elsa laughs, too, making squeaks and yelps, her eyes fast on her mother. Elsa is so wrapped up in her mother now. She thinks this is all so wonderful, this sharing, this laughing with her mother and no one else in the whole world understanding it, because it is only they who know.

Isabel reappears. Noticing that her seat has been taken by Elsa, she plonks herself rudely into the empty seat and gives a suspicious sideways look at both mother and daughter. She seems put out by their private joke.

The wicked old woman onstage bursts into song and Katherine and Elsa get taken by a fresh bout of laughter because the song sounds so ridiculous. As Katherine watches, she is struck by something familiar about the actor who is playing the wicked old woman and, as her shoulders shake, she holds up the program in front of her, squeezing her eyes slightly to see better in the dark, and finds the name Charlie Copeland mentioned in the playbill. It is enough to wind her laughter down.

'Oh, it's Charlie, my goodness—!' She looks up at the stage and then turns to Elsa. 'Imagine that!' she says with a great sigh.

Katherine feels filled with fresh air after the laughing. She looks at Elsa as though Elsa is her saviour.

'I love you, Elsa.'

'I love you too, Mummy.'

When the performers take their bow at the end of the show, the children are too busy searching for dropped sweets to applaud them. Katherine decides to go backstage to say hello to Charlie Copeland. The narrow corridor eventually leads Katherine, with Elsa and Isabel in tow, to the makeshift dressing rooms, where, as she knocks and slowly opens the door, she finds Charlie Copeland sitting in a tiny room. The room is filled with boxes, rows of stacked chairs, and a large bingo board. Charlie Copeland lifts his head to look at Katherine as she enters. His lids glisten peacock blue, his lips are scarlet red and his eyes are rimmed in thick raven black. His wig lies on his lap like a dead cat.

'Charlie, remember me?' Katherine holds out her arms to embrace him.

Charlie Copeland jumps up. 'Oh, of course I do, of course I do. My lovely Katherine, oh my goodness, what a delightful surprise!' Charlie smiles broadly at Katherine and throws his arms around her. 'Katherine Fallon! How are you?'

'Just fine, Charlie!'

'And these are your beautiful children!' Charlie pulls back to take in Elsa and Isabel.

'This is my daughter Elsa and her friend Isabel.'

'Two beautiful girls.' Charlie has now folded his hands under his chin, shaking his head in admiration at the two girls and staring in disbelief.

'How are you, Charlie? Are you well?'

'Oh, as well as can be expected. Oh, what a lovely surprise.' Charlie's eyes are filling up as he looks at Katherine. 'What a lovely, lovely surprise! And look at you, just as beautiful as ever! After all these years! My goodness! And tell me' – he speaks quickly now—'are you still living over the chip shop?' Charlie turns to Elsa and Isabel and laughs. 'I used to love it when your mother came to rehearsals smelling of fish and chips – always made me hungry, so it did.'

Katherine laughs, too. Elsa smiles. There is a look of slight disgust on Isabel's face.

'No, Charlie, I'm living up on Hillfoot Crescent now, just beyond Hillfoot Road.' Katherine smiles at Charlie.

'I know Hillfoot Crescent well. Oh, and you're looking as glamorous as ever, Katherine. Look at your mother, girls – isn't she beautiful!'

Isabel slips another hard sweet into her mouth and, crunching it loudly, brushes her hair back from her face with her hand.

'And you Charlie, still living up on Ridgeway Street?'

'No, dear, I've moved back in with Mummy. She's not at all well.' Charlie Copeland shakes his head a little, as though pitying himself.

'I'm sorry to hear that, Charlie.' Katherine's concerned tone disguises the fact that she is genuinely amazed that Charlie's mother is still alive after all these years.

Then, suddenly he says, 'Come here, Katherine, and tell me, have you seen anyone else from the group. What about that Rosemary Wylie one, where is she now?'

'I've no idea, Charlie. I've lost touch with everyone.'

'I know that your fella, what's his name . . . your Don José! . . . Hugh Drummond – he's doing very well for himself. Runs a catering business and has hotels and all, all over the place.'

'Oh, very posh!' Katherine laughs.

'And James McCauley took over his father's furniture shop.'

'Oh, very good.'

'And Cissie McGee went to America.'

'Charlie, it seems you know everybody's business!'

'And of course there was that young tailor.' Charlie Copeland's pace slows a little. 'You remember him, don't you, Katherine? He made your costume for *Carmen*. A lovely young man.'

Katherine bleeds white and cold at the mention of Tom. 'Yes, Charlie, I remember.'

'Terrible, wasn't it?' Charlie Copeland gives a large sigh. 'Do y'know – now this'll tell ye how odd I am – I still think about that young man. I do. Funny that, isn't it. After all this time, I still think about him – as if that would do any good for him! That was such a terrible shame, that whole thing . . . such a lovely young man . . .' Charlie Copeland's voice trails off almost to a whisper.

'That's nearly twenty years ago, Charlie.' Katherine says, her voice shaking.

Charlie nods. 'How time flies, eh!' he says, and he hunches his shoulders to show that there's nothing he can do about the time flying. Then he makes a funny face at the two girls. He is aware of Katherine's sudden disquiet. He wants to lighten the mood. 'There you go!' he says, and smiles a wide smile.

Katherine visibly steadies herself and looks Charlie firmly in the eye. 'And George is still a civil engineer and still works part-time for the Fire Service,' she says briskly.

'George?'

'George Bedford. Yes, we got married.'

'George Bedford. You married George Bedford after all? That big brute of a man! Oh, for goodness sake.'

'And he took me to Mexico for our honeymoon.'

'He did not?' Charlie Copeland has an astonished look on his face. 'Mexico! Well, isn't he the bee's knees!'

'And we've four children.'

'Four. How wonderful. And are you still singing, Katherine?'

'Oh, no . . . no, not anymore.'

'Oh, that is a shame. And you could've taken the world by

storm!' He looks intently at Elsa and Isabel. 'Your mother, girls, your mother had a magnificent voice. The voice of an angel.'

'And you, Charlie, how's the printing business going?'

'Still good. People still want their calendars I'm glad to say. And, as you see, I'm still doing this amateur stuff for my sins!' Charlie screws his eyes up as he smiles, his red lips spreading. 'You know, we should get everyone together again – have a reunion!'

'Yes, we must.'

'Sure it's great to see you.'

'And you, Charlie.'

'Any of these young girls gettin' married soon?' Charlie turns to Elsa and Isabel again. Elsa smiles in response. Isabel glares at the ceiling.

'Charlie, we'll leave you now and let you get organised. Perhaps we'll catch up soon?'

'I certainly won't leave it for long now that I know where you live!'

'Please, Charlie, call in if you're ever passing, number ninety-two. I'd love to see you.'

Katherine gives Charlie Copeland another embrace.

'Good-bye, Charlie.'

'Good-bye, Katherine. See you soon.' Charlie turns to Elsa. 'This little one looks so like you, Katherine. Another Katherine Fallon, imagine that!' He rubs the top of Elsa's head. Isabel has already moved to the door. Then turning to his makeshift dressing table, he gives Elsa two toffees from a paper bag.

'Thank you,' says Elsa. She looks into Charlie Copeland's face. It is a child's drawing.

On their way through town after *Hansel and Gretel,* Katherine, Elsa, and Isabel pass St. Mary's Church on Chapel Lane. The two girls chat. Katherine is so preoccupied with the thought of having met Charlie Copeland again after all these years, a concrete reminder of when Tom was still alive, that as she passes the chapel, it happens automatically. She blesses herself – in the name of the Father, and of the Son, and of the Holy Ghost

– lifting her hand unconsciously and gracefully to her forehead, her chest, and her shoulders. So deep in thought is she that she is unconscious of how deliberate a display it is. Elsa and Isabel look up at Katherine in disbelief, wondering if she is aware of what she has done. And then it happens. Instantly across her cheek a splat of warmth, a thick, wet stink, shocking in the cold air of the night. Someone's spit is on her face.

Katherine turns, confused, to look at who would do this, expecting a jeering child, a scut of a boy, an unruly adolescent who will run away as soon as he is spotted, but instead she sees a well-dressed, tallish man in a long haired tweed coat, carrying an umbrella. He has a face like a bird. The man looks directly at her, unflinchingly holds his gaze on her with his black eyes, then silently mouths the word *Fenian* as though he could be blowing her a kiss. His head remains angled toward her as his body moves forward. She feels the glob of spit move slowly down along her skin. The man walks on casually. She searches for a handkerchief in her handbag. She is shaking. She emits a sound that Elsa has never heard from her before, a high, soft groan. Elsa looks up at her mother, startled. The man turns the corner of the street and is gone. A shadow that's crossed her soul.

The incident over, Katherine tries to make light of it, but she can see the girls shrink from her, as though they are completely embarrassed by her and want to pretend that it never happened. So instead, Katherine quickly switches to talking to the girls about *Hansel and Gretel* as they make their way home. After they disembark from the bus they leave Isabel at her door, but Isabel's father wants to show Katherine and Elsa his lamp stands – wine bottles over which he has painstakingly arranged a layer of seashells – and Katherine says what an interesting use of wine bottles and seashells and how did he ever find the time to make them, but the conversation tires her. When at last they get home, Katherine washes her hands and face and then decides to change out of the tweed skirt she had put on that morning. The elasticated waistband of the skirt feels loose and she has become conscious of how it keeps slipping from her waist down onto her hips. As Katherine changes out of her skirt, her chest feels tight and her back feels sore. She stops to take a breath, spreading one hand in front of her upon the dressing table and leaning her upper body forward in an attempt to loosen her frame to take in air.

She tries to put the 'incident' out of her mind. She won't tell George: he'll get too upset over nothing. There's no point, she reassures herself, for by tomorrow it will all be forgotten. It was an isolated incident, just one of those stupid things that could happen anywhere. She gets a flash of the man's birdlike face and his lewd curling lips. She straightens herself to see if that will help her breathe. Just one clean breath, just one sensation of air going all the way in. But her lungs seem to cheat her, as though they are plugged. So she fixes her thoughts on meeting Charlie Copeland again, of how lovely it was to see him, of how she hopes that he will hold to his word and call to see her sometime, of how, undeniably, her meeting him has only served to intensify her thoughts of Tom.

The shock of Tom's death had, at the time, served to affirm for Katherine what she had known all along but had chosen to ignore, that her feelings for him, no matter how genuine, had indeed been inappropriate. That teetering down the path of illicit romance had been foolish and irresponsible. It served to show her to herself, her lack of moral fibre, her selfish indulgence, her disrespect for any religious mores her mother may have attempted to instill in her. Her total disregard for George. But there was also a darker shock to weather. The question that had turned over and over in Katherine's mind – for weeks, for months, for the two years that George had waited for her to set a wedding date, a question that still, after all these years, had not been answered, and in truth never could be – had she been responsible in any way for Tom's death? Was it her rejection of him that had, in a manner of speaking, pushed him over the edge into the swollen river? Had she caused him such distress that he had lost all common sense that night and, regardless of the storm, had walked the river's path? Had his distress marred his judgment, caused him to fall to his death? Had he died in any part because of her, died for her?

The weight of this burden took its toll. For months after the accident, Katherine's behaviour was tempered by an extreme caution, as though there was a constant pressure on her, physically and emotionally, as though something was pressing her in, limiting her; her words and actions rationed by need until they were only just enough, her moods shifting uncannily slowly, seeping through the days. For weeks on end, she would often appear preoccupied, distant, almost anesthetized to the world around her. Then for periods after that, she would appear agitated and restless. Only occasionally would she be angry, and usually over the smallest thing, a forgotten appointment, a mislaid belonging, something she had spilled or broken, but even then there was no sense of real release. Her anger would rise up and then would hang around her until she simply tired of it. To her mother, Vera, and Frank, Katherine always seemed to be on the brink of a fever or a flu. Her mother had advised her to see a doctor on several occasions, which Katherine never did, choosing instead to stay in her room. She couldn't sleep at night and would walk the house while everyone else was in bed. At work, she would be exhausted. She ate little and had no interest in going out. She had retrieved her engagement ring from the jewellers in Smithfield Market, paying back the money owed and not mentioning anything to George about how it had been used as security against the purchase of the statuette – but then she wouldn't wear it. George would call at the flat, only to be told by Vera or her mother that she was resting or that she was not feeling well enough to see him and that she would telephone him later, which of course she never did. At other times, George would call at the offices of the Ulster Bank, only to be told by her colleagues that she had left early to go home.

But George had waited for her patiently all that time, his only aim being that she would be happy again, that she would finally agree to a life together with him, that she would set a wedding date. The two years of their engagement he had found difficult. Katherine knew this. He found her anger easier to handle, he had told her. At least then there was contact between them, albeit edgy. But when she pulled away from him, he said that he despaired of ever winning her back. His mother, Anna, had disapproved of Katherine's behaviour. No woman respected a man who spent his time walking on eggshells around her, she had said drily. She urged him to be firmer. But George was content to count his blessings, as he put it. He loved Katherine more than anything in the world, he had said. She had agreed one day to be his wife, and to him that was all that mattered.

And in the end, George's love had indeed brought her back, offered her a new beginning, allowed her to let go of the past. Hadn't it?

Why, then, has the past been haunting her again, as though there is unfinished business?

Is it because the world is trying to catch up with her? For, for her, it has been winter for quite some time. Since George rescued her from the sea, since she encountered the seal, the coldness hasn't gone away. It has been her constant white companion, travelling at her elbow with an earnest expectation. It hangs around her now like an invisible hoary skin that she must shed. While she goes about her daily household chores. While she sleeps. While she dresses her children for school. While she embraces her husband before he goes to work. It hangs around her.

Whenever Katherine wakes up to the call of her children or to the rousing streaks of the winter's yellow dawn coming through the bedroom curtains or to the telephone ringing for George, she feels exhausted. There is no sense of regeneration in her sleep. Tiredness fills her body and she carries the heavy dryness of it all day. It seems as though it is suffusing her whole body, circling in her blood until it reaches every fingertip, every cell, every last piece of her, reaching right into the insides of her, synapse after synapse. The children think she looks puzzled or confused, as though she is constantly trying to remember the name of something or decipher the sound of a distant voice. The blue-ridged veins along her hands feel tender and sore and seem to have grown bigger than they need to be. Her hair hurts where it joins her scalp. Her back hurts.

Nights are broken by the bad dreams of her children, who, while in their jittery somnambulant daze, can walk directly to the mother smell in the next room. Their bad dreams do not coincide, but stagger from one child to the other at different times during the night on different nights, as though each has taken it in turns to slumber-read a chapter of the same anxious story. Then there are the colds and coughs, the teeth hurting, the leg cramping, the snot-blocked noses, the aches of growing. Katherine comforts and rubs and reassures but finds herself, by breakfast time, a mere shadow. Nights that the children sleep right through, she is ill prepared for, and she wakes regardless, expectant and listening.

The tiredness calms her by disorientating her. It makes her selective. I can go shopping for groceries or I can take the children to the park, not both, she thinks, I can cook the dinner or wash the curtains, not both.

At its most intense, she is only hearing. A dog barking in the distance gives her a sense that there is life.

And then there is a nausea that beleaguers this calm. A nausea that sweeps periodically through her body. She feels herself falling down inside herself, slipping down, back down, into the red ochre sludge that her blood has become.

Since the summer Elsa and Elizabeth have had to consider the two alphabets. One alphabet is Catholic, where the letter *h* is pronounced *haiche*. This alphabet they have finished with for the day at school and so have packed it neatly back into their schoolbags. The other alphabet is Protestant, where the letter *h* is pronounced *aiche*. Even though things have quietened down in the city, they still routinely arm themselves with this particular alphabet on leaving school. As they have to walk through a Protestant neighbourhood on their way home, chances are that Protestant children will stop them, and this semantic ammunition may work in their favour. All other clues that they are Catholic are, as usual, covered over by their navy coats.

They take the familiar route home, cutting across the junction on the Woodstock Road and then making their way along Jocelyn Avenue. Elsa spots them almost as soon as she and Elizabeth have rounded the corner: four boys, dragging their schoolbags along the pavement, looking for trouble.

'Elizabeth,' Elsa says quietly, 'will we turn back?'

'No.' Elizabeth keeps her head down. 'It'll be all right.' The foursome slow their pace. Then the oldest boy in the group, a thin, wiry, long boy of about eleven, his hair shaved close to his head, makes a dash across the road toward them.

'Where d'ye think yer goin'?' His discoloured teeth point inward. Ink streaks his cheek. The two girls remain silent and carry on walking. Within a matter of moments, the other three boys join the long boy with the shaven head. They form a ragged semicircle around Elsa and Elizabeth, blocking their way forward.

'I said, where d'ye think yer goin'?' The questioning is ritualistic, a way of searching for provocation in the least response, a question demanding the right answer. Elizabeth mutters, 'Home,' her head bent low. Elsa says nothing. Then Elizabeth starts to cry.

'Are yous Fenians? Did yous hear me ask ye where ye fuckin' live?' The long boy grows longer with the prospect of giving out a good beating. 'Say the fuckin' alphabet, yous wee fuckin' Taigs. Say it!' Elsa and Elizabeth remain silent. Elizabeth wipes away the tears that are running down her face. 'Have yous gone fuckin' dumb or somethin'?' The long boy stands glaring at them. 'Say the fuckin' alphabet!'

Elizabeth lifts her head and is just about to start with the letter *A*, when suddenly, out of nowhere, a figure runs up from behind the group and pelts Elizabeth with eggs. Two, three, thrown at her face, another at her legs. The *splat-splat* against Elizabeth's head confuses her. She raises her hands in protection, thinking someone has thrown stones at her, but then she feels the globules of egg white and yoke running down her face.

The group whoop and jeer, delighted with this surprise gift, satisfaction spreading over their faces like an infectious rash. The perpetrator hollers into the air and then scoots off across the road, gone perhaps to get more of his friends to gloat over his target. The long boy backs off. 'Fuck yous,' he says. 'Yous wee dolls need a hair wash.' He cackles wildly with his cohorts, leaving Elizabeth and Elsa alone.

Elizabeth stands sobbing, her face and hands slimy with egg white, a burst of egg yolk splattered on the crown of her head, shell caught in the strands of her hair, bits of eggs spotting the front of her coat. Elsa finds two egg spots on her sleeve. She rubs them off, then looks at Elizabeth. Passersby look, too, but make no remark, nor offer help.

Elsa wants to leave Elizabeth there and run away. But she doesn't. They stand on the street, Elizabeth sobbing quietly, Elsa unable to comfort her.

Eventually, they shuffle onward, toward the bus, toward home.

On the bus, no one makes any comment, not even the bus conductor, who only shows some reluctance in taking the money from Elizabeth's sticky hand. The egg in Elizabeth's hair has a rotten smell. It feels like cool orange blood on her scalp. She sits on the bus with Elsa, still and quiet, holding her bus ticket, her schoolbag, and an unused alphabet.

When they arrive home, Elsa goes upstairs to find her mother and tell her what has happened, crawling up the stairs like a sherpa carrying a bagful of pitiful news. On reaching the top stair, she is halted by the sound of deep, low voices behind the closed door of her parents' bedroom.

After a few moments, the bedroom door opens and Elsa, overcome with a sudden feeling of guilt, flees.

Now a stranger follows her down the stairs and stops to use

the telephone without even asking. The stranger smells like a doctor. His shoes are shiny and his glasses have a silver chain that loops around the back of his neck. He speaks with a serious tone on the telephone, he writes something in his notebook, and as he turns to go back upstairs, he catches sight of Elsa. He smiles at her, nodding his head all the while, as if he is agreeing with himself. He looks as though he is trying to squeeze the smile out of his face.

'Ah . . . yes,' he says simply, and goes back upstairs.

Elizabeth sits quietly in the kitchen. She has made no move to wipe her hair or face. Elsa had gone upstairs to fetch Elizabeth a towel from the airing cupboard in the bathroom but had come down again empty-handed in her sudden departure after the doctor had opened the door. Now, at least, Elsa shows Elizabeth some concern.

'Are you all right?'

'Yes, thank you,' Elizabeth says politely. 'Where's Mummy?' Elizabeth blows her nose on a crumpled tissue from her coat pocket. Snot and egg white are indistinguishable.

'She's upstairs.'

'Who was that on the telephone?'

'A man.'

'What man?'

'I don't know. A man.'

'What's Mummy doing upstairs?'

'I don't know.'

'Is she asleep?'

'No. She talking to Daddy.'

'Oh, Daddy's home?' Elizabeth, for the first time since the incident, manages a small smile. 'I didn't even see his car.'

'It's parked on the street.'

'Why is it parked on the street?'

'I don't know.' The conversation comes to a natural halt. Both of the girls realise how strange it is for the house to be this quiet when they come home from school. Whatever is happening upstairs seems to have cast a spell over everything.

Elizabeth and Elsa hear heavy movements on the floorboards above them. There are footfalls on the stairs and then the front door of the house opens and closes. The two girls remain sitting in the kitchen. Elizabeth begins to shiver.

Upstairs in the back bedroom, everything, in a single moment, reduces itself to a point of nascent panic when the word *cancer* is mentioned. The doctor has advised George that Katherine be taken to the hospital for treatment immediately, for as far as he can tell, the cancer, wherever it started, has spread to her spine. George cannot hear anything the doctor is saying after he hears the word *cancer*. The doctor's mouth is moving, but George cannot decipher sound. The doctor is writing something on a piece of paper and showing it to him, but George cannot make sense of it. It is as though the furniture in the room is rapidly being sucked, piece by piece, into a vacuum and that any second they, too, George and Katherine, will be sucked away.

Finally, the tiredness that Katherine had been feeling is explained to her, and the nausea is explained to her, and the breathlessness, and the back pain.

Now Katherine is moaning in disbelief and shaking her head, a gentle grimace on her face. She cannot comprehend it. She is staring at the doctor expectantly, as if she is waiting for him to change his mind. But the doctor doesn't change his mind. After a few moments, he leaves the room to make a phone call, and as he opens the bedroom door, he finds Elsa scurrying away down the stairs.

Strange to say that, after this, Elsa will not have any memory of her mother leaving the house. What she will remember is her father coming into the kitchen, looking agitated and white-faced, and she will remember his gentle, if somewhat distracted, concern over Elizabeth and the eggs in her hair and the long boy. She will remember how, eventually, she helped Elizabeth out of her stained uniform and helped her to wash her brown-black hair in the bathroom sink. How she dried Elizabeth's hair by the two-bar electric fire in the back room, Elizabeth's cheeks getting overly hot and flushed, and how she brushed Elizabeth's hair until it was beautiful again. She will remember Isabel calling at the house and sneering at Elizabeth on hearing about the egg incident, and she will remember telling Isabel that that wasn't a very nice way to behave and then Isabel leaving with her head down. She will remember that later she and Elizabeth joined Maureen and Stephen at Nanny Anna's, and that she and Nanny Anna and Maureen and Elizabeth sat playing cards at the little round table in Nanny Anna's front room, and that they lifted their heads occasionally from their game of cards and caught Stephen, wrapped up in his woollen coat in the garden, pulling leaves off the winter shrubs and laughing.

# 11

*December 1969*

KATHERINE NOW SHARES A WARD with six other women, all suffering from cancer. She wears a lilac nightdress and a pink dressing gown. She feels the nightdress is too short, but it was all that was available to her – she had pulled it hastily from the airing cupboard – and she tugs the hem of her dressing gown once again to cover her bare knees.

George is with her now. He has managed to secure two days off from work to get Katherine settled. He can leave shortly to get Katherine whatever she needs, toothpaste, tissues, soap, a longer nightdress.

The consultant's registrar has already been on his rounds and has taken some details from Katherine, confirming her age, the name of her G.P., which medication she has been on, if any. The questions from the registrar had been innocuous enough, but to Katherine they were able to stir within her a deep sense of anxiety and panic. The registrar had written down her details on the sheet of ruled paper pinned to his clipboard, writing them down as she spoke quietly or George spoke for her. The registrar was a young man, no more than early thirties, his registrar's coat just a little too big for him. He had spoken to Katherine and George with the acquired veneer of authority. He had informed them that shortly Katherine would be taken down to the Radiology Department on the ground floor for a chest X-ray and then Mr. Kentworth – He had stopped to ask if they'd met the consultant, Mr. Kentworth. No, Katherine and George had replied. Well, after the X-ray Mr. Kentworth would be able to get a clearer picture of Katherine's condition and then decide how best to proceed with treatment. The registrar had left them, a self-satisfied look on his face, cocking his head sideways as he passed the nurses' station in the assumption that there would be an admiring audience. But the nurses' station was empty.

Now Katherine and George wait. They say very little to each other because talking seems like a frightening thing to do. It does not help them forget. It does not help them pass the time. It merely serves to draw their attention in, to copper-fasten their terror.

George holds Katherine's hand, absentmindedly stroking the elongated soft hollows between her knuckles and rubbing the tips of his fingers across Katherine's nails, which have begun to curl back over and around her fingertips. Both Katherine and George look around the ward. They are out of their depth. The smell of the ward and its muted sounds blend to become one awful, indistinguishable thing.

The other women in the ward lie propped up in their beds, assuming the shapes of women. Only one woman sits on a chair, rocking slightly back and forth with her hand across her mouth, her hair just two small tufted bunches on her head.

Katherine looks at George.

He does not exist in her mind. He is real. Her marriage to him does not exist in her mind, but comes from real things. Has always come from real things. It is more than love, is it not? It is the sweet pattern of compromise. It is love and more than love. She has suspected this. Suspected it long before her illness ever distilled her.

And as she watched George then, the night she stood on the little veranda of their Mexican hotel, she had felt that the sky was too big to be true. Looking up, it was the widest expanse she had ever seen and still blazing, although the tyranny of the daytime sun had waned. Incidental clusters of cloud, bathed in a burning sunset orange, broke the foreverness of the sky and helped her feel less overwhelmed by it, gave her eyes something to latch onto. These clouds felt almost merciful to her. She had never seen anything like this before.

She stood on the wooden veranda, which faced onto a broad stone courtyard. Shadows fell from the yucca plants and the bougainvillea. Behind her, the town square, out of which a church spire stretched elegantly over the surrounding low buildings with their ugly loose-hinged shutters, was quiet. She could smell the resin from the wood beneath her bare feet. The wood was warm. The air was warm. And from off of her skin rose the faint, and not unpleasant odour of her perspiration.

She turned from the sky to look through the open door into the room beyond. She watched George. He was inside, sitting on the bed and fixing the strap of her sandal, which had snapped during their walk back to the hotel that evening. He was quietly and intently working with a needle and thread.

Beside the bed, its plain covers of limp cotton crumpled from their lovemaking, sat two sombreros, one on top of the other, on a squat cabinet. She and George had bought them when they had stopped to get their bus at the border town of Nogales. The markets there had been full of street sellers crouched on the ground, selling sweets and flowers, some offering little wooden images and idols of baked clay. Mangoes had spilled from plaited baskets. There had been papayas and bitter cucumbers, too. She and George had both felt the flush of inelegance when one street seller, a man with a deep-set jaw and coal black eyes, had reached out to take their camera and had gestured to them to pose for a photograph in their new hats. They had stood for what seemed like an achingly long time while the street seller pointed the camera this way and that, their arms slung around each other, motionless in their vulnerability, smiling into the sun, and had felt obliged to give him extra pesos.

The trip to Mexico would symbolise a new start for them, George had said. And after Katherine had finally agreed on a wedding date, he could think of nothing else. His plan was for them to travel by boat from Belfast to Liverpool and then take the transatlantic liner on to New York. Arriving in New

York, they would board the Southern Pacific Railroad Golden State train to Phoenix, Arizona, stopping overnight in Kansas City. In Phoenix, he and Katherine would stay with Mildred, his mother's sister, until he had secured a job and a small flat to rent. His job prospects at home with the Belfast City Council were modest, to say the least, and he felt fervently that America promised them a better life. Mildred had assured him in her letters that there were plenty of opportunities in the burgeoning electronic and clothing industries in Phoenix as long as he was prepared to accept any position to start with. She already had a list of employers for him to contact when he arrived. So George and Katherine's wedding was also a wake. They said their good-byes to family, friends, and colleagues to begin their new life together, a strain of anxiety visible in both their faces, despite the obvious excitement of the day.

Their journey from Belfast to Phoenix would take them almost twelve days, and they had put aside enough money to then celebrate a week's honeymoon together before George would begin looking for work. Being so close to the U.S. border, Mexico had seemed the obvious choice for a honeymoon. It had also seemed exotic to them, dangerous almost. Clearly the start of something new. But as they set off on their trip out of Phoenix, they suspected that their honeymoon had been ill planned. A little too much to take on in a week. They had already felt the journey across the country to Arizona very long and tiring, and then here they were almost immediately setting off again. They took a Greyhound bus from Phoenix to Nogales, which was comfortable enough. However, the bus journey onward from Nogales had been long and hot (the only 'air conditioning' was the fleeting rasps of still-warm air sucked in occasionally through the open windows of the bus). The bus had rattled along the rough sandy roads through scrubland, infants sleeping on the floor, the driver chewing coca leaves in an attempt to keep himself awake, and it had taken almost six hours to reach their final destination, Alamos. It disheartened them to realise that after only three days in Alamos, they would make the return journey, stopping once again at Nogales to catch the Greyhound bus back to Phoenix.

Despite all that, the time spent together in the heat and the uncomfortable confinement of the bus had reduced them. It had disabled their quick judgments and their small talk and had induced a kind of sleepy acceptance of this harsh new world through which they moved together, watching the mountains push majestically toward them as they travelled south.

When they arrived at Alamos, they had walked from their cheap hotel through the town, crossing the almost colourless central arcaded plaza, catching glimpses, here and there through half-open doorways, of the small patios beyond filled with marguerites and with carnations of yellow and white. They had talked and walked holding hands. They had sat waiting patiently in the heat at an empty bar just off the central square, where, eventually, they were served seasoned pork sandwiches and refried beans, which they washed down with glasses of lime water.

Refreshed, somewhat, they had walked back through the town and across the Plaza de Armas, where they had found a small museum – they were not sure whether it was even open, it seemed so empty and quiet, but it was – which had retouched photographs of the town in its heyday. The photographs showed Alamos's rise to substantial wealth in the seventeenth century, following the discovery there of some of the richest silver ore in Mexico, a stark contrast to the sleepy town they now saw around them. The mine workers stared out from the photographs with a fearsome intent, their large moustaches ringed in white dust. There was a little model of the mine itself and of the homestead of the Alamada family, who had governed the region after its independence. Someone had stuck a parakeet's feather down into the chimney of the little house. A feathery plume of green-and-yellow smoke. Katherine slipped the feather out of the little chimney, thinking she might keep it as a memento.

'*My* turn to put the fire out,' she had said to George, giggling a little, and then had blown her breath upwards, through her pursed mouth to cool her face.

There was little to do in the town. Within an hour and a half, they had walked from one side of it to the other and back again and had had their modest meal and their visit to the museum, but it was just this sense of idleness which, they were suspecting, was enriching them.

And the way in which George had held her hand that day as they'd walked through the square of the small Mexican town, is the way in which he holds it still, now, among the drip trolleys and the dying women in the hospital ward. He holds her hand now the same way in which he has always held it, with love.

A porter arrives with a wheelchair to take Katherine to the Radiology Department, and with the porter is a friendly young nurse. When the results are examined by Mr. Kentworth, he will make a particular visit to Katherine and explain to her that, in his opinion, operating on the cancer is not an option. He will suggest radiotherapy and chemotherapy as a way forward. He will not inform Katherine to what extent the cancer has spread, but he will tell George. He will tell George that Katherine has, at most, six months to live and his lips will fall in a slight pout, as though he is about to say 'Sorry.'

George had come from the room and had joined her on the veranda of the little hotel, wrapping his arms around her body and kissing her lovingly on the side of her face. They had stood together, watching the evening close in. In the gentle light of the sky, a stark white swollen Mexican moon had appeared, as though it had been switched on. And as the moments passed, they had stood and watched the sky grow darker and the milky rays of moonlight grow more intense, until their shadows were black and their skin was painted in lines of wet silver. Our honeymoon. I have never seen anything like this before, she had thought to herself.

And so it had seemed the most natural thing in the world to do.

She had turned her body around to George and had looked at him with the openness of a child. The long sigh she had given had signalled that she had felt within easy reach of herself. She had stroked the side of George's face with the back of her hand and then, smiling at him as though she were slightly drunk, she had talked quietly and sweetly to him.

'George,' she had said. It had all seemed so perfect. 'George, I want to tell you something.'

George had raised his eyebrows softly to indicate that he was listening to her.

'George, I want you to hear what I have to say. I want you to understand. I . . .'

'I'm listening.'

Their faces had remained close. They had held their gaze on each other and the swollen moon had continued to bathe them in its generous light.

She had smiled. The moment to redeem herself had come.

'George, while we were engaged . . . I have to tell you that . . . well . . .' It had felt as though there was a bubble of air in her throat. 'Well, you see . . .' The bubble broke. 'Well . . . you see, George – I was in love with someone else – I had fallen in love with someone else – I—'

George looked puzzled. 'What did you say?' he asked as though he had misheard her.

'George, it's important that you understand that this has nothing to do with us now, with what we have together now,' Katherine said, trying desperately to compose herself.

George remained silent, watching her. His face still held a questioning look.

After a few moments, Katherine spoke. 'It's something that has passed, is over,' she insisted. 'It's something that *had* meaning, but I know now . . . it doesn't mean . . . .' With this, she slowly ground to a halt. She looked up at George. For a moment, George stared back at her and then he said quietly, almost imperceptibly, 'Fallen in love? While we were engaged? Engaged to be married? In love with who?'

'I want to explain . . .' she continued, hardly knowing what to say.

George slowly repeated his words in a feeble attempt to assimilate what he had heard. 'What in God's name—'

He rocked slightly back from her, his face fixed in a grimace, his arms still enclosing her, his eyes searching her face. But from the polite, quiet way in which he had spoken, from the way in which his words had been hinged with disbelief, she realised instantly that she had made a dreadful mistake.

'In love with who?' he insisted. She could feel his body tightening beside her. 'What – Katherine – in God's name do you mean?'

'George – it's not what you think. It's—'

'And what am I supposed to think? While we were engaged? What kind of thing is that to say?' George loosened his hold on her. 'So what does that make me, then? Eh? What does that make me? Some kind of – bloody – some goddamn – bloody – fucking – joke! What have our years together meant!' George eyes blazed. 'Who was it, for Christ's sake?'

She began to backpedal then, tears streaming down her face, talking fast, trying to dilute the effect her words had had on George, and it was all ugly, every syllable of it. She was not even sure what she was saying anymore – gushing apologies, thin explanations, trying to make George understand. She shook her head in complete despair, more tears coursing down her face. 'Someone I met – a tailor who – when I was playing Carmen – he died – he died George – he drowned – I couldn't stop thinking about him – I'm so sorry – I tried, but I just couldn't stop – but we're married now, George – we're married and it's all different and—'

'Are you over him?' George's voice had a vicious edge to it. 'Are you?'

'Yes, George,' she said weakly, 'of course I am.'

'I doubt that.'

It was an impulse she should have checked. An unguarded moment she herself should have understood. Rooted in the selfish desire to release herself from her guilt and eased forward by the heat and by the gentle thrill of her new surroundings, she had sensed a new beginning. She had wanted to put everything behind her. She had wanted to forget Tom. She had felt herself opened and lightened and, as a consequence, had foolishly thought that George would somehow understand all that and see something new in her to love.

And she could not undo what she had done. She could not unsay it. What had she been thinking? How was it possible that she had thought for one instant that George would not be decimated by her words? How cruel to cause him such pain. If she could have had that moment back again, she would have sealed it all in. She would not have opened her stupid mouth.

They stood for a few more moments on the veranda of their hotel, both of them silent and altered, and the night sounds surrounding them – a shutter being noisily closed, the complaining bark of an old dog, the clicking of some insect somewhere.

But George had understood, he said, he had understood what she had said to him, and he did not want to hear anymore. Then he turned away from her and walked slowly back into the bedroom.

*Don't walk away from me like that.*

It had been the casualness of her impulse to confess that had hurt him deeply. She knew this. The terrifying ordinariness of her opening tone, she knew, had crushed him beyond belief. It was as though she had been telling him about what she had just seen, a lizard in the courtyard below, among the bougainvillea, under the swollen moon.

Elsa has never been inside a hospital. She had only ever been in the hospital car park at the time when Stephen was born. Stephen had developed jaundice, and so Elsa, Maureen, and Elizabeth hadn't gone into the hospital, they hadn't even gotten out of the car, but instead had pressed their faces against the car's back window, waiting expectantly for their new baby brother to appear. George had gone into the hospital to tell Katherine that the girls were out in the car, and moments later, although it had seemed like an age to Elsa, mother, baby, and father had stood framed in the hospital window. The girls had waved excitedly at the vision. Mother was mother in a white robe. Baby was a little yellow Pope in knitted skins, his face the size of a yo-yo. Father had his arms proudly around them both.

Now Elsa has brought a comic with her. It is an old edition of Twinkle but there are at least two stories in it which she could certainly read again. She likes the story about the vet's daughter. She would like to be a vet when she grows up. That's why, Elsa is saying to her father as they walk together from the car park, the hospital will be an interesting place to visit, because doctors are a bit like vets, only people can talk to them and tell them what is wrong with them and animals can't, and that really means that to be a vet, you've to be even cleverer than a doctor, because you have to work out what is wrong with the animal yourself.

George holds Elsa's hand and listens to her chatter as they walk through the main doors of the hospital. The doors in the hospital corridors are made of a heavy semitransparent plastic. Nurses busily flap through them on the way to Emergency, trolleys push against them, and doctors casually feel them yield under their touch. The plastic doors surrender to the traffic on either side, like the epiglottal folds on a giant throat.

But the smell of disinfectant and excrement frightens Elsa, and now she stops talking. George takes over the conversation, explaining to her where they have to go to find Katherine's ward. People are passing Elsa in the corridor. Patients are walking forlornly in their dressing gowns.

They find Katherine. Elsa looks at her mother only briefly, feeling, for some reason she cannot explain to herself, that it would be rude to stare at her. Her mother is a grey shape in the bed. Her head is tilted back and her eyes are only slightly open. Her hair is different – there is less of it, or maybe it has just been brushed back. The sides of her mouth are caked a little with creamy saliva.

As George takes Katherine's hand, she begins muttering and her head lolls from one side to the other. She looks like an old woman. She looks like an old drunk woman in the bed, her body drinking bitterly from a nearby drip.

George kisses Katherine's forehead gently and pulls over a chair for Elsa to sit down on at the side of the bed.

'Your mother's just a bit tired. She'll say hello in a minute,' he says gently to Elsa.

Elsa sits on the chair and opens her comic. She stares at the pictures and listens to the particles of conversation between her father and her mother. When Katherine speaks, she does so in clumped phrases with a rising pitch, which makes her sound as though she is whining. The words are disconnected in short, intense bursts. George's tone is always reassuring.

They stay for a while together, sitting like three points of a triangle. Katherine is saying something now about a wig and beginning to cry a little, her eyes still half-closed, her head still lolling from side to side, and Elsa pretends to read while she eavesdrops on her mother dying.

There are other people in the ward. They sit as disparate shapes. The patients are in their nightdresses and dressing gowns, pale and gaunt. They look as though they are wrapped in cloth, half-mummified. They are stripped of the everyday. They are patients now and their job is to wait, wait for biscuits and analgesics and the knowing nods from a passing consultant, to whom they routinely nod back, having understood nothing of what he has said.

The visitors sit waiting with the patients who are waiting. The visitors wear clothes that allow them to go out into the wind. They hold grapes and newspapers, and all their voices blend together into one low rumble, which vibrates across the damp sheen of the hospital walls.

Elsa hears a trolley clacking along the corridor, the occasional high rattle of cups, and the shrill peal of a nurse's laughter. Elsa looks around the ward.

On the bed next to Katherine's sit a mother and daughter

with noses of identical shape and size. They are the younger and older version of each other. As they turn to look at each other, they create a perfectly symmetrical space between them. Across on the other side of the ward, a patient sits alone on her own visitor's chair, looking at the empty bed. She now dips her head and begins rummaging in a plastic bag. Every so often, she quickly pops something small into her mouth from the bag, gnawing at whatever it is like a wily squirrel with an acorn. Her bed jacket has fallen open, revealing a thin slice of breast. At the bed nearest the door, a group of young men in white coats are surrounding the slim shape of a sleeping woman covered with a blanket. They are talking cheerfully, as though they are at a luncheon and are eagerly waiting to see what they will have to eat.

George reaches over to touch Elsa on the shoulder.

'Would you take out the things for your mother from the bag, pet?' he says, attempting to coax Elsa to engage with her mother. Elsa lifts the bag up onto the bed. Out of it she lifts some fruit – two apples, two bananas – a neatly folded facecloth, a magazine, and Katherine's mule slippers. Elsa hands them to her father. George places the fruit and the magazine on the bedside locker and then, pulling open its creaky tin door, puts the slippers and the facecloth in among Katherine's spare nightclothes.

'Has Vera been up to see you, Katherine? Or Frank?' George is tidying the contents of the locker. Katherine groans in response, lifting her head from the pillow and looking past both her husband and her daughter into the air beyond.

'Elsa has just come from swimming.' George continues calmly, as though there is a conversation. 'Monday already. And we got Mass yesterday at St. Mary's, you'll be glad to hear – we haven't all become heathens since you've been out of the house!' George turns to Elsa with a smile. Elsa bends her head and pretends to read her comic.

Suddenly, Katherine pushes herself up in the bed, pressing her fists into the mattress to raise her chest, her arms like thin stilts.

'Swimming,' she says clearly.

George turns to Katherine, surprised at her voice.

'Yes – swimming on Monday.' George's reply is cautious. 'Tell your mother about the swimming today, Elsa.'

Elsa says nothing.

George reaches over to help Katherine settle in the bed. She arches her back in distress. 'Where?' she asks.

'The Templemore Baths, Katherine, with the school,' says George.

'Yes. Yes, I know.' This time, Katherine's voice is a calm day. She looks kindly at Elsa and then slides through George's hold to rest back on her pillow. George fixes the blankets around Katherine and turns to pour water into a glass from the jug on the locker.

But Elsa doesn't want to talk about swimming. Talking about swimming makes her stomach sore, for every Monday Miss Fairley takes the whole class to the Templemore Baths like lambs to the slaughter. Today was just like every Monday, Elsa thought to herself. And every Monday it's the same thing. When they reach the flat grey steps of the baths, all the girls are marshalled through the heavy stained-glass doors, which then swing tightly closed behind them. Miss Fairley orders the girls to move in a dignified manner to the cubicles. Some girls rush ahead to get the best changing rooms – the ones nearest the showers. Elsa inevitably ends up with the cubicle at the end with the broken door, so she always feels on view. The floor of the cubicle is wet and scummy and the grouting between the tiles is green and dirty. Elsa hates when the swimming teachers shout, which they do all the time. When she tries to put on her swimming cap, her hands fumble against the resistance of the rubber. It thwacks stubbornly each time she tries to push more hair in underneath it. The cap tugs at the hair on the nape of her neck and creates little spindles of pain each time she moves her head. Every Monday, she walks to join the rest of her classmates who are always already standing by the edge of the pool, a strand of her hair snaking its way down the back of her neck, marking her out as different, marking her out as the worst swimmer in the class. This Monday was no different from all the others. She had stood, as usual, cold and frightened, shaking in her little black swimsuit. So, no, Elsa doesn't want to tell her mother about the swimming.

Another trolley clacks along the corridor and a nurse bustles into the ward carrying a tray of medication. George reads this as a sign for them to go. Elsa is relieved. She feels uncomfortable sitting at the side of the bed of a mother who seems unfamiliar to her. She folds her comic and listens as her father speaks quietly to her mother, as one would speak slowly and calmly when leaving a nervous child. He strokes her head. He tells her she has beautiful hair. Her mother has sunk into her half-unconscious self and groans as though to acknowledge their leaving. Elsa and her father make their way out of the hospital and walk back across the car park.

The sun, like a huge copper penny, had suddenly dropped out of the cloudless evening sky and was gone. Blocks of purple shadow were cast by the surrounding terraces onto the courtyard of the hotel. Fireflies flitted orange-red across the blue stones. The night grew quickly cold.

George had turned away from Katherine and, having made his way hurriedly down the wooden staircase and out through the back door of the hotel, now sat on the edge of the dry stone trough in the middle of the courtyard. As she approached him, he was a still, dark shape, his head bent low, his hands splayed on his thighs. His anger hung around him like a hungry dog.

They remained silent. She stood there, dressed only in her cotton nightdress and still barefoot, the stones giving back the daytime heat beneath her feet. Her arms and legs shivered slightly in the slim evening breeze. She stood there, not knowing what to say nor how to go about repairing the hurt she knew she had caused George. Why had she told him? Why had she been so foolish? Would she ever be exonerated in his eyes?

After a few moments, George released a small sound, something like a groan, only thinner and tighter, as though acknowledging a point of no return. When he finally spoke, his voice was measured and low.

'I found him, Katherine.' George's head remained bent.

'What, George?' Her voice was a tremor.

George talked slowly, deliberately, as though he was spelling out every word to her. 'Your tailor. . . your lover . . . whatever you want to call him . . . I was the one who found him.'

'What?' Katherine spoke as though in a trance. 'What do you mean, George?' A keen breeze ruffled the hem of her cotton nightdress.

George lifted his head suddenly, his eyes, black pools, glaring out into the night. 'For God's sake, Katherine—' A dark breathlessness was creeping into his voice. 'I knew exactly who he was. I knew – you and he – had been – I had seen you both the night I waited for you – I had seen you from your mother's parlour window – the night I asked you to marry me' – he dug the heels of his palms into his thighs as though in pain and squeezed his eyes tight momentarily as though he was trying to block something out—'and then I saw you two in town together – walking – and the way he placed his arm around you – I knew – I just knew.' He widened his eyes briefly, struggling to retain composure. 'And people talk, Katherine. You know. People talk.' The darkness of his eyes intensified. He took in an enormous breath. 'And then when I saw him kissing you that night – backstage – that night of Carmen – I had come to tell you I had been called on duty that night, but when I saw – I couldn't bear it – I couldn't bear to be anywhere near – so instead of talking to you, I wrote you a letter and I left – I wanted to deny the whole thing was happening – I thought that I would die – I couldn't bear it Katherine – I couldn't bear it.'

'You knew?' asked Katherine.

'For years it feels I have been waiting for you to come back to me.' He lifted his head to the night sky. 'You were lost to me, Katherine – my fiancé – a ghost of a woman.' He gasped between tears. 'All I longed for was that he would not matter to you anymore – that you would love me with the same passion that you loved him – that you would throw your arms around me finally as though I meant something to you.' He cupped his head in his hands and through his fingers she heard him say, 'I didn't mean to – Katherine – oh God, Katherine, I didn't mean to.'

'What are you talking about, George?'

George let his hands fall from his face. When he spoke, his voice seemed hollow, and his eyes were wide and needy. 'That night a call came in – someone had seen a man fall into the river beyond the foundry. We spread out on both sides of the bank – the swell so bad, the current so strong, the water so cold that none of us expected to find anyone alive – the rain and wind making it almost impossible to see anything' – George swallowed hard—'and I had moved upriver, away from the others, away from the foundry – I don't know why – some reason – instinct – perhaps – coincidence – and just beyond where the bank broadens at the distillery – tucked away in under a clump of reeds' – George struggles to keep talking—'caught on a bolt from an old metal girder lodged in the riverbed – there he was – the collar of his jacket hooked onto the bolt – his head only half submerged' – George stared into nothingness as he recounted the events to Katherine—'he was breathing – he was still alive.'

Katherine spoke with a quiet exactitude, her body shivering with the increasing night. 'They said that he was dead when they pulled him from the water.'

'Yes, he was.'

'But you're saying he was still alive when you found him.'

'Yes.'

'I don't understand.'

For the first time since he had spoken, George turned his head to look at her with a helpless despair. Then tears began to choke him. 'I did nothing, Katherine, I did nothing. I just watched him.'

Katherine stood motionless. Then in a small, broken, voice she said, 'You let him die?'

George said nothing.

'You let him die!' she repeated in disbelief.

George looked at her, this time pleading for succour, asking for forgiveness with the eyes of a ruined man.

'Katherine,' he said softly amid his tears. 'Oh Katherine.'

A lizard scuttled out from behind the dry stone trough at their feet and disappeared soundlessly across the courtyard. Fireflies darted once again in the gloom, illuminating only their own infinitesimal world. The swollen moon was hanging above them as though from a silver hinge.

They checked out of their hotel in the cool of the early morning. They had not slept. Left behind on the squat cabinet beside their bed were the sombreros they had bought only two days before. By the time they climbed aboard their bus in the plaza, the sun was burning the world. Their long journey back to Nogales was wordless. The intense heat this time made them feel solid and heavy. Once again, the bus rattled along the roads of orange-brown dust, the tall trees on either side offering little shade. As they left the town, the endless fields of sugarcane spread out before them, taller than the tallest man, soft green and yellow-streaked, their tips falling backward, as though they were fainting from the heat. Hedges of organ-pipe cacti with gnarled, robust skins hemmed the outlying villages, threatening the volcanic orchards and cutting the cruel blue of the sky. The fields gave way to vast plains of arid scrubland, where a lone farmer walked a desolate cow, a rope looped around its horns. The bare mountains loomed oppressively in the distance, the same mountains that, on their journey in, had elated them.

When they disembarked at the border, the street seller who had taken their photograph approached them once again. Seeing that they had no sombreros, he tried to sell them more, holding his arms open to them, smiling at them with a wide, handsome grin. But they had walked past him without a word, their faces sombre, their heads bent. Alone, together.

Their new life in America didn't happen. As it turned out, Aunt Mildred's connections were not as solid as she had led George to believe, and the jobs were not as plentiful in Phoenix as her letters had suggested. Their savings were disappearing week by week and the hope of creating a new life for themselves in America became more and more of a distant dream. George applied for whatever jobs came up. He wasn't choosy, taking work for a time as a school janitor until he could secure something with better prospects, but he didn't find anything. Even the state Fire Department had little to offer him. After four months, they made the decision to return to Belfast. They departed Phoenix on a balmy summer evening, the air heavy with the scent of orange blossom, and boarded the train back to New York, their hearts filled with a mixture of defeat and relief.

A few days after taking Elsa on her own to see her mother at the Royal Victoria Hospital, George takes all three girls, but this time the usual chatting is absent from the back of the car. The three girls seem isolated and in their own space. They sit looking out of the car window. There are plumes of smoke rising up to the cold sky at the end of their street. There is the smell of burning rubber. Then Elsa sees it – a black shell, a strange black cave. The large front window of Mr. McGovern's shop has been completely demolished and Mr. McGovern's groceries – his neatly stacked packets of tea, his thoughtfully arranged fruit and vegetables in their baskets, his appetising selection of cooked meats – have all been hauled through the gaping hole and left smashed and spattered and burned on the pavement. The 'open' sign hangs desolately from the edge of a shard of glass on the door of the shop. Smoke still rises from the burned wood. The words TAIGS OUT have been painted in large red letters on the outside wall.

'What happened to Mr. and Mrs. McGovern's shop?' asks Elsa, alarmed. 'Are Mr. and Mrs. McGovern alright?' Maureen and Elizabeth turn to look out of the car window.

'Apparently, someone threw a petrol bomb into their shop last night. I was just talking to Isabel's mother before we left.' Elsa makes a face at the mention of Isabel's name. 'She had heard about it this morning,' George continues, 'and, yes, they're alright, thank God, they're alright.'

'But who would do that?' asks Maureen concerned. As George drives on the girls hear him muttering 'Thugs' to himself and see him shaking his head.

Elsa now imagines what it might have been like for Mr. and Mrs. McGovern in the burning shop. Her father had always told her how quickly a fire could spread, how it could destroy a whole room in seconds, how the smoke could choke and kill you before the flames would even reach you, how you would never have time to collect and bring with you all of your favourite things. She imagines Mr. and Mrs. McGovern sleeping soundly between their crisp sheets in their full nightclothes. She in her seersucker nightie and rollers, he in his plaid maroon pyjamas and his cotton bed socks. His thorax rattling and cracking under the strain of his great snores and then the sound of the smashing glass. What in God's name?

The smash, Elsa imagines, is followed by a low thud, and then all falls flat and quiet. In her mind she can see Mr. McGovern jump up from the bed and in a cold confusion grab whatever clothes he can find, pulling his trousers over his pyjama bottoms, struggling to find his shoes, calling to his wife. Now Mrs. McGovern groans, but she still remains a large static lump under the blankets. Mr. McGovern thumps her in panic, telling her to wake up! He reaches for his teeth in the glass beside the bed, spilling the water everywhere, hurting his gums as he thrusts them into his mouth.

And then he smells it, the acrid, foul smell of smoke. Mr. McGovern shakes his wife harshly. Mrs. McGovern stirs. Voices can be heard on the street. He pulls at his wife until she is at last upright. Then she is wide awake, staring wildly about her, bewildered and frightened. *Quick! Get out! The bloody place is on fire!* He is almost screaming now. Mrs. McGovern goes to grab her dressing gown, but her husband pushes her toward the door. Mrs. McGovern, terrified, waddles, as quickly as her stiff hips will allow, down the narrow staircase of their flat into the parlour. Black smoke is streaming in under the rim of the closed door that leads from the shop. Inside the shop, everything is catching fire easily, the wooden shelves, the linoleum floor, the paper blinds. The new glass fronts on the shelves are cracking loudly. Mr. McGovern's white nylon shopcoat, hanging on the door at the back of the shop, is a blazing beacon torchlighting the demise of a livelihood.

Elsa imagines it all.

Mrs. McGovern is making small moans and shaking her hands at everything she cannot take with her as she moves toward the back door – her new settee, her documents, the photographs of the grandchildren. Mr. McGovern slips on the stairs as he trundles down them, banging the back of his head on the wooden handrail, like he is in a cartoon. Then he is beside her, twisting at the lock on the door, desperate now. Mrs. McGovern is giving out a childlike whine. The smoke is easing into the parlour, filling it up, engulfing them. They are coughing and spluttering, pulling at the safety chain, twisting at the lock.

*Dear God, this bloody door!* And then the door opens. They stagger out onto the laneway at the back of the shop, coughing loudly. They stand there, bewildered, wondering what they have lost.

And in the back parlour, its door wide open to the night, the paper-thin Christmas-red, vinyl tablecloth on their parlour table dissolves in the flames.

And the jars of sweets are cracking and splitting. The rock-hard clumps of sticky sweets all melting, Elsa imagines. The chocolates, the raspberry ruffles, the black jacks, the bonbons, butterscotch, caramels, lollipops, Jujubes, the Sugarmines and the flying saucers, all melting in the blistering heat to become one huge molten mass of glistening, sugary, burned sweet lava flowing through the sweet shop like an enormous sweet, sticky river. A gorgeous sticky river.

'Look at that!' Elizabeth nudges Elsa as she sits beside her in the back of the car. Elsa rouses from her daydream and stares out of the car window to where Elizabeth is pointing. By this stage, they are close to the hospital, but there is a large burning bus ahead, splayed across the middle of the road like a great steel carcass. It sits like some petrified, cornered circus animal bleeding fire and smoke. More things burning, thinks Elsa, everything's burning. She wonders if anyone has been burned in the big bus.

'Is it an accident?' she asks her father.

'No,' says George. The annoyance in his voice at having to find another route to the hospital is mixed with concern. 'Just some trouble ahead. Just an isolated incident.'

'What's an "isolated incident," Daddy?' asks Elsa.

'Something that there's just – one of – just one thing that's happened. It's fine. It'll all settle down again and be forgotten about.'

'But that's two things I've seen burning in the one day – that's two isolated incidents,' continues Elsa.

'Will you have to put it out?' Elizabeth is suddenly taken with the realisation that her father may have to step out of the car and try to put out the fire single-handedly.

'Of course not, love. I'm sure the machines are already well on their way.'

But there is no fire brigade in sight.

Now around the burning bus, clusters of young men are wielding sticks and holding beer cans, stoking up the temperature of newly found intentions, whooping with each stone that they hurl into the burning bus. The stones rattle and split the last slivers of glass left in the window frames and drop into the belly of the fire.

As George begins to reverse the car, two youths lurch off the pavement toward them. George makes his manoeuvres in the car very deliberate, reversing as far as he can in order to swing the car around. The two young men suddenly backtrack to follow the car. One of the men has the leg of a table in his hand, and as George turns the car, the man hits the car with the table leg on its rear fender. The girls jump.

'Daddy, I'm scared.' Elizabeth starts to cry.

'It's okay, love. It's all right. We'll be out of here in a minute.' George rotates the steering wheel to straighten the car, and as he turns his head to check clearance from the curb he finds himself looking straight into the face of one of the young men. The young man glares at George, his vengeance resting on a cusp, waiting for a trigger.

George places his foot on the accelerator and, turning his head away, moves the car quickly forward. He sees the young man in his rearview mirror staring after the car, surmising whether he has just missed an opportunity to make a point.

Over the weeks and months to come, George will make his journey back and forth to the Royal Victoria Hospital, sometimes alone, sometimes with the three girls in the back of the car, rarely with Stephen in tow – a pilgrimage to the woman he loves – wondering to himself if there would come a time when such a young man would need no such moment of deliberation, no such moment of weighing up before he brought the broken bottle down upon a face, or pulled the trigger of a gun, or smashed the window of a car and dragged out the driver and beat the driver in front of his children.

Katherine has been discharged from hospital to spend some time at home. With her treatment here has come a remission and Katherine has appeared stronger, but she is still far from well. However, the hospital team feel that it would be a good thing for Katherine and the family to spend Christmas together and they have talked George through the administration of her medication.

Katherine's bedroom has been prepared and readjusted to cater to her disappearing body. New pillows have been settled at the headboard to provide a spine for her so that she may sit up. All clutter has been cleared away from the bedside table so that her reach, feeble as it is, will not become easily confused. On the table George has placed a glass and a little jug of water, tissues, and Katherine's morphine and laxatives.

A few magazines and books are placed on the shelf of the bedside table, and around the picture frames that hang on the wall in the room some golden tinsel has been draped. On the windowsill stand three 'Welcome Home' cards.

Elsa can see that her father is greeting Katherine's homecoming with a mixture of excitement and dread. He is at sixes and sevens. He takes the little paraffin heater from the garage up to the bedroom, now worrying that the oily fumes that it releases will aggravate Katherine's breathing. But the room will be too cold without it, he keeps saying. He has moved Stephen's cot into the girls' bedroom, which is now cramped for space. To the grey woollen throw on the back of the sofa in the back room, her father has also added a blanket in case, he says, his presence in his own bed beside Katherine is too uncomfortable for her.

But now on the day of Katherine's return, amid her slow dance from one room to another, she insists that she sleep in the girls' bedroom at the front of the house and that the girls and Stephen sleep in the back bedroom.

As her father moves the furniture, Elsa can detect that his anger has a distinctive disappointment to it. He is stretched to his limits and has no tolerance left. He appears angry with Katherine for wanting the furniture moved, angry with her for moaning and complaining, angry with her most of all for being sick. He pushes the children's beds together sharply, the carpet buckling underneath from the rough movements, and then he squeezes in Stephen's cot just behind the door. It is all awkward and wrong. The door cannot open fully now and there is no room to move. He has upended their double bed on the small landing and now struggles to angle it through the door of the front bedroom. It lands with an unmerciful crash. He arranges all the bits and pieces Katherine needs, once again, on the table beside the bed. He stops for a moment. He is breathless and tired, but he turns to Elsa and nods his head and gives her a small smile, as though to say, 'Thank God she's home. Thank God your mother is home.'

When Christmas morning comes, the three girls keep their

voices down lest they disturb their mother. It is four o'clock in the morning and still dark. In the cramped back room, there is a conspiratorial air among them as they slip their hands into their stockings to find what Santa Claus has left them. A mandarin orange, bubbles, chocolate coins, a skipping rope. They giggle quietly and communicate in fast, fractured whispers, only to fall guiltily silent as they remember – and remind one another – that they must not wake their mother.

The day moves by as though it were a strange story unfolding. They are enjoying Christmas Day, but it has never been this static, nor this careful.

Later that afternoon, Katherine is lying on the brown leatherette sofa in the back room. She is wrapped in the grey woollen throw with its mint green edges, and the two-bar electric fire is on beside her. Maureen, Elizabeth, and Elsa play 'What's the time, Mr. Wolf?' in the back garden. Their voices are crisp and light as they play. Elizabeth and Elsa are poised and ready to run and Maureen is ready to catch them. The snow that had fallen during the very early hours of the morning is still powdery and soft and the world appears to have been made quieter by it. Stephen has so many layers of clothes on him, he totters around like a little snowman. His woolly hat has slipped down over his eyes and his arms are stretched out in front of him. Together the children are an oil painting of a winter scene. The snow graces their Wellington boots, their cheeks glow crimson, and Katherine is now not at the kitchen window to watch them.

But soon the children come back into the house, as though they sense that without their mother there to offer witness, their play means nothing. George helps Stephen out of his coat and boots while the girls quietly collect their model village of Applewood Green from their bedroom to bring downstairs. They settle together in the back room and begin to arrange the painted plastic houses and people.

'Mummy, can we use your legs to make hills and things?' Elsa asks.

'Give your mother some space, girls. Let her rest.' George is concerned the children will tire Katherine out.

'No, really, it's fine,' Katherine reassures George.

With Stephen watching, his lips pouting in concentration, the girls gather around Katherine as she lies on the sofa and lay out the village on top of the grey woollen throw. They push Mrs. Dainty's post office into a small dip in the blanket and rest Dr. Broom's surgery on top of their mother's knee. They place Mr. Fennel's fishmonger shop near their mother's abdomen, where the blanket flattens slightly, and put Willy Miller's mill down near her toes. Soft channels in the blanket provide roads on which the villagers can travel. And all roads lead to Her. The villagers can bring Katherine anything she needs now. Micky Muffin, the baker, is on his way with fresh bread and scones, and Tommy Topper brings milk and cream. A road curves down from Katherine's thigh, which, although too narrow for the motorcar or the truck, allows Mrs. Cinnamon's width. The chemist's wife glides toward Katherine, holding her baby at her breast, and brings cough mixture, some perfumed bath salts, and gossip from the village.

'Did you hear poor Mrs. Dainty has lost her puppy? Oh dear, isn't it awful. And then there's Private Dooley, whose mother bought him a different-coloured glove for each hand so that finally he can tell his left from his right. How about that? And then of course Dr. Broom, who is away on an emergency call at the moment, said very clearly that you're going to be as right as rain. All you need is some of Farmer Meadows' lovely fresh eggs. And can you believe it – here comes Farmer Meadows right now.'

Farmer Meadows approaches, courtesy of Maureen, with his wonderfully fresh farm eggs and offers them to Katherine.

'Thank you very much, Farmer Meadows,' says Katherine.

'No eggs,' Stephen says with a frown on his face, pointing to the little plastic figure of Farmer Meadows.

'We're just pretending,' explains Elsa patiently. 'Here, you bring Willy Miller over to see Mummy.' Elsa hands Stephen the figure of Willy Miller.

'Wil-ly,' Stephen says with a huge smile, and immediately he wants to see what Willy Miller tastes like.

'No – don't eat him! Bring him to Mummy!' Elizabeth laughs.

A humpback bridge suddenly appears on the road as Katherine shifts her position a little on the sofa.

'Let's put a barricade on the bridge and a burning bus,' says Elsa. She lifts Micky Muffin's bread van and turns it on its side. 'That'll have to do for the bus.'

'What are you doing, Elsa?' asks Elizabeth.

Elsa continues. 'Now' – she stops Farmer Meadows with her finger—'do you have any identification, Farmer Meadows, in order to pass the barricade?'

'Don't be stupid, Elsa,' says Maureen. 'Why would you need to ask Farmer Meadows for identification if you know it's Farmer Meadows.'

Elsa looks blankly at Maureen. Maureen promptly removes Micky Muffin's bread van from the bridge and allows Farmer Meadows to continue. Farmer Meadows weathers the humpback bridge nicely.

Then Willy Miller arrives beside Katherine wet with saliva, as though he has just been caught in a shower of rain.

'For Mummy,' Stephen says, and smiles at her.

'Thank you, my love,' Katherine says. George comes over to the sofa and sits on its edge. Katherine looks at George. She looks at her children. *To have all this.*

⁂

Only once since that night on their honeymoon in the bluestoned courtyard had they mentioned Tom. The day George was helping Katherine move out of her mother's flat into their new home together, George had spotted Katherine packing a small statuette and had asked her where it had come from. When she told him, he had exploded in anger. 'A fucking shrine – that's what you've made for him, is it?' Startled, she had let the statuette slip from her hands. It had fallen onto the parquet floor and had broken into two pieces, the smooth bald head rolling off under the table as though the statuette had been guillotined. Outraged at the viciousness of George's attack, Katherine had screamed back at him, 'His name is Tom, for Christ sake! His name is Tom!' The sound of the name pitched in the air like that, so much in the present tense, shocked them both. His name, that name, transforming right in front of them into something rich and strange and terrifying.

On their honeymoon, she had offered George a confession, in the hope that it would set her free, and he had, in turn, handed a confession back to her. Their wedding gift to each other. A gift they had rewrapped and then carried silently throughout their married life. They had both been frightened that talking through their feelings about what had happened would have unravelled the hurt caused, would have demanded something of them that would have been too much for them to bear. Would have demanded that they look together at the frayed threads of their lives spreading out in front of them like an ancient tapestry. Each of them then having to discern exactly which one was the thread of guilt and where precisely it had twisted around the fibres of their love. Each of them asking how easy would it be to find the thread of infidelity? Its silken weave so difficult to trace and capture. And which the illusive thread of betrayal? Where did it follow the warp and where the weft? Which the thread of culpability? And where the threads that had unravelled from doing nothing until it was too late? But in the state of forever searching for the other's forgiveness and never asking, they had both kept Tom alive. The way we continually keep the dead alive in an attempt to repair the past. The way we carry the dead through life and so forget to live.

However, losing each other they had never wanted. She sees this now.

Something within Katherine is softening – whether of her own volition or not is hard to tell – as though a veil or a skin is falling from her. And it seems perfectly obvious to her now, only she just hadn't been able to see it. That holding on to her memories of Tom, burying them deep within her, detail after detail, in a vain effort to protect herself and George, had in itself been an endless infidelity. An infidelity to the here and now. Even though she had not been able to admit it to herself, she had held on to it all in her attempt to make sense of Tom's death. Perhaps make sense of the loss of a baby, too – if there ever had been one. Most of all, to try to make sense of what George had done – or not done – out of love for her.

Then, since her cold encounter in the sea with the seal, since she had faced a kind of drowning of her own, all those memories of Tom had risen to the surface, risen in a bid to be released, risen in a bid to release her.

George had been tortured by his own ghosts, too, she had no doubt, interminably tortured, had turned pieces of memory over and over again in his mind, wondering how he could have made things different, or possibly, even secretly, grateful that he hadn't. The pain of that keeping, she feels it now. Such a weight for him to carry. George waiting in the dusk of his life, like a child waiting for the big snow, so that it may ease the world with its white promise. Wasting himself with an ill-defined hope. Wondering how, in the eyes of the world, he could possibly justify his actions on the night of Tom's death. Wondering how, in the eyes of his wife, he could possibly compete with the perfect dead.

~

After their play, George makes something to eat for the children, then goes upstairs to prepare Katherine's bed. Katherine gathers up Applewood Green and all its inhabitants in the grey woollen throw to keep them safe, leaving them on the sofa, and then touching each child tenderly on the head as they sit at the kitchen table, she moves to the hallway and begins to climb the stairs. George comes down the stairs and meets her halfway. She looks up at him.

'It's bad luck to cross on the stairs,' she hears herself say to George.

'Is it, now?' George replies with a smile. 'I never knew that.'

Then he bends down and lifts her in his arms. 'I'll have to carry you, then,' he says.

He lifts her up and cradles her against his breast. Her frame is as light as a child's. Her hair is soft against his cheek. He rubs his cheek against her hair. He breathes her in. He carries her up the stairs, still the groom he once was, still the man who loves her, the man who has always loved her more than anything in the world. This big, generous man, showing pride in his carrying, as though he has just discovered his talent to win her back. She takes to him, allows herself to yield to his carrying, though she laughs and tells him she does not need to be carried, that she is strong enough. This is sweet, sweetness itself. This acceptance. She had imagined it as a melting, but instead it feels like a falling, a cascading. Now that it has all begun to surface, it is, ironically, an easy spilling, a welcome release. This acceptance of what they were together and what they are. He carries her into the bedroom and sits, still holding her, on the end of the bed, as though he sits on a large rock staring out to sea, her head still resting on his breast. Picture them together. She is a limpet on his body. He will not let her go. His arms encircle her. She has found strength she did not know she had. The arc of her bent body keeps them both weighted to the rocks.

It is not forgiveness. Forgiveness seems irrelevant now, too haughty a thing, too opinionated, too sure of its own step. Too dependent on negotiation. This is something other. This is a recognition, a reclaiming. A much more delicate thing. It has the kind of cleansing purity that weeping can sometimes bring, although they are not weeping. They are sitting together on the end of the bed. In each other's arms. Trembling with tenderness.

# 12

*March 1970*

ELSA SLIDES HER HAND PENSIVELY along the dim silver bar at the end of the hospital bed. She is in a bad mood. All three girls have come up to visit Katherine this time. George has left Stephen with Nanny Anna, who will already be teaching him how to play rummy and soak salted peas for the next day's soup.

After Christmas, Katherine had taken a turn for the worse. Although George had followed the instructions that the medical team had given him to increase the amount of morphine for her should he need to, he rapidly lost confidence, phoned the hospital and had been advised to bring Katherine back in.

Six weeks later, and she is now in a different hospital closer to home. This hospital caters to cancer patients with different needs. Their care is palliative, they say. They are past offering any promises now.

The sun seems inappropriate in its brightness as it shines in through the hospital window, painting all their faces in a creamy orange light. It makes them all look like their faces have been buttered. It makes the little ridges on Elsa's frowning brow stand out in relief.

Elsa is in a bad mood today because her mother has forgotten her name. Her mother is not like an old drunk woman anymore. She is propped up in the bed by firm pillows, the green candlewick bedspread covering the two bony sticks that are her legs. She is quiet and she is staring at Elsa, her eyes like deep brown pools, as though Elsa is reminding her of someone she once knew. But Katherine has not remembered any of their names, Maureen's, Elizabeth's, Elsa's, or George's. Her large eyes suggest a confused tolerance of the strangers in her room.

They have brought her flowers and homemade birthday cards, each letter of 'Mummy' written in a different colour. The cards have been decorated with glitter, which has rubbed off onto their fingers. Little pieces of glitter can be seen, here and there, on their faces where they have scratched themselves absent-mindedly or anxiously and on Katherine's face where the girls have kissed her, spreading the glitter like a love infection. They all twinkle now in the cream-filling buttery sunlight, a microscopic firmament watching the mother star grow dimmer.

Elsa turns to give her mother a look, but it is a timid challenge. She wants her mother to know she is annoyed. She *ping-pangs* her fingers against the steel bar at the bottom of the hospital bed. Her mother is staring at Elsa, her lips a tight, thin line and she is saying nothing, her eyes like two saucers of submission, like the eyes of a Biafran child, Elsa thinks. It is now difficult to tell which is the greater enemy, the cancer or the medication, as both are eroding her mother piece by piece.

No one talks. The strange figure in the bed has put a stop to all that. The birthday wishes have been given. The flowers have been arranged in the bulbous-shaped vase that sits on the bedside locker. The vase too squat to hold the full length of the long, elegant stems, the flowers have immediately outgrown their welcome.

George has filled in for all the things Katherine might have said to the children, about the cards, about school. He is father and mother now, an interpreter of sorrow and a guide to the stranger in the bed. These sights before you are the daughters you love, he might have said to Katherine. Don't let their bad mood bother you. They are unable to change the story of their lives, which is unfolding before them.

The door opens and a nurse steps in, smiling and apologising for interrupting them. She talks loudly to Katherine and checks the drip that feeds into the cannula on Katherine's hand. She talks softly to George, telling him that the consultant will be on his rounds very shortly, if he'd like to talk to him. She lifts the sputum bowl from beside Katherine's bed and leaves the room. Her shoes squeak against the hospital floor, making a rude noise.

A new silence and then *ping pang* against the bar.

George speaks.

'Let's go out for some orange juice. Would you like that?' Elizabeth lifts her head quickly from the magazine she has been reading, startled in the belief that her father has said this to her mother. However, George is not looking at Katherine as he speaks. He is looking at his three daughters. Maureen, who has been sitting nearest to her father, utters a simple 'Yes.' Elsa turns to them with a scowl.

'I don't like the orange juice here. It tastes soapy,' she says.

The strange woman in the bed still stares at them.

'We'll see what they have.' George beckons to them to move. They kiss the strange woman in the bed briefly, not really wanting to touch her skin, but that's all she has to offer them. That's all she is now. Elsa looks at her mother's hand, the fingers of which are still holding one of the homemade birthday cards. Her mother's fingers are the glittery twigs of a tree, with fingernails like large spoons.

Has she woken up or is she now falling asleep? It is difficult to find the one detail that can confirm for her which it is. Like sometimes on waking up in the morning it is, momentarily, impossible to remember what day it is or what important things have to be done. The struggle, on these occasions, is a mere glitch. Now ill, now sedated with morphine, Katherine's consciousness does not have the same ability, nor the same interest, to discriminate anymore between what is real, what is memory, and what is simply wishful thinking, and the glitch is almost all there is. She exists in that space now as though on an ocean swell that might never end, where the horizon offers her glimpses of other worlds, which vanish as quickly as they appear.

Sometimes, though less and less now, she experiences a moment of searing clarity on the rising arc of this ocean, knowing who she is and where she is and why she is connected to tubes and monitors. Everything comes into focus. Definite, precise, sensual. These moments can stay with her for minutes at a time. And then slowly the clarity fades. She hears words in her brain that confuse her but might carry with them the sense of home, or of a doctor's face, or of the taste of chocolate, or all of these at the same time. She takes the downward sweep, or it takes her, and once again, she cannot tell whether she is awake or asleep.

Now she turns her head slowly on the hospital pillow and sees George beside her. He sits on the chair next to her bed. His eyes are closed. The room is full of oyster light as the sun is dipping in the sky. And she knows what the sun is and where it is and how soon it is to its setting. All is clear to her. She looks at George. She looks how the light from the sun falls on the black hue of his hair, intensifying it, and illuminating the streaks of grey at his temples until they appear almost blond. She looks at how his brow furrows deeply even while he sleeps. The shadows of worry on his lids. His broad shoulders hunched against the back of the small chair in which he sits. His arms folded around his chest as though he is giving himself a gentle hug.

Katherine sees it clearly as the sun slips farther down in the sky. She sees it as she looks at George sleeping in the chair beside her bed. How her love for George and George's love for her has held everything together. How the threads of their love for each other are deeper and more entwined than any dream or any nightmare. A love lived, not imagined.

George stirs for a moment from his sleep. He slowly raises his head and rubs the back of his neck with his hand. Then he turns to look at Katherine. He smiles when he sees that she is awake. In her eyes he can see that she is with him.

'I love you,' he says, and he takes her hand.

It could never be more real than this.

'I love you, too.' Katherine's medication brings her suddenly on a downward sweep. Her eyes close. She is hearing her father's voice now. He is talking to her of summer, as though he is the sun that warms it. His voice is the light of summer. He is there on the horizon, lighting up the world.

And her beautiful children. Beautiful. Never did a word carry so much. The very essence of them. So many horizons now as Katherine moves on the swollen sea.

She sees them, her beautiful children. She sees them living their lives like emotional detectives, far away on the blue horizon, searching for and assimilating signs and symbols and using every shred of evidence to compile their own individual dossier of affection. They are tirelessly and privately obsessive in their foraging for clues, measuring, recording, interpreting the temperature, the gradient, the circumference, the unconditionality of their mother's love for them. And, like points of light luring ghost moths in the dusk, they even set themselves as traps to try to capture her, to keep any bit or piece of her that might be hovering loose in the night air. All signs, no matter how trivial or inconsequential – the residue of a dream, the accidental hearing of her namesake in a supermarket, the catching of a familiar song on the radio – is given weight and importance beyond the norm. Love that is not lived but only constantly sought. Becoming something of and in itself. A narcotic that numbs them against the world that is, and fills them with the delicious and continuous surge of expectation as they surrender to the fantasy of her return. She sees them.

So many horizons now. There, over there is Maureen, taking on the mantle of responsibility, a paisley robe too big around her shoulders, protecting her siblings from what she does not yet know or understand. Surrogacy assumed of her whether she is ready for it or not. On her horizon, Maureen is watching a sports event on television, an opening ceremony, and her own children are teasing her for weeping at the underwater sequence where giant fabric fish swim in the charged, milky air of the arena as though they are speaking to her. Katherine sees this. And there on another horizon, there is Elizabeth, Elizabeth sitting listening to the radio, her hair cut short now, wearing a tartan blouse and black jeans. She is listening to the radio and wondering why so many times she does not offer her opinion on things she knows so much about. She has not been prepared for just how quiet sorrow has made her. Oh, and Elsa. Elsa is there, too. Elsa's twin girls, gorgeous little things with golden hair, beside her at the dinner table and she is feeding them. But they are easily distracted, and react with bewildering panic at the sound of a door closing or a too-quiet kitchen. Their mother tongue is the language of checking, *Are you there? Where are you now?* as though they have inherited the expectancy of abandonment. And there is Stephen. Stephen. What a beautiful man he has become. Look at the dark wave in his hair just like his father's. Look at his broad shoulders. He is alone, happily working on a remote island. Another blue horizon. Imagine. How extraordinary. But soon he will resent the visit of a group of students to his one-man anthropological station. While their company will enliven him, the sense of loss when they leave will be so unbearable, he will wish that they had never come.

And George. Where is George? What horizon is his? Is that him, tiring himself out from trying to make the world as real as possible? Holding his breath as though he lives in a state of constant fear? Is that George there, watching the goodness of his city crumble in front of him like dirty, dried earth falling through his fingers? Uttering his city's place names in bewilderment. George, in an awful, endless winter, reassembling, in his sleep, the pieces of a body he has found, the remaking of a beautiful child? Trying to make sense of loss. But there is no sense to it, George.

The downward sweep takes her again, but this time there are no more horizons, as though the ocean covers everything. Now everything appears reduced and intensified. In the distance a dark, wide head appears. It moves towards her. The ocean begins to part and then disappears. The dark, wide head moves closer. Up out of the invisible sea. Closer and closer it comes. Katherine stares at it. Then she sees what it is. This dark wide head is the head of a woman. The eyes of the woman hold on her. The heft of her body now remarkably still, her bulk buoyed by the invisible sea. That big grey head. The woman now walks toward Katherine. She wears what looks like a Quaker's bonnet covering her hair, the bonnet so simple, it is a black-and-white arc around her face, its black ribbon elegantly tied under her chin. The woman is standing looking at Katherine, her body slightly twisted away from her, her head turned toward her, a look of soft intent upon her face. A moment and then the woman taps her hip censorially with her left hand and then begins to slip her right hand under the belt of her long skirt. She pulls a little muslin pouch out from under her belt. She opens the pouch with a challenging look on her face. In the little pouch, a swell of yeast. The woman folds the muslin once again and returns it to the warm skin of her hip. She turns away from Katherine and walks out toward the infinite arid scrubland that now spreads out before her, which has arisen out of the sea. Then the woman stops after only a few paces. She stops and turns her head and the whole sequence starts over again. She is simplicity at its most eloquent.

But they have met before, she and this unnamed angel in the bonnet.

The association of his touch as he had brushed her hair away from the back of her neck to measure her and Katherine's sighting of the framed photograph of Princess Elizabeth and the woman in the bonnet had somehow fixed itself somewhere in Katherine's psyche. A moment regarded. He had measured her from her neck to the centre of her back and her spine had taken it in, had registered it, just as in the same way, in the same moment, her eyes had taken in the woman's face. Now, Katherine's spine, as it disintegrates, begins to release what it has been holding on to, like the last fizz of a dying insect's wing against a flame, like a last skin, and the woman returns to Katherine in her disease as though to offer her possibility. As though to offer Katherine the song lines of the wide, open plains, where, in the faint cracks of the baked, hardened landscape, love survives.

*How do you stay awake to see the thing that eats you?*

Now the woman is gone and everything is bleached white.

Where is George?

She finds him.

*I can feel your hand in mine and mine in yours, George.*

'George,' she says to him.

Elsa sits up on the edge of her bed. She sits as though she is on a wall watching the sea, or watching people playing in a park, or watching for a thrush to return to its nest with worms for its young. She sits in her long white cotton nightdress with the blue *m* embroidered on the cuff. Her arms hang by her side, the heels of her hands press lightly against the mattress, her legs swing loosely over its edge and her shoulders and her back slope casually downward. Her eyes slowly scan the darkened room. Is it early or is it late? She does not know. She sits quietly with the remnants of her recent dreams, allowing fragments of thoughts to drift, settle a moment, then wander again.

The blind of the bedroom window has been left up. Elsa slips out of bed to look outside. Tiny lights, headlights of cars in the distance, wind their way down the hills behind Stormont. Elsa is able to determine their curious paths as they dip into the half-black and out again. Broken pieces of light, they relentlessly follow the twists of road all the way down, blotted out only for a brief second, then satisfyingly reemerging to complete their journey. Night-weary. Black-swallowed. Home. These are the hills where the big white building sits. The big white building, which is full of angry men, all shouting for the playgrounds and swimming pools and cinemas to stay closed on a Sunday, all yelling for the curbs and streets to be painted red, white, and blue, all asking for the nonbelievers to be brought to retribution. But no big white building now. It is obliterated in Elsa's picture window, where everything looks dark and shades of dark. All black, all safe. Elsa looks out at the night through the window of her bedroom, as one single piece of light moves down the hills behind Stormont, trickling down the indefinable black, disappears and, this time, does not reemerge.

Elsa can see the reflection of her face in the window, can see the small shape that is her mouth. Behind her, the outlines of her sisters' bodies in their beds, like mountain ranges in the distance.

Elsa leaves the bedroom. As she passes her father's room, she checks to see if he is there. There is only Stephen in his cot, fast asleep, lying on his back with both knees bent, as though he is sunbathing. Elsa goes downstairs. She cannot tell what time it is. There is not a sound in the house.

'Dad?' she calls tentatively.

'Yes, love, I'm in here.' George appears in the doorway of the front room. He smiles at Elsa. 'Can't you sleep?' he says gently.

Elsa doesn't reply but stretches and yawns. Her hair has become tangled with every twist and turn she has made during the night and now sticks out all on one side, a semaphore of her restlessness. Elsa looks past her father, who still stands in the doorway, and into the room behind him. Suddenly she sees it. For the first time. Her mother's coffin. She had heard the commotion of the coffin being brought into the house the day before, late in the afternoon, but she had stayed in her room. And when Maureen and Elizabeth had both gone into the front room to see their mother laid out, she had refused to go in with them. Elsa's eyes dart quickly away from the coffin to the empty air in front of her. But too late not to realise that now the world is utterly different.

'Are you all right, darling?' George is concerned. How does he explain to Elsa? How does he help her understand?

'Dad, Isabel has a chocolate machine and it makes real chocolate.'

'Really?'

'And she can make chocolate anytime she wants to because it never runs out.'

'Very good.'

'Dad, I'm hungry.'

'Well, there are some sandwiches I've made for later, but you can have some now if you want. They're on the kitchen table.'

Elsa stands rigid by the doorway.

'Elsa, there's something I want to show you.' George moves over to his dead wife and delicately lifts a small golden locket that is hanging around her neck.

'Look,' he says to Elsa. Elsa does not move. 'It's okay darling, it's okay,' he reassures her.

Elsa moves hesitantly toward her father.

The locket is the size of a threepenny piece and is engraved with a delicate wandering design, like a tiny garland of still-moving threads. The gold of the locket is slightly tarnished. Elsa now stands on tiptoe beside the coffin, beside her mother's skin, catching its creamy pallor out of the corner of her eye, taking in the overwhelming smell of aging lilacs. George opens the locket. Inside are two photographs. Elsa recognises them immediately. They have each been cut from the photograph that used to sit on the mantelpiece, the one of her parents on their honeymoon in Mexico. Both her mother and her father are squinting into the sun. Each of them wears a Mexican hat. The way the photograph has been cut, her dislocated father's hand rests on her mother's shoulder. Elsa thinks of her father using the huge kitchen scissors to cut her mother's face out of the photograph, as though he is cutting out a paper doll on the back of a comic, feeding her head and shoulders to the heavy working blades, sensing the point of no return as soon as he starts. She wonders why he chose this photograph to put in the locket. They look so silly in their Mexican hats.

Elsa now closes the locket and hears a delicate click. Then she opens it again almost immediately. Has she caught them unawares? No, there they are, still squinting into the sun. Still wearing their big silly Mexican hats. She closes the locket again and thinks about the two of them in there and how they would be like that forever. Smiling at each other in their big silly Mexican hats, forever.

'There'll be lots of people coming to the house tomorrow,' George speaks quietly. 'It'll be a hard few days, love.'

Elsa remains quiet.

'Why don't you stay here with me for a while, Elsa? We don't even need to talk.'

Elsa still says nothing.

'It'll be okay,' George says, putting his hand on Elsa's shoulder.

Elsa looks up at her father. 'Can I go now?' she asks.

The vacuum cleaner has sounded relentlessly in the house since Katherine's death, sonorously sucking the moments of love that have fallen over time onto every carpet in every room, until the house is different. Mother memories disturbed, collected, disposed. *Leave the bits of flaky life, the strands of hair, the crumbs of bread eaten when there was hope. Leave the fibres of love and life as they are.*

It is Saturday evening. Outside, the grey-black March sky promises sleet. Its hazy blanket of cloud is covering the whole world, not just the end of this one life, in this one house, in this one street.

A solemn swarm of people have gathered in the back room, talking in low voices and exchanging head nods and shakes as though trading in the currency of grief.

Elsa looks around to see if Isabel is there. No. Probably wading deep in seashells with her father off some windswept coast, dusk rippling on their earnest pursuit.

Elsa's Aunt Vera, her mother's sister, appears and, wrapping her arms around Elsa, hugs her tight. So tight, in fact, that, for as long as the hug lasts, Elsa cannot breathe. But her Aunt Vera smells lovely. She smells of roses and toast. Vera lets go and stares at Elsa. She says nothing for a while.

Elsa looks up at her Aunt Vera. It is like looking at her mother. Vera has the same warm red-brown tones to her hair that her mother had and the same ring of hazel around her eyes – although now her eyes are tired and the skin around them slightly puffed and flecked with pink – and when she speaks, it is as though it is her mother speaking, so similar are their inflections. Vera is casting a spell over Elsa.

'Now, my love, can I get you something to drink? Would you like some lemonade?'

'No, thank you, Auntie Vera.'

Elsa thinks her Aunt Vera looks so elegant in her red tweed suit with its tiny handmade wooden buttons. She watches as Vera clicks open her shiny brown handbag – which matches her shiny brown shoes – and, searching through its contents for a moment, pulls out a crumpled cotton handkerchief. When she opens the handkerchief, there is an amber brooch inside.

'I was just looking through some things I had. And I remembered this. It used to be your mother's, then she gave it to me, and I thought it might be nice for you to have it.'

Elsa looks at the brooch nestled in the handkerchief in the palm of Vera's hand. The brooch is shaped like a marigold, its petals golden, its centre an amber glass heart.

'Would you like to have it?'

'Yes, thank you, Auntie Vera.'

Elsa lifts the brooch and then holds it to her eye and squints through it. It is an automatic reaction, to lift it to her eye, to want to sense the world through the light it promises.

'You're the image of your mother, d'you know that?' Vera remarks tenderly, stroking the side of Elsa's face.

But Elsa does not answer. She thinks it funny that Vera, who *is* the image of her mother, should say this to her. Elsa turns her concentration now on what she sees through the glass centre of the brooch. The amber warms her. Its uneven glassy surface makes things appear hundreds of times beside themselves. Elsa now views the room through her trinket periscope, delighted to find, suddenly, such abundant life beached before her. There, from her warm and watery den behind the coloured glass, she can see Nanny Anna shaking all of her one hundred heads in unison while one hundred of Uncle Frank's hands gently pat all of her shoulders at once. One hundred each of George's twin sisters, Heather and Susan, sit still and quiet at the table together in the centre of the room, and Aunt Vera has now conveniently multiplied one hundredfold to be able to fill all of the one hundred cups of tea requested by the abundant sea of faces.

And there is her father, hollowed, one hundred times hollowed at the very least. Elsa swivels the brooch around in her fingers and watches every one of him sparkle and glint like gold milk-bottle tops in the sun before the birds have pecked them.

She turns her head with the brooch to her eye, continuing to peruse the curious life upon these sanded shores and now wishes she could submerge herself and completely disappear from them all. She moves her head a little to look at the lighted lamp on the table beside her, like a moth irresistibly drawn. A fist of sunsets bursts through the amber-coloured glass and Elsa feels she is in Heaven.

Elsa moves through the subterranean landscape of the long room like a deep-sea diver, her walk slow and deliberate, her periscope placed firmly to her eye. She needs to find something special in which to put her amber brooch, like the blue box she keeps for her pennies.

Elsa makes her way out of the busy kitchen, her hair tousled by some tea-warmed hands, and moves quietly along the hall past the 'good-front-room,' where the coffin ticks. If she steps quietly enough now, the door of the room will stay as it is, she thinks, solemnly half-closed, and she will make it to the end of the hall. If, however, she lets herself be heard, the gape of the door will swallow her and the room will suck her in. Elsa holds her breath and moves quietly to the end of the hall.

There are some boxes and small bags in a corner at the end of the hall. Her Aunt Vera had been looking for some personal mementos belonging to her mother to place in the coffin and had left them there, either to be kept or disposed of. Amid the bits and pieces Elsa spots a small box wrapped very loosely in a cloth. She pulls the cloth away and opens the box. Inside the box is an object wrapped loosely in paper. She opens the paper, to find a small broken statuette. She puts the pieces of the statuette back in the box and looks at the paper. The paper is lovely, she thinks. It has lots of writing on it and lots of music notes and lots of colourful orange-red lipstick smudges, as though someone has kissed it over and over. Elsa wraps her amber brooch in the paper and takes it upstairs.

She finds Maureen and Elizabeth, sitting on Maureen's bed, story-picking from the *Bunty Christmas Annual 1969*. Maureen and Elizabeth are reading 'The Four Marys,' and when they finish the story, curiously at exactly the same time, they flick over the page to begin 'Pansy Potter.' Elsa sits with her two sisters on the bed, listening to the murmur of voices rising from the room below them. It is like some melancholic music, she thinks, that someone has piped around the house, making everything 'The Four Marys' and 'Pansy Potter' do seem much more serious than usual. Even the obligatory celebration in the tuck shop appears to be a sad affair.

Elsa looks at Maureen. She watches as Maureen slowly reaches down and fixes the curve of her slipper around her heel. The movement of her hand is soft, soft and desperate. Elsa follows the arc of it. She then moves to her bedside cabinet and, trying not to raise her sisters' curiosity, reaches into the back of the cabinet and takes out the little blue box fastened with an elastic band. She slips the amber brooch wrapped in the piece of music paper with the kisses into the box without taking its lid off completely and replaces it firmly. Then she finds her place again upon the bed.

Just then, a gentle knock comes on the door. The girls lift their heads to it but say nothing. The door opens, revealing their father. George looks tired and cold.

'Just coming in to say good night, pets. Everyone will be leaving soon, so try to get some sleep.'

'Yeah, we will.' Maureen answers first with a commanding air, which belies her desperation, and resumes comic-flicking.

'We promise, Dad.' Elsa smiles at her father.

George remains straight-faced, as though he is wondering about how he should be saying good night to the children. All through Katherine's illness and hospitalisation, it had, ironically, been simpler. They had had a purpose. They had prayed for her every single night before going to bed, prayed for her to get better and for her to come home. And George had, of course, told them that their prayers would mean something. What else could he have said? But now what was there to pray for? So, before he closes the door of their bedroom, he says quietly, 'And in your prayers tonight, ask God for good weather for the funeral on Monday.' His face is stings red from the pathetic realisation of the words he has just heard himself say.

'Okay, we will.'

George leaves.

Maureen turns to Elsa. 'You can't wear my navy hairband to the funeral.'

'Oh, okay, then.'

Monday morning, the morning of the funeral, and from the front window Elsa sees Isabel coming up her driveway. Isabel is dressed in her school uniform. She looks plain. Her hair is tied back in a low ponytail. She walks as though she is counting her steps, her head bowed, her pace regular and deliberate. She is holding something in her hand. A few moments later and Isabel knocks on the front door. Elsa opens it. At first, nothing is said. Isabel is looking down at the front step and is beginning to tap one of her shoes against the other one. Elsa is looking above Isabel's head, as though she has noticed something of great interest in the far distance. Isabel begins to chew on her bottom lip.

'I brought you some chocolates.'

The box of chocolates is not wrapped, so Elsa can see that they are chocolate-orange matchsticks, which she likes.

'Thank you' says Elsa politely.

'And a card.' Isabel indicates for Elsa to turn the box over. Elsa turns it and sees a white envelope taped to the base of the box.

'I didn't draw it or anything, I bought it,' Isabel continues quietly. 'The card's for everybody, but you can have the chocolates.'

'Thanks.' Elsa gives the box of chocolates a little shake. There is a soft rattle. 'You can come in if you want to.' Elsa now looks at Isabel.

'Can't,' Isabel replies. 'Got a note from school on Friday. There's nits goin' around. Mummy said just in case.'

'All right.'

'Did ye see Dana won the Eurovision song contest? Did ye watch it on the telly Saturday night?' Isabel sways back and forth on the step.

'No. We had people over.'

Isabel stands for a moment. 'I'm sorry about your mum.'

'Thank you,' Elsa says politely.

'When are you going to the church?'

'Not for another hour and a half. Are you going to school?'

'Yeah, soon.'

'See ye.'

'See ye.'

Then Isabel trots down the front steps of Elsa's house, and when she reaches the gate she attempts a smile and a casual wave back to Elsa. Elsa closes the door. She moves into the kitchen, where Nanny Anna is tidying up. Elsa puts the box of chocolates on the table and begins to help her grandmother.

'That was Isabel.'

'Yes, and she brought you something nice.' Nanny Anna nods at the chocolates. 'That was very good of her, wasn't it?' Nanny Anna turns to Elsa and gives her a hug.

'Yes,' Elsa says simply, and goes over to Stephen, who is sitting on the floor. He holds a biscuit in one hand, a slice of apple in the other. He has no agenda, no plan for the day. He is nodding his head in his own time to a tune on the radio. When he talks now, he sounds polite, precise. 'Go, go, go,' he is saying. He is looking at the apple in his hand. 'Go, go, go!' Since Christmas, his hair has grown into long, soft, dark curls. One of them falls down onto his forehead. He is a child always eager to be happy. 'Look, Nana,' he says proudly, 'look!' He shows Nanny Anna the apple slice from which he has taken a bite.

'You're a great fella!' says Nanny Anna, watching him. 'Now darlings, we'd better get ourselves organised and get ready. I'll check how Maureen and Elizabeth are getting on upstairs.'

There is a knock at the door again.

'More flowers!' Nanny Anna adjusts her pinafore and goes to answer the door. Elsa follows her and stands at the doorway of the kitchen, looking down the hall. When Nanny Anna opens the door, there is a man, perhaps in his early fifties, of medium height, and wearing glasses, standing before her holding a piece of paper in his hand. His hair, greying at the temples, is brushed neatly back from his forehead. It is as though Nanny Anna has startled him slightly on opening the door, perhaps a little too quickly, as his lips are curled in anticipation of what he has to say. Although he appears grave, his face breaks into a broad smile.

'Have I got the right house?' he says.

Nanny Anna looks at him and replies simply, 'I don't know.'

'Oh, I'm sorry, I'm looking for Mrs. Fallon, Katherine Fallon. I'm an old friend of hers. She's Bedford now, of course,' he adds correcting himself quickly. 'I know she lives on this street. I'm sure I have the right house.'

Nanny Anna cannot believe how awful the man's timing is. So fresh in her own grief, she does not know what to say. After a moment, she asks the man to step inside the house.

Elsa watches Nanny Anna and the stranger standing in the hallway. She looks at the two of them silhouetted against the glass of the front door. She cannot make out what they are saying to each other, as they are speaking in such low tones. The man had appeared animated at first, but now his movements are smaller and slower. Elsa now sees the man lower his head and put his hands up to his face. Nanny Anna is still talking. Elsa sees the man's shoulders shaking and then she hears a strange high bubble of sound. The man is crying. She has never seen a man cry before. She wonders who he is. Nanny Anna has placed one hand over her mouth. Elsa moves a little closer to Nanny Anna and the stranger.

'I am so sorry,' the man says to Nanny Anna between sobs 'Oh, I am so, so sorry.' He takes out a handkerchief from his pocket and, lifting up his spectacles, wipes his face roughly and then blows his nose. He makes a sound like a cow anxious to be milked.

'And now that I look around me . . . what with the flowers and all . . . and the blinds are half-pulled . . . but I didn't . . . I . . .' Here he sucks at the air sharply. 'I only came with some details about mutual friends of ours . . . When I met her last, only four, five months ago. My name is Charlie Copeland.' He is shaking his head in disbelief. 'I have names and addresses here. I thought she might like to know.' Charlie Copeland raises the envelope that he has been holding in the air and then lets his arm fall like a hammer. 'And I brought her a calendar, too.' With this he gasps a little at the inanity of his gift, 'I make . . . calendars you see . . . but it's of no consequence . . . no consequence.' His voice trails off into nothing.

Charlie Copeland stands like a man at the edge of a cliff, looking downward, slightly stooped, shaking his head at what he sees washed up on the rocks below him. He cannot believe that Katherine is dead. He cannot take it in. He does not know what to do with the envelope and the calendar in his hand. They are an embarrassment to him now. His hand is shaking. He does not know whether it is more inconsiderate to take them with him or to leave them behind. Either way, it now feels pathetic. Charlie Copeland awkwardly places the envelope and the calendar on the hall table.

'Ach, my God, my God' is all he can say.

Nanny Anna and Charlie Copeland stand quietly together

in the hall for some moments. Nanny Anna then offers him a cup of tea. Charlie Copeland takes Nanny Anna's hand and squeezes it, shaking his head as a 'No, thank you.' Charlie Copeland then quietly says good-bye and moves slowly through the front door.

Elsa runs to the door to watch Charlie Copeland walk down her driveway. She remembers now that he is the man they saw at the pantomime, the man who played the wicked old woman. Charlie is lifting his spectacles and rubbing his face with his handkerchief again. He wears a bright canary yellow jacket with broad orange stripes, and parrot green trousers. But then, his is a surprise grief.

As she comes back through the hallway, Elsa sees Charlie Copeland's envelope and calendar lying on the table. She lifts the envelope and, seeing that it hasn't been sealed, opens it. Inside there is a letter and a newspaper clipping. The letter, written in an irregular hand, begins, 'My dear Katherine. So wonderful to see you again. You haven't changed a bit. I hope you don't mind my saying, but I always had a soft spot for you.' At the bottom of the letter, there is a list of names and addresses: 'Hugh Drummond, Rosemary Wylie, James McCauley.' The letter ends with an invitation to a reunion at the Grand Central Hotel in Royal Avenue at the end of March. She sees that Charlie has signed the letter with what looks like a small heart above the *i* in his first name. She opens the newspaper clipping that accompanies the letter. The headline reads A CAPTIVATING CARMEN. Underneath the headline is a photograph of a group of people in costumes, in the centre of which stands a woman wearing a dress that spreads out so elabourately around her that it looks as though it goes on forever. And under the photograph it reads 'The Rutherford Musical & Dramatic Society present a tale of passion and despair in this tragic, romantic melodrama. Carmen, a young woman not careful with her love . . .' Elsa is immediately drawn back to the photograph again and realises that the woman in the centre is her mother. Her mother links the arm of the man beside her as though they are married. She has a haughty look about her, as though she owns a secret. Her hair is pinned up. Her head is held at a defiant tilt.

Nanny Anna calls Elsa from the kitchen. A sandwich and a glass of milk are ready for her. Elsa stuffs the newspaper clipping and letter back into the envelope and places it back onto the hall table. As she turns from the table, she notices that Charlie Copeland has marked 'Reunion at the Grand Central Hotel. See you there, Carmen!' in tiny handwriting on the calendar.

The coffin had been slow to move out of the house. And people had hovered around it silently, so silently. And all the people dressed in black had looked like little figurines, all moving together, as though stuck to one another. Elsa watches the black bits of people now through the back window of the black car. The black car follows the hearse. The people follow the black car. Inside the black car, the smell of the new leather seats intensifies as the car heater is switched on. Elsa sits in the backseat of the car beside Maureen and Elizabeth. Nanny Anna sits in the seat in front of them with Stephen on her lap. Their father walks with the people behind the black car. Elsa has never seen him look as sad as this. Tears are rolling down his face and dissolving him, spilling themselves upon his skin and burning him. After never having seen a man crying before, now she has seen two in one day.

Everyone in the car is quiet, even Stephen. He is unaccustomed to his new look. His hair has been brushed and tidied and he wears a little navy jacket and a pair of navy trousers. Elsa thinks he looks sweet and a little bit funny. He keeps kicking his shoes off. They are a too big for him and he doesn't like them.

'Now, darling,' Nanny Anna says reaching for his shoe on the floor of the car, 'you've got to keep your shoes on.'

'Here, Nanny' Elsa leans over the seat to get Stephen's shoe. 'I'll put it on him.' She tickles Stephen's toes before she slips his shoe back on. 'Your toes'll get cold, silly.'

Stephen gives Elsa a big smile. He starts to laugh. 'Put shoe on,' he says, and jiggles his legs up and down.

Elsa leans farther toward Stephen and pushes her face close to his. 'You look like a little monkey in that suit.'

'Elsa, stop that,' Nanny Anna says gently.

'Monkee!' Stephen laughs. Then he says, 'Li-li looks like a monkee!' and he points at Elizabeth.

'I don't look like a monkey. That's a rotten thing to say,' Elizabeth says dolefully.

'He's only joking,' says Elsa in his defence. Then, feeling the need to humour Elizabeth a little, Elsa says to her 'Would you like to play "blue car, brown car"?'

Now Maureen starts to cry. She draws her long hair over her face so that no one can see.

Elsa sits back into her seat. She looks out of the car, squeezing her nose against the glass. From where the car is now, on the steepest part of their road, she can see the city spreading out below her. It reminds her of the burning bus, of the two alphabets she needs coming home from school, of the angry man with the stick in his hand and the look of vengeance on his face. As the car turns around the bottom of the street, Mr. McGovern's shop stands empty and black. Someone has painted a new slogan on the side wall of the shop above the words TAIGS OUT. The new slogan is painted in big white letters and it says The Past Is Not Quite Past. Elsa wonders what it means. Then she puts her hand up against the window and blots it out. Now she can no longer see it.

With her hand against the glass, Elsa turns to look at the hearse in front of her. The woman in the coffin did not look like her mother, she thinks. That woman was just a little grey bird. The woman in the photograph that Charlie Copeland left on the hall table did not look like her mother, either. But her eyes were bright and her lips were pretty. She was dangerous and lovely at the same time, Elsa thinks. So which is she? And where is she? Where is her mother now?

Elsa looks up at the sky. There is a flat fluorescent light upon the day. Gently, a thin curl of sunlight slips through the pearly grey clouds above, as though someone is gingerly pulling back a curtain in the sky, and soon sunlight falls on the cortege. Elsa drops her hand from the car window and rests her head against it. The sunlight widens and intensifies as the clouds continue to separate. Elsa feels the sun on her face like a warm caress. She sees her reflection in the car window. Where the sun falls on her face, it looks as though there is a light coming from her mouth and she feels her breath like a light rising up inside her. She hopes that calling her mother a bitch at the blackberry bushes didn't make her sick or make her die. She feels the hot air blowing from the car heater and warming her ankles. She thinks for a moment. She knows what she will do to find her mother. She knows what she will do. She closes her eyes. This is her plan. She imagines herself at her bedroom window, the headlights of the cars in the distance dripping like raindrops into a black pool, and she sees herself walking quietly through the door, leaving Maureen and Elizabeth still asleep. There is no light on the landing. Her father has switched it off on his way to bed. She moves past the bedroom where her father and Stephen are sleeping, down the stairs, and through to the kitchen end of the back room, where she feels the cool linoleum under her bare feet. She is wearing the white nightdress handed down from Maureen with the tiny blue *m* embroidered on the cuff. Her hand reaches up to pull back the curtains of burned honey revealing a key hanging on a little hook. She lifts the key off the hook and inserts it into the lock of the back door. It turns easily and she leaves the house.

Outside, a thin drizzle has just begun to fall and she can feel the fine needlepoint droplets delicately cool against the skin on her hands and feet. The air smells only of rain, all other scents suppressed. The night is calm and cold and the moon obscured by clouds. Elsa sees herself walking down her driveway and through the front gates, turning upward to the top of her road. *Nicotiana, honeysuckle, night-scented stock* runs like a song through her head.

She joins the main road and walks along it, past the power

station, past the blindman's house, until she comes to the blackberry bushes. There she steps into their midst. There is not a sound, not a person. All dark and all shades of dark. A mysterious world of no colour through which she moves.

Now it is the feel of earth beneath her feet, and now, faintly, she can hear the tiny trickling of the little river. Light falls from the nearby streetlamp on the main road. It is her electric moon. She winds her way through the bushes, along the little pathways, and crosses the river by the stepping-stones, three rounded boulders, each one a lover's stone chapter, one – two – three. On the other side of the river, the ground opens out into a grassy meadow where the flowers grow. These are the plants that attract butterflies by day and moths by night. Where children run breathless with nets on the ends of long bamboo canes to catch the butterflies and moths on balmy summer afternoons and in the summer evening dusk.

She sees herself walking through the grass, the hem of her nightdress skimming the wet blades as she goes. She finds a spot where the ground dips. She lies down on her back and spreads her arms and legs out on the earth.

The earth feels silver under her body, as though it is smooth, curved metal she is lying on and not the earth. She is nestled in the slight hollow in the ground, her throat exposed to the tilt of the dark above her. She hears the gentle *glip* of the night water from the river. Her long white cotton nightdress is now spread out as wide as a tent. Like a great white skin. I will be irresistible to them, she is thinking. She looks up at the night sky and everywhere there is cloud. Everywhere there are dense indefinable purple-grey folds and curves, whether moving or not moving, she is not sure. I will be irresistible to the ghost moths, she thinks, in my white nightdress among the night-scented stock, among the honeysuckle, among the nicotiana, nestled in the hollow.

All she has to do is wait. Wait even until she will perhaps wake up in the grey-lime dawn. She will wait and she will lure the hovering moths and trap them and take them home. The souls of the dead. *Wait, wait, they will come!*

She lies in the grass amid its inky black blades and, guided by her electric moon, looks up at the night sky, which is not there. She is a child trap for the ghost mother and she is cradled in this small hollow of the world. She will lure her and trap her and take her home. *Wait, wait, she will come, she will come!*

Elsa opens her eyes.

Acknowledgements

My sincere thanks Christine Dwyer Hickey for all her support and advice; to Anne Enright and Declan Hughes for their encouragement. To Sara Hollwey, Sara-Jane Scaife and Rose Henderson for their responses to early drafts. To my editor Leslie Hodgkins at Bellevue Literary Press for his commitment to this novel. Thanks also to Erika Goldman, Kent D. Wolf, Molly Mikolowski, Joe Gannon and Carol Edwards. My thanks to Peter Straus. To Sophie Buchan, Elizabeth Allen and the wonderful team at Weidenfeld & Nicolson. To Breda Purdue and Edel Coffey of Hachette Ireland; Matt Hoy of Hachette Australia. To John Killen and Ita McGirr from the Linen Hall Library, Belfast. To Belinda McKeon, Bert Wright and Vanessa O'Loughlin for all their help. To Jack French for his digital wisdom. To fellow travellers and treasured friends Hilary Fannin and Maureen White. Thanks to Ebony, Robert, North, Winter, Persia, Daniel, Amelié and Michele Campbell. To Nicky for the Vaio. To Ernie, Mary, Roma, Errol and Lisa for all their love and for sharing the journey. To Owen, Megan and Ethan, for your constant faith in me, thank you. And to Eleanor – missing you still.

*blog and newsletter*

For exclusive short stories, poems, extracts, essays, articles, interviews, trailers, competitions and much more visit the Weidenfeld & Nicolson blog and sign up for the newsletter at:

**www.wnblog.co.uk**

Follow us on

and twitter

Or scan the code to access the website*

*Requires a compatible smartphone with QR reader. Mobile network and/or wi-fi charges apply. Contact your network provider for details.